ABLAZE

INDESTRUCTIBLE TRILOGY: BOOK TWO

EMMA L. ADAMS

I dream of a world ablaze.

The sky's a vivid red like the inside of a wound. The outline of a dark figure approaches me. I lie on the ground, the earth rough to touch. A Burned Spot.

As the figure gets closer, my heart skips a beat as I recognise the man.

"I thought you were dead," I whisper, my voice ragged, my throat drier than the parched earth.

"Did you, now?" Cas gives a soft laugh. "You know I don't die that easy."

The dream wavers before my eyes, Cas's face fading, and I awaken and remember Cas is the enemy's prisoner.

It's the third day since I saw him, and I have no idea if he's alive or dead. Common sense tells me he's alive. He's an almost-invincible warrior created in a lab. But I can't forget the image of his face distorted by pain. Pain from the tattoo marking his arm, a mark that binds him to the enemy. Something tells me his time's running out.

For the first time since I came back to the base, my body feels like mine again. Three days I've lain here in the dormitory in a haze of exhaustion, listening to the others tiptoe around me like ghosts. Murray told me that I over-taxed my powers when I battled the fiends' leader. I pushed myself too far, beyond what even a Pyro can usually stand. What I did wasn't normal for a Pyro, though. Not by a long shot.

Then again, *I'm* not normal for a Pyro.

There's nobody in the dormitory now. The others are probably patrolling. Murray doubled up on security after Jared broke into headquarters. He's still out there some-where. And Cas is with him. The man who saved my life by healing me with his blood. The man who gave me his cursed blood and hated himself for it. Now Jared's prisoner. Jared, who'd have done anything to defeat the fiends, experi-menting with fiends' blood to create his own twisted monsters. Even experimenting on Pyros.

And he wanted *me*.

The thought makes me shiver all over. By going back to rescue Cas, I'll be delivering myself into his hands, exactly as he wants. Murray will never let me go. I had a narrow escape last time already. Just as I'd accepted I had powers far beyond a normal human, Jared shattered that notion in a second when he tortured me. Not only that, he hurt Cas to make a point, and finally forced me to abandon him to close the bridge over the divide before the fiends could invade again. *I did that.* I don't *feel* superhuman, though I feel much more alive compared to the past few days. I'm not broken, though I went to hell itself. I stared into the fiends' infernal world, and faced one of their leaders.

I killed a Fiordan. I'm not sure even the others know what I did. As for *how*, I wish I knew. Even though I know more than I ever thought I would—than I ever *wanted* to know—about where the fiends came from, how they wiped out the human race. But my own powers? I don't know nearly enough. I might have beaten the Fiordan, but I was powerless to stop Jared taking Cas away.

I sit up, looking around the dorm. Nobody's here, so it must be the middle of the day. Only Elle's come to talk to me, chattering away as I lay in a delirium. The others tiptoed around me. I was too out of it to catch their whispers, but I can guess. I don't know how much Murray told them, but even Poppy and Tyler, my dorm-mates, would be freaked out to know I blasted one of the Fiordans to pieces.

I just hope they forgive me when I walk away without saying goodbye.

I head to the bathroom and take a proper shower to wash every trace of the fiends' world off me. Then I change into combat gear, plain black clothes. I hesitate before picking up one of the Pyros' infamous bright-red coats. Generally, Pyros want to draw the fiends' attention, but that's not my mission. I leave the coat behind.

The door opens. I freeze.

"Leah?"

It's Elle. Small, delicate-looking, and smiling at me.

"Hey," I say, trying to make my tone strong and cheerful as though I haven't been in a coma for three days.

"You're leaving, aren't you?"

I guess she's not always naïve.

I bow my head and look away. "I have to," I say, softly.

"Cas is probably dead, Leah."

I stare at her. Words jump into my head—he's invincible, he *can't* be killed. And Elle's not normally so morose.

"I mean," she goes on, "dead to us. To you. He's Jared's."

I wince because I know she's right. Jared has Cas's life in his hands. Yet I still can't give him up. Not after what I saw in his memories.

"Sorry, Leah." She walks over and puts her small arm around me. The mark's still there, where Nolan cut into her

3

wrist and transferred his own blood in order to make her susceptible to Jared's control, too, like the other Pyros Jared marked so they'd obey his every command. Pyro blood is powerful, and even from a distance, he can kill anyone marked with his tattoo. Nolan was acting out of desperation when he marked Elle, because he wore Jared's mark himself and if he didn't get me and Cas to go with him, Jared would inflict horrible pain on him.

That doesn't mean I forgive Nolan. Cas had the same marking and he didn't even mention it. Instead, the pain struck him down at the last second, forcing me to leave him behind. Even though Cas *told* me to leave him, I can't get his pain-stricken expression out of my head. What good is being indestructible if I couldn't prevent that happening?

"Wait," I say. "You said Murray found a way to stop the tattoos working, right?" *Even Cas's?*

Very little can harm Cas. But the tattoo had the same effect as Nolan's. Agony without end. Even for Pyros.

"My dad's looking into it," she mumbles. "But Leah… he's been with Jared three days already, and you know he'll be raving mad. Furious. He'll have been taking it out on Cas." She trembles all over, and I hold onto her, trembling, too, trying desperately not to picture what Jared might be doing. I've seen flashes of it in visions since I passed out, but I can't always tell the difference between vision and dream.

And that's another problem I have to contend with. Another reason to seek out Jared.

"Maybe," I say, my voice shaking, "but I have to try."

I know the war and the potential invasion should be my priority, because the fiends will be furious with me for closing the bridge. Two years ago, the fiends' first invasion killed three billion people and destroyed civilisation as we knew it. The Pyros, the only people with the power to fight against the fiends, failed to stop it. This time, I don't know if my killing the fiends' leader means they can't break through again, but I don't dare even consider forgetting our mission. But neither can I abandon a—friend? I don't know *what* Cas and I are.

"Leah," says Elle. "Murray needs you. We all need you. Don't go."

Cas needs me. I think. Even he can't fight Jared alone, nor escape as long as their lives are tied together. I killed Jared once already. He ought to be dead. And... Cas and I are tied together. Somehow. He can't be dead if I'm seeing his memories. Right? He's one of the Pyros' best soldiers. We're outnumbered already, even without Jared's threat as well as the fiends'. If we're to beat the fiends, we need to be rid of Jared. I tell myself that's my real motive for leaving—not just because I want to save Cas.

And not because Cas is the key to undoing whatever damage seeing his memories is doing to me. All the other experiments who experienced the same connection lost their sanity and died.

But if I leave without getting as much information as possible, I'll be wasting my chance and running the risk of ending up at Jared's mercy once again. Sighing, I turn back to Elle. "I'm not going yet, but I will," I say. "But first I have to know how to stop the tattoo from working."

She visibly relaxes. "Ask my dad. I think he's on patrol. He's been working double shifts to make sure Jared doesn't come back."

My throat closes up. Jared's invasion shook everything out of sync, even for Elle. She might be Murray's daughter, but her mother was an ordinary human, and she never awakened as a Pyro like the rest of us. So Murray tried to shelter her. Now she's seen how ugly the real world is.

I nod. "Okay. I'll speak to him."

Elle looks at me with a solemn expression and leads me

to his office. Murray's door lies open. He's talking to another Pyro, a tall woman with her hair tied into a ponytail. Val. She turns to me, eyebrows lifting.

"Leah?"

"Sorry I ran off," says Elle. "I wanted to see Leah."

"Leah," Murray repeats. He runs a hand through his hair. Lines underscore his eyes, and he seems somehow older than before, even though it's three days since I last saw him.

"Will I be able to go outside again soon?" I ask. The words come out before I can stop them. He looks at me sharply, as though he knows exactly what I'm thinking. But he also knows I'm not like the other Pyros.

An ocean of unspoken words swirls between us, as I meet his stare defiantly.

"Soon," he says. "We need to give you a medical evaluation at the very least. You've been unconscious for three days. Delirious."

"It might just have been exhaustion." Val smiles at me. "I'm looking forward to getting our best warrior back in training."

Something cracks inside me. Cas is supposed to be the best warrior. And I feel guiltier than ever for considering abandoning these people.

I hesitate, torn in two. "I have to go back in the field eventually," I point out. "The fiends broke through the divide once. It could easily happen again."

With a glance at Elle, he sighs. "I know. But if we lose you, Leah, we've truly lost to them."

Please. Don't depend on me. I was nobody when I was human, and now… I'm expected to save everyone. It's a responsibility I never asked for, nor do I deserve it. It's moments like this when I wish I was human, anonymous, again. If Cas hadn't found and healed me, he wouldn't be Jared's prisoner.

I shake my head, like that'll help me forget it. "What about removing the tattoos?" Screw not speaking about it in front of Elle. Everyone has to know, because other people have the tattoos. That was Jared's edge over us. He never activated them before, but that doesn't mean he won't if it means he'll get his way. "I thought you were working on a cure."

"We were trying," says Murray, "but we hit a snag. Corrupted blood was used to bind the victims to Jared. I managed to stop Elle's because it was recent, and your blood neutralised it. But I can't guarantee the same would work for the others. I tried to get answers from Nolan, but he doesn't know."

"Or so he claims," says Val.

Nolan. Hate surges beneath my skin. He betrayed us, marked Elle to force Cas and me to go and join Jared. It's his fault Cas's gone.

If I see him, I might kill him.

Elle lets out a choked sound, apparently seeing something in my expression, and steps back. "Leah, you can't talk to him. What if he marks you, too?"

I blink. I've never even considered the possibility. Would his mark work on me? Or does it only affect regular Pyros? I store the information away—maybe I can use it to my advantage. If my blood neutralises the tattoos… there's no way I can let this go.

I scan my surroundings, at the heart of the supposedly-extinct volcano where the Pyros made their home. The railing's slightly bent out of shape from when Cas and I fought the fiends that came in here. The image of Cas standing on a rock in the middle of the lava rises unexpectedly, and tears prick my eyes. *Dammit.*

Val hauls me off to the nurse for an appraisal. It comes as no surprise to hear that I'm fine. Not at all like I effectively burst into flames three days ago. Murray himself hovers anxiously in the background, paying more attention than usual to the bright-red samples of my blood collected in test tubes. I'm not keen on the idea of them being left lying around, if I'm honest, especially considering how Jared created the blood-tattoos.

Stupid. No one here would betray you.

But after Nolan, I'm not sure I believe it anymore.

"Right, she's healthy," says the nurse. "Better than anyone has the right to be, after what she's been through. I'd suggest bed rest, but—"

"I'm fine," I say quickly. "I've had more than enough bed rest already."

"I thought you'd say that," says Murray, with a hint of amusement. "You remind me of Cas, after—" He breaks off, guiltily.

A lump sticks in my throat. "Are you just going to leave him with Jared?"

"We don't know where Jared *is*, Leah," says Murray. "In fact—that reminds me. Do you mind giving me a more detailed account of what happened? In my office."

Val comes along, too, as she's my supervisor. I'm guessing he'll tell the other senior Pyros as well. I'm restless, a large part of me wanting to scream that Jared's tormenting Cas right now. Not that I know for sure. But I nearly killed the guy.

Swallowing my impatience, I give a quick account of our brief stay at Jared's place. Or, the Pyros' old headquarters. The escape, the almost-invasion, Cas's capture, and the fight with the Fiordan. They seem more interested in that than Jared apparently coming back from the dead. I stabbed him, and there was a *lot* of blood. The memory makes me wince slightly, but I don't regret it. I wish I'd aimed for the heart.

"So the Fiordan," says Murray. "We've sent out a patrol to the divide since you came back, and it doesn't look like there's been any kind of disturbance there. More energy blasts nearby, of course, but few people are left in those areas anyway."

Because they died. Or ran away. The divide appeared at the time of the fiends' first invasion. Energy blasts rippled along the length, killing everyone in their paths. The same thing almost happened again. But I stopped it.

"The divide's definitely closed?" I frown. "I don't get how that works, actually. There was this... bridge. It fell to pieces when the Fiordan died."

"Fiordan?" Val blinks at me. "That's their name, right?"

Murray gives a tight nod. "Yes, it's the name of the dominant species on Fior—that is, the fiends' world. We haven't seen one since the war, because the divide sealed them off. For one to break through—it might signal another invasion."

My heart sinks, and Val's mouth falls open. "Invasion?"

"The Fiordans are clearly attempting to break through to our world again," says Murray. "We've no way to see what's happening on the other side, of course, but if one almost got through already..."

"I should be out there," I say. "And—and Cas." I place emphasis on the name. Murray *can't* give up on him so easily. There are less than two hundred of us, and how many fiends? Millions? We haven't even managed to kill all the fiends already here, let alone the countless enemies on the other side of the divide. "How does the divide keep the fiends out, anyway?"

"My theory is that it's partly a wall," says Murray. "The two worlds are permanently melded together. I don't know whether that was the fiends' goal when they invaded, but that's what happened. We had no way to undo it."

"That's messed up." I shake my head. "And the people on the other side? You've never crossed?"

"It's like running into a barrier," says Val. "Cas tried once, of course."

Of course he did. "Is there a way to lock the fiends out? Permanently?"

Murray hesitates. "Yes," he said. "We believed so. That was the eventual goal…"

"Of the Transcendent," I say quietly.

Murray nods. "But the earthquakes and energy blasts make it dangerous to go near the place, even for a Transcendent. The last…" He looks at Val, his face tight. "When the last Transcendent died, the bridge the Fiordans were using closed, but the divide remained open. Ever since then, the fiends' world has slowly been leaking into ours—you can see it in the red sky, the energy blasts. And now the Fiordans have a way back here as long as the divide exists."

"So we need to close it." I nod, though my chest feels tight and part of me shrinks away from the responsibility. Closing the bridge and defeating the Fiordan exhausted me so much I passed out for three days. How can I permanently remove the divide, when the last Transcendent died in the process?

I draw in a breath, watching Murray carefully. *"I* need to close it. I'm the only one," I add, interrupting Val when I sense she's about to protest. "I'm the only one who can. Right?"

Murray's mouth presses into a line. "We never did find another way."

"I need more training," I say, with a glance at Val. "I've no idea how I beat that Fiordan. It was all instinct." Like I turned the energy blast against it. But the memory's little more than a blur of white light, the Fiordan exploding before my eyes almost before I struck. And Cas told me the last Transcendent accidentally caused the first energy blast here on Earth when Jared killed her in the middle of closing the breach.

I can't risk going near the place until Jared's gone for good.

"Most fighting is, for us," says Val. "It's in our DNA. But of course you can come back to training. Just… don't do anything rash."

She's not stupid, and neither's Murray. They must know I've at least considered rescuing Cas. He might have been an asshat, but he doesn't deserve to die. Or to be tortured at Jared's hands. I've seen it before—more than Cas wanted me to know. I've seen what Jared did to him, pushing him to his limit against the fiends, torturing him, and giving him no escape, even death.

To know he could be going through that again, right now, is more than I can take. I *will* get him back.

2

V al insists on dragging me to the cafeteria to eat something. We're joined by Poppy, the dark-skinned girl my age I met on my first day and Tyler, the boy with dreadlocks who shares our dormitory. They're as astounded I'm alive as Elle, and I'm the centre of everyone's stares. There's no chance to talk privately and tell my friends what really happened, so I just pretend I got lucky. Val must have told them not to mention Cas, because no one brings him up even though his name passes unspoken throughout the recreation room when I walk there with Elle, Tyler and Poppy, doing my best to ignore the stares.

"So," says Tyler, with a grin, settling on a chair. "Want to go wall-punching?"

Poppy hits him in the arm. "As if. The back way's out of bounds. There are people there almost all the time."

"They think the fiends might get in that way again?" I ask, frowning. "Or—Jared."

"So it's true?" asks Tyler, glancing over his shoulder. "He's really Murray's evil brother?"

Poppy and Tyler exchange glances.

"More or less," I mutter. "He's like Dr Frankenstein, but with freakish fiend technology." I instantly regret speaking, and stand, unable to bear the restlessness burning through my veins. "No wall-punching, but are either of you up for some sparring?"

"Are you sure?"

"I'm discharged," I say. "No injuries. I want to be able to fight again."

"I'll spar with you," says a voice from behind. Val. "I'm your supervisor. I can have you declared fit for the field again."

Gratitude floods me. "You mean that?"

"We'll come watch," says Poppy, with a grin. "See how your new badass powers work."

So Elle did tell her something. At least no one else is in the practise hall. Obviously, I can't use my real blade, but Val and I have a couple of hand-to-hand bouts, most of which end up with me on the floor. I don't mind too much. I'm out of practise. Fighting the fiends is different to battling a Pyro. The fire leaping from my skin, the surge of energy, the way my body feels light and weightless as though gravity itself doesn't matter anymore—nothing can match it. But I can't use the extent of my powers here.

I know what being a Pyro is. But *Transcendent* is like a label that doesn't belong to me. I'm none the wiser about how I killed that Fiordan.

There are more of them. They might be coming to Earth, again.

Fire surges from my hand without warning, and I stumble back over my own feet to avoid hitting Val. "Oh, crap. I'm sorry."

"Don't worry about it." Val wipes her forehead with her sleeve.

"You okay, Leah?" asks Poppy from the side lines. She and Tyler sit with their backs to the wall, near the alcove where the targets and training dummies are set up. Where Cas used to hang out.

"Yeah," I lie. "Sure, I'm fine."

But I don't feel much like talking for the rest of the evening. I make an excuse to have an early night, but the other three follow me back to the dorm. There's no one else around, thankfully. I've had enough of the stares.

"I'm glad you're all right, Leah," says Tyler, lying back on his bed with a paperback. "For real. We thought you were a goner."

"No, we didn't," says Poppy, throwing a pillow at him. "I knew you'd pull through."

"Right," says Elle, yawning. "You're like a phoenix, remember?"

I forgot the nickname. "Ha ha," I say.

Tyler watches me. I almost guess the question before he speaks. "So it's true that you… went over to the fiends' world?"

I nod, sitting on my bed with my arms wrapped around my knees. "Yeah." There's no point in lying to my friends.

"So does it mean there's going to be an invasion? Like, soon?"

I hesitate. "I don't know." *Yes,* I think. It's just a question of who makes the first move: Jared or the Fiordans.

"Damn," says Poppy. "I hope not."

"Murray'll have a plan," says Tyler, with bravado that doesn't quite fool any of us. "He always has."

"Yeah, but we weren't old enough to fight the last time," Poppy reminds him. "Don't you remember how he shut himself up in his office all the time?"

"He blamed himself for the fiend invasion," Elle says quietly, surprising me. "He said he shouldn't have pushed the Transcendent—" She breaks off, almost guiltily.

"And he doesn't want to do the same to me," I say, getting

it. "But if I *am* the only person who can close the divide, I'd do a lot more good outside. Besides, I'm ready to fight again."

Please. If not for the safety rules, I'd run outside to clear my head. I've been trapped inside too long.

And I'm not alone in my head. Cas's memories await every time I close my eyes.

———

I'm standing on a plateau, a jagged piece of rock protruding over a river of molten lava. The river churns, red and steaming, and my feet inch closer to the edge. Looking down, I can see an arm that's not mine, hanging limp at my side, marred with livid red scars.

Cas's.

He's alive. A surge of relief rises like a tidal wave, even though I'm not here, I'm seeing through Cas's eyes—and I don't even know where *here* is. It looks like the divide, judging by the gap in the earth stretching away to either side as far as the eye can see—but I'm limited in my perception, seeing through Cas's eyes, as he stares down into the river of lava.

Pain prickles my right arm, sharp and intense, like a needle. But it's a mere aftershock compared to the pure agony when Jared uses the tattoo to inflict pain on his victims. I've felt it before, twice, when lying exhausted in the dormitory—a blaze of crippling agony, like every nerve in my body is on fire. Nothing matters but escaping the pain. But the pain isn't mine, it's Cas's. I'm not here. I'm not…

Cas lifts his arm, painfully, and my heart drops when I see that the scars converge at a point above his right hand, over the veins.

It's another tattoo. Harsh black lines crisscrossing one another, a meaningless scribble rather than a particular

15

pattern. Blood seeps from underneath, mingling with the dark ink.

The fist clenches and pain shoots up my own arm.

———

My vision flickers and I'm back in my own body, gasping for breath. My heart pounds in my ears, each beat sending a sharp pain shooting up my arm from my hand, even though there's no mark there to hurt.

Another mark, a second one. Was that real? It wasn't a vision of the past. I'd have seen if there'd been a second marking. Did I see the present? If the pain transferred to me… it feels like a sign. A bad one.

I'm restless all day, again. At least Val lets me back in training, and I practise hitting a dummy with careless abandon until I realise I've drawn an audience. I let my hands fall to my sides, pretending not to see the stares, and run off to practise with weapons instead. I'm still not used to being around people, not after two years outside, tiptoeing through the wilderness.

But those skills will come in handy when I leave to find Cas.

"Wow, you're making up for lost time," says Val, watching me with gleaming eyes as I pretend to decapitate a dummy. "I'd feel sorry for that fiend. Almost."

I manage a faint smile. "I imagined it was Jared, actually." *I should have killed him before.* What did he do to himself that he recovered from a wound that should have been fatal?

Not Cas. It can't have been… But he might have taken blood from either of us while I was unconscious, and used it to heal himself or… *no. He can't have done that.*

"Good," says Val. "You're definitely back on form. Much faster than I expected."

I just nod, not wanting to bring up being Transcendent with everyone watching me. "Can I talk to you outside?" I glance meaningfully at the people making no effort to hide that they're listening in.

"Sure."

We find an isolated part of the corridor easily enough, since following us out of the training hall would be *too* obvious.

"I wondered... How much have you and Murray told the others about what happened? I mean, the important parts. Like... the Transcendent. Poppy and Tyler know."

"Everyone knows the word," says Val, "but we didn't tell anyone you were Transcendent after you left in case Jared found out—in the end, it didn't matter, because he knew anyway. Some people guessed because of the rumours, but we couldn't risk it."

Like the tattoo marks.

"So they don't know I killed the Fiordan? That's not something a normal Pyro can do, right?"

The root of my problem. If I knew *how* I did it, I'd feel a lot more secure going after Jared. Because he's only human. Well, Pyro. If my powers can take one of the fiends' leaders, surely they can take Jared, whatever experiments he's performed on himself.

The dream of Cas's new mark is fresh in my mind. My hands knot into fists.

"No, we didn't broadcast it," says Val. "But Elle would have found out from Murray, and she probably told your other friends."

I nod. That makes sense. "Okay. Because being everyone's saviour is a bit much, considering I beat the enemy by total accident. And Cas..."

What can I say? Few people here actually liked him. Okay, nobody, except possibly Murray, and only in the way he cares about all of us as the leader. Not that Cas himself helped that impression. But for them to just forget about him...

"I'm sorry," says Val. "He wasn't the easiest person to get along with, but he always... fought like a true Pyro."

I don't answer. He saved my life, more than once, and towards the end...

No. It wasn't the end. I won't accept that. "What about Jared? Do the others know?"

"He made a scene impossible to cover up," says Val. "Murray's been telling the others some of it, but not how he experimented on fiends."

"Why?" *Because he wants to defend his brother?* That can't be right.

"Because it'll cause panic," says Val. "The fiends are scary enough without imagining jacked-up versions. Of course, if they become a direct threat, he'll change his mind. I know Murray. He hates deceiving people."

"Seems like he did a good job covering up what his brother did."

I don't mean to be so harsh. Or maybe I do. But then, I wasn't here two years ago. The fiends invading and destroying the world, and the Transcendent dying—that was more than enough for the Pyros to cope with already without adding betrayal into the mix. Especially when everyone thought Jared was dead, and the truth buried with him.

"He has his reasons. He cares about all of us."

"I know." That's why he has her keeping such a close watch on me. Maybe I'll be able to get back on missions soon, but *how* soon? Cas has been with the enemy four days already.

And Nolan? He's still locked up. *I need to talk to him alone.*

Because if there's anyone who might know what Jared's doing, it's the latest betrayer.

"So do the others know the fiends might invade again, soon?" I ask.

Val nods, her face grim. "It's always been a possibility."

The Fiordan was a sign. They're coming back.

Whether Jared provokes them or not, I have to make sure he's taken care of. We have enough enemies out there already. I no longer doubt whether I can kill a person. *He's as bad as the fiends. Easily.* I've been used to doing everything alone, despite the past few weeks of working with the Pyros. It might be unfair to leave the others out, but I'd never forgive myself if anyone got hurt because of me.

"Do... you think Nolan might know something?"

A head-shake. "He pleaded ignorance."

"Can I talk to him?"

"You'll have to ask Murray."

Great.

Val apparently reads reluctance from my expression. "I shouldn't, but I have a spare key. You can handle him, right?"

"Of course. I just don't want to draw attention. He might not talk if Murray's around, so..."

"I thought so. Murray always goes on the early evening patrol," she says. "I'll hand you the key after training, and I'll wait out in the corridor."

I head back to the training hall and try to forget. Eventually, when everyone else is in the recreation room, I manage to slip away, pretending I need to fetch something from the dormitory. Val casually strides past and nods to me.

Pushing back all doubt, I grip my dagger tight. Rust-red metal gleams in the firelight. It's made from the ashes and blood of dead Pyros, which is kind of creepy, but Pyro blood has special properties. It's what makes us different. And given the way Jared can control anyone thanks to his possessing their blood, it's not always an advantage.

But I'm not facing Nolan unarmed.

I pull in a deep breath and ease the back door open, my dagger half-drawn.

Silence.

The door's creak makes my heart skitter. Another door at the back leads to the spare room Murray locked Nolan in after he betrayed us. I slide the key into the lock and turn it.

Click.

The room behind is dark and dusty, and bigger than I expected—twice the length of Murray's office, and filled with glass cases and long tables. A row of filing cabinets blocks my view of the back of the room. I edge inside, lifting the dagger.

A light flashes, and without warning, someone hurtles towards me. A hand grabs my wrist before I can swing the dagger, and the momentum sends me crashing to the floor. I kick blindly, and my foot connects with something solid. Nolan curses, his grip loosening slightly—and I'm on my feet and have my dagger at his throat.

"Don't even think about it," I say, through clenched teeth.

"I knew you'd come back." Nolan's pale face is crusted with dried blood, and his nose looks broken, though it's hard to tell in this light.

"I didn't come to set you free," I say, pressing the dagger to his neck as close as I can without drawing blood. "I came to ask you something."

"What?" Nolan asks, one eyebrow raised. "You want something from me?"

"The tattoo," I say. "Murray's working on a way to stop them affecting people."

"He what?" Disbelief is etched on his face. I guess no one told him.

"It's true," I say. "He stopped Elle's." *Using my blood.* Why? Perhaps it's because I'm Transcendent. I don't know. Apparently, Jared used fiend blood in the original marks, and Transcendents can make mincemeat of the fiends.

"Murray didn't tell me that."

"You probably never gave him the chance." I tilt my head. "I don't suppose you want to tell me who else Jared marked?"

"I have no idea."

I narrow my eyes at him. "How'd that go down, anyway? Did you see him mark you?"

"See him?" Nolan gives a hollow laugh. "He told me it was a rite of passage. He took his time. God. I still feel it." He rubs his arm, lifts the sleeve to expose the tattoo, scabbed over from where he sliced it open to pass onto Elle. "You can't imagine it, Leah."

"Oh, I can," I say. "You know what being Transcendent means? I feel what Cas does. Including... that."

Why did you tell him that? Maybe it's because Nolan looks so defeated, slumped under my dagger point. Maybe it's because I'm sick of being angry. Or maybe it's because Nolan, of all people, knows what it's like to be at Jared's mercy.

"No shit?" Nolan shakes his head. "Damn. You're something else."

"At least I'm not a liar."

I have to say that, to remind myself he's the enemy. Who was he pretending to be before? Was it all an act?

Does it matter? Get your answers. Get out.

"I didn't lie to you, Leah, not at first. We all thought he died. That's why none of us went back to check the old place. It was crawling with fiends, too, the ones he was experimenting on. They got out when we lost the war."

I hold back a shudder at the image. "And the tattoos? They stopped working afterwards?"

My blood counters it, I think. My blood. If I use my own blood on Cas's tattoo…

Nolan dips his head, confusion pulling his mouth down at the corners. He holds up his arm, letting the sleeve fall down to reveal the crisscrossing lines. Like a sketch of a flame.

"Right," I say. "Jared has Cas prisoner. I'm the only one who can get him out of there. So I need to know where he is."
'

Nolan blinks. "You're going after him? I thought you hated Cas." For a second he sounds like his old self.

Now I'm angry. "Yes, and thanks to you, the enemy has him. I'm going to stop Jared provoking the fiends into another invasion." *And if I don't save Cas, I die, too.* The words are like bitter-tasting dust caught in my throat. Jared as good as said so. The visions will drive me to madness, like the others. Even being Transcendent doesn't change anything.

"Right." It's plain he doesn't believe me. Not that it matters. "How am I to know where he is?"

"The old lab was destroyed," I say. "So he won't be there. I need a guide."

"You want me to come with you? No thanks. I'd rather stay here, thank you." He compulsively rubs the tattoo again, but his gaze remains on the knife at his throat.

"You think you're safe from him here?" I ask. "You know he can hurt you wherever you are. I don't think Murray has any intention of letting you go… or removing *your* mark."

Nolan blinks at me.

"I killed Jared," I say, softly. "I killed him once already—stuck my dagger right in his chest. I don't know how he survived, if he did, but I'm more than happy to finish him off."

Nolan stares at me. It's the first time I've acknowledged what I did aloud.

A long pause stretches out between us. Finally, Nolan says, "I'll come back to the lab with you."

"He might not be there," I warn him. "The fiends broke in before. If he's not, is there any other place he's likely to go?"

Nolan shakes his head. "The other labs were destroyed when the fiends broke through. The divide opened right over our training ground."

The divide. I think of the river of churning lava, Cas standing on the brink. A horrible suspicion rises within me, but I can't say it to Nolan. Not yet.

"Okay," I say. "That'll have to do for now."

I pull the dagger back, and he breathes out. I actually frightened him.

Nolan doesn't take his eyes off me as I back away. It's like he thinks he's looking at a stranger. *You and me both.* I don't trust him.

I withdraw the blade. How I'm going to explain this to the others... I've no idea.

"Tonight," I say, guilt already rising. But I can't wait around for approval. I've wasted enough time already. As horrible as it is, Nolan's my one link to the enemy.

This time, I *will* kill Jared. For real.

———

Of course, it's harder than I anticipate, acting normal while planning to abandon everyone. I lie in bed fully-clothed in the full uniform of a Pyro, complete with the deep-red flame-resistant coat. The dormitory quietens as one by one, the others fall asleep. At midnight, I slip out of bed and tiptoe to the weapons room. Murray doesn't sleep in his office but it's locked anyway. Luckily, I know how to pick a lock. One of the skills Randy taught me in the wilderness, in case we had to steal from an abandoned house. It takes longer than I'd like. Then I have to repeat the process with the back door.

"I thought you'd gone." Nolan appears from the gloom, close than I'd expected. His hand moves towards one of the weapons in my hand. I took as many as I could carry.

"Don't you even think it," I warn him.

"I know better than to mess with a girl with a dagger. Or thirty." The corner of his mouth quirks up. I shake my head at him. I wish he *had* attacked me, or at least been hostile. It'd be easier to hate him. But he's not a bad guy—just a coward.

Except I'll never forgive him for what he did to Elle.

"Come on."

Guilt tails me every step of the way. I asked Elle about patrol routes earlier, but I still expect someone to sneak up on us as we leave the back way, through the tunnel Murray declared unsafe after the fiends got in that way and tried to bring the ceiling down. The rocks blocking the path are nothing to my powers, though I do take the time to push them back into place afterwards. The fiends aren't sneaking in again if I can help it.

But there's no sign of them out here, even though night has fallen. I tread carefully on the platform, knowing too well how easy it is to fall. The path leads downwards, and I can't help but pause besides the entrance to the cave. Now I know the truth, I'm guessing it was where they kept old experiments. Those winged skeletons.

Transcendents.

"We should move," says Nolan, and I nearly spear him when he appears from the shadows beside me. Apparently I'm more on edge than I thought.

"Yeah." I continue down the path. "Just thinking. I could fall from here and not break. Like a superhuman."

"Superhuman? You're not human at all, Leah. Have you no idea what you can do? I guess you haven't been around here long enough to hear all the tales of the Transcendent. The last one could run faster than a cheetah and tackle a wall of solid concrete and survive. Before the end, back when we lived in hiding, she used to track the fiends miles away. She'd have this instinct, a sensitivity to the fiends that none of us could match up to. It was like she could smell them or something. Her whole body lit up like a beacon when they were nearby."

I shake my head, feeling slightly dizzy. "I can tell you now, that's never happened to me."

"It didn't for her at first," he says. "She was like us to begin with—she was a Pyro, anyway. And then she got seriously injured in a fight with a fiend. The doctors did their best, but she was on the verge of death. Jared set Cas on her. He didn't want to—he protested pretty loudly about it, but next thing you know, she's walking about, on her feet again in a day. Never seen anything like it." He sighs. "But Jared took a fancy to her. I don't know what he did to her in there, but she became distant and stopped talking to the rest of us."

"You knew her?" I ask quietly, thinking of Cas. He was her bodyguard, the one supposed to protect her.

And the one who made her Transcendent.

"Not well. I'd only been living there a few months, and she was miles ahead of everyone. She hated that we lived in hiding while the fiends kept breaking through. She said if we could take the fight over to them, we could destroy them forever."

Take the fight over to them. To the fiends' world.

"That didn't work out so great." He scrutinises me. "I'd have expected you to ask more questions about her before now, Leah."

"To who? No one would tell me a thing." I cross my arms defensively. "Look, I'm still getting used to being a Pyro. Now it turns out I'm something else, and I nearly died for it.

So you'd better tell me everything you know or I can't promise I'll protect you when we go up against Jared."

"What I know?" Nolan's shoulders slump. "Nothing. I wish I did. I don't know how she got her powers, I don't even know what happened on the front line. I was lucky, so were all of us survivors."

"So you've not seen the fiends' leaders?"

"I'm not convinced they exist," he says. "Why aren't they attacking us now? I admit I used to think there must be some kind of driving intelligence behind their attacks, but I guess they're just mindless killers."

I open my mouth to tell him about the one I fought, the shape-shifter who looked like Jared—but hesitate. He's dead right that there doesn't appear to be a reason for their attacking us. Ever since they first invaded, the first quakes, the attack that killed my sister, I've never had time to wonder *why* they did it. What the history is between them and the Pyros.

I haven't tried to use my powers since the battle, but the flames burn still, underneath the surface. I draw in a deep breath like in one of the meditation sessions in training, and focus. I need to understand if I'm to beat Jared. He's not Transcendent, whatever he might have done to himself. I imagine his smirking face right in front of me, and raise my clenched fist into the air.

A surge of heat almost knocks me off my feet. Light flares around me, and Nolan backs away, shielding his eyes. But to me, everything looks sharper, every speck of dust in the air stands out, defined. Every crack in the stone walls. Every curl of smoke from the lava.

And my dagger, which I hold amongst the others, gleams bright red like burning coals. My nerves stand on end, except it doesn't hurt, it's more of a tugging sensation, like the need to find food or sleep. Part mental, part physical. I turn around, half-involuntarily. It's coming from nearby.

"What the hell?" Nolan says, as I step forward.

A fist crashes down without warning, sending rocks tumbling towards me. I dive out of the way, dropping half the daggers, and land on my feet, skidding on the wet path. The ground vibrates as the fiend lands in front of me. Wide as a small car and built like a mound of rock, its skin gleams russet-red in the rain, its ugly, flat face twisted in a scowl. It bares its long teeth at me and roars.

Behind me, Nolan curses.

Despite myself, a grin steals onto my face. I'm more than ready to fight again.

3

The fiend might be twice my size, but I'm a Pyro, and built to be stronger and faster than any fiend. My body moves almost without conscious thought, hand forming a fist, fire-coloured light flaring as I smack the fiend's clenched hand aside. Its tiny eyes screw up against the light. In my other hand, a frisson of heat burns from the dagger to my skin, but it doesn't burn me. The fire's an extension of myself.

This is what I was meant to do.

I lash out with the dagger, see the flames dance over the edge of the blade, feel the connection between the weapon and me. Brownish-red blood sprays from the wound. I slash again, keep my feet a width apart. There's not enough space on the platform to manoeuvre, but more than enough to strike. The weapon's bonded to my blood, and I can channel the fire right through it. I slash at the fiend again. The smell of burning rises from the blade as the fiend's skin begins to crumble on one side of its face. I leap back, out of range, as it swings its fists clumsily. *Too slow.*

My weapon is a burning blaze; a filter of orange-red

hangs over my vision. But I'm out of practise. The fiend's wide shoulders hit the cliff walls, sending pieces of rock raining down on me. Unbalanced, I don't dodge quickly enough and the fiend's fist slams into my shoulder, knocking the spare daggers from my hands. Instinctively my hands move to grab them and the sharp point of a blade leaves a trail of agony up my arm. I gasp, staggering back.

The other weapons slide from my hands and clatter on the ground. Except my dagger, which remains attached to my hand. But when I try to move my arm, the pain almost makes me pass out. My vision goes fuzzy.

The fiend aims another blow at my head. I drop to a crouch, ignoring the pain in my right arm, and hit it from the side.

Suddenly, Nolan's beside me, and he aims a punch of his own. The fiend's wedged in by the cliff walls and can't run. Between us, we pummel it—me using my free hand. One hit. Then another. Its skin starts to smoke all over, and cracks spread over the surface like breaking rock.

With a thunderous roar, the fiend drops to its knees. I pull back, my arm aching furiously, and my eyes meet Nolan's. I look away, down at my arm. Already, the pain's faded to a bruise-like ache.

The fiend's crumbling before us, pieces of it breaking away into fragments. I move back out of range, and so does Nolan.

Silently, I bend down to retrieve the other weapons.

"Want a hand?" Nolan picks a sword up before I can move.

I spin around, half-expecting him to put the blade to my throat, but he simply sheathes it. I give him a suspicious look.

"I'm not going to hurt you, Leah. I don't want to hurt anyone. I just want this damn curse off me."

"Yeah, well, the others might not get that," I say. "Not after what you did."

"I just helped you, didn't I?"

He indicates what's left of the fiend, little more than a heap of stones. As if it never lived at all.

Despite myself, I bend down beside it, turning one of the rocks over. Thick blood stains my hand, and a strange sensation passes over me. The blood feels more like fire—Pyro fire, not painful. At least, not to me.

My mind replays the image of the first fiend I saw. The fiend that clawed its way out of a building as I watched, terrified, trying to get my sister away. It had an axe embedded in its side, presumably from some desperate person trying to defend themselves. The blood spraying from the wound looked unreal, cartoonish, but it burned holes in clothing, and Randy got a blister on his hand from where some of it touched him.

These things are deadly to humans, but not Pyros.

Why?

The question won't leave me alone. It's trivial in the grand scheme of things, and yet three days asleep have raised too many questions from the depths of my mind. What *are* the fiends, and what do they want with humans? What makes their blood different?

And what are the Pyros?

A voice whispers in my ears, soft, taunting: *"I needed their blood for my experiments. Cas himself carries it within him, and that same blood now resides in your veins. You are part of one of the monsters you so despise, Leah."*

No. It's not true. Jared's the real monster. Blood doesn't mean a thing. I still *look* human. I still feel it.

I stare at the blood on my hand, and a dull pain vibrates up my other arm.

"Leah, come on," says Nolan.

"Wait," I say, hoarsely. I flex my hand and move the dagger, and this time, there's no pain.

I've healed.

My heart drums in my ears. I stare another moment—I've never seen the healing work on my own body before, and my thoughts—*I'm human, I still feel human*—seem less certain. But I stand up, backing away from the remains of the fiend, and give the tunnel one last cursory glance. No more weapons lie on the ground.

Nolan and I walk down the mountain in silence. I stride ahead, like it can erase the guilt at abandoning the others. Am I as bad as Nolan now?

As we reach the crossing, the place where the sea swirls inland, Nolan pauses. "I want to know what I'm getting in for," he says.

"I thought you just wanted to be free."

"That won't help if we both get captured. What's this cure?"

I start to say something, but the low, distant sound of thunder interrupts. Followed by a familiar roar.

Another fiend.

"Crap," I say.

"You know we're exposed out here, don't you?" Nolan asks, but I ignore him and jump onto the first stepping stone. The sea's higher than before, and my heart starts beating fast. I've never liked open water *or* stepping stones. Salt spray stings my sunburned hands and face.

"You know, Leah, I thought you knew better than to go rushing off on a whim."

Despite the slippery rocks under my feet, I whirl around to face him. "Don't you start," I say, in a low voice. "You think I meant for any of this to happen? Blame Jared, not me."

"I wasn't blaming you, Leah."

My foot slips, and I awkwardly jump to the next rock before I lose my balance.

"Sure," I say. "You're the one who signed me up in the first place, in case you've forgotten."

No response. I've got him.

I jump again, wildly, and my feet don't catch the next rock on time.

I'm falling.

I can't breathe. I choke and gargle, spitting out sea water, arms flailing in instinctive revulsion. My eyes burn; I can't see anything, but a rough hand grabs me. Another few seconds of flailing, and then there's suddenly solid ground beneath me. I roll onto my back, gasping, and open my eyes to a squint. I'm not on the stepping stones anymore; but on the other side. The blurred outline of someone stands nearby —Nolan.

I blink furiously. He pulled me out of the water?

"Thanks," I cough, not meeting his eyes as I get to my feet. My cloak's sodden and heavy, but there's a lightness I didn't expect—*oh, no.* I've lost the other weapons, except the one melded to my hand. *My* weapon. It's part of me—and apparently, even falling into the sea wasn't enough to dislodge it from my hand. Pyros can fight with any weapon and channel our power through it, but usually only bond to one, or so I've heard. I slump back in relief. If I'd lost *that* weapon, I'd be screwed. I shiver, tossing the coat's hood back and squeezing water out of my sleeves.

"It was nothing," Nolan says flatly. "You okay to move?"

"Yeah." My throat's hoarse, my ears feel waterlogged, but I can't focus on that now. "Come on. We should move."

Nolan throws me a concerned look, but doesn't say anything. We head down the nearest path, but I don't want to get too close to the divide.

"Leah!"

I stop. A dark shape hovers in the sky above us. Nolan pulls me down, but there's nothing to shelter behind.

It's one of Jared's engineered monsters. And it's spotted us.

The fiend drops from the sky, bat-like wings spread wide, long tusks protruding from its jaws. I tense, dropping into a defensive stance. Claws swipe past me and I duck and stab upwards. My knife catches it in the arm, but barely breaks the skin. Dizziness from my near-drowning slows me down.

I duck another swipe, getting into position to strike. The fiend dives, headfirst this time, teeth bared. I roll underneath its claws and swing my fist, fire lighting as I punch it in the mouth.

The impact vibrates through my bones, but the fiend's tusk breaks in two, and its face crumples inwards where I struck it.

Breathing heavily, I move back, out of the way of its stumpy legs. The fiend raises a hand to its ruined face and bellows in pain, feet stamping, sending ripples across the ground. I stumble, blood spilling from the cut on my arm again. The fight has torn it open.

Not good. The fiend takes another swing at me, and I don't have time to think. I duck, hitting its arm with a well-aimed left hook. It's twice my size and too slow to catch me as I slide under its feet and slash at its ankles. Once, then twice. I come upright and kick it square in the solar plexus. The fiend's all muscle, but I'm made of different stuff to normal humans, and my kick drives it down, gasping for breath.

I've forgotten about the wings. Without warning, leathery wingbeats carry it into the air. The fiend hovers out of reach, then dives at me. Fire flickers along my blade as I swipe at its outstretched hands, but not before one of its claws catches my already-injured arm. Pain turns my vision red.

No. Through the haze, I see my dagger burning,

33

surrounded by red flame, held high. The fiend takes flight again, claws ready for another dive. I sway on my feet but keep the dagger ready, aiming for the killing blow. As the fiend's weight comes crashing down on me, I aim right for its heart.

The impact slams me onto my back. I feel wetness and know it's the fiend's blood soaking into me, but my arm's slick with my own blood, too. The world's slipping away, even as the fiend crumbles to rock, even as I know I've won.

No...

The world falls apart in pieces, and I'm gone.

4

I'm sitting in a metal chair in what looks like a lab, though the walls are made of stone like the inside of a cave. Someone sits opposite me, smiling.

Jared. Of course.

"I do wish you would be more cooperative," says Jared, with a melodramatic sigh. "You know there is no easy way out for you."

"It was worth a try." The voice comes from my own mouth, but it's not mine. Cas.

"Worth a try." Jared shakes his head. "To think you had the audacity to try to take your *own* life."

"I told you, I didn't," says Cas, with a touch of impatience. "Don't you think I'd have done that years ago if it wasn't pointless? I couldn't do a better job than you, anyway."

My heart twists, reminding me I'm not really here. What Jared did to Cas—tortured him to test his limits as an unkillable Pyros—was just sick. If I hadn't seen it myself through Cas's eyes, I'd never have thought anyone would be capable of something so cruel and depraved.

But where am *I*, and how am I supposed to get out of here?

"Do I detect a hint of resentment? Cas, you alone walked away from the war unscathed. You'll never be able to repay me for what I did for you."

"Oh, believe me, I'd like to try."

"We've been through this already," says Jared. "So, if you didn't try to commit suicide, then what…?" He trails off. "The girl."

"What?"

"The girl did something. Let me see."

Cas makes an impatient noise. "It's stopped bleeding already." But he bares his left arm, and my heart skitters.

A long, ropy scar cuts right through the middle of his tattoo. It's mostly healed, but blood streaks the skin either side of it.

Shock pulses through me. I did that. Somehow, through our connection, the wound transferred over to him.

The impact jolts me awake, in my own body. I gasp, sitting up, sending crumbling rock flying every way. Dust clouds rise up and obscure everything. I make out the shape of the fiend as the dust clears. Its eyes are screwed up, and pieces of it have already broken away. But a horrible, gurgling laughter comes from its throat, and I realise with horror that it's trying to speak.

"You Transcendents… all monsters at heart."

Blackness clouds my vision again, and suddenly I'm somewhere else entirely. I'm in front of another fiend, one with two long, clawed hands and two sets of bat-like wings.

A knife's in my hands, blazing like the sky above.

"Play nice," whispers a voice. Jared. "Don't break each other too badly, huh?"

Rage fills me, thick and burning, and—

"Leah!"

My forehead's pressed to the ground. I look up, and Nolan's crouching nearby.

Is the same thing happening to Cas? If he can somehow channel my pain, like the cut on my arm, maybe it is. But if I get drawn into Cas's mind, who's going to save him?

Don't think about that. I know how to remove that tattoo. When I find him, I can stop this.

I focus on that. Something I *can* do.

"You passed out," Nolan says, unnecessarily.

"It happens." I shudder. I don't want to tell him the truth, but my life's in his hands if it happens again.

Am I making a huge mistake?

Common sense tells me I am. I should at least have asked some of the others to help. But I wanted them to be safe. I can't save both them and Cas at the same time, much as I wish I could.

"I get… visions," I say. "Cas and I are linked, and I sometimes see through his eyes."

"You're joking." Nolan stares at me.

"No," I say. "We need to get a move on, anyway."

I don't relax even as we put more than a mile between us and the fiend. Nolan isn't as fast as me, but we can far outpace regular people. We run until there's nothing but sea on one side and empty fields on the other, with the occasional Burned Spot marking where there might have once been a village or town.

The energy blasts. They came when the fiends did, and were almost as effective at killing. Anyone within a ten-mile radius of one is vaporised.

Anyone except the Pyros, that is.

Even now, the memory of that day is seared into my mind. The first time I saw an energy blast. The same day I lost my parents, my friends—everyone in my town. The fiends took everything from me. But it's Jared's grinning face I see now, when I think of the evil that's invaded the world.

"Wait up!"

I pause. I was so preoccupied in my own thoughts, Nolan's been left behind. He hurries to catch up, looking around uneasily. Guess he thinks we might run into the fiends again.

Unless they're attacking the others, back at the base.

No. They'll be fine. We're the vulnerable ones out here. And Cas? If there's a way to stop the tattoos working, is there a way to sever our connection, too? Short of one of us actually dying. Jared implied it was too late. Yet he hasn't hurt or killed Cas yet.

My mind spins with the possibilities. Even three days of rest aren't enough to make up for the horrors I've been through lately. It feels like the slightest push, another trip into Cas's memories would make me fracture like glass. Forget who I am, lose myself in the madness of memories. It almost happened when I lost my sister, before I made the decision to carry on living for her sake.

I made the same decision for the others. To fight.

I'm not about to back down now.

———

The sky never really gets dark anymore, but the sun dips out of sight beyond the horizon, turning the sea to blood-red. It seems ominous, and I think of the river of lava I saw Cas standing near. Is he on the other side with the fiends? But Jared was with him, too. Something doesn't add up—I've no way to tell if the visions are happening right now, or in the past. And the urgent look Nolan's giving me suggests we're running out of time to make a decision. Hide out for the night? I don't need to sleep, but he probably does, and in any case, the fiends will be swarming everywhere soon. The closer we get to the divide, the more likely it is that they'll find us.

"Leah," says Nolan, as we pass by a stretch of trees. "I know you're Transcendent, but I'm not. I'm not going to be in any shape to fight anything if we keep going at this pace. Let's head for the woods."

I remember the last time I was in a forest with vivid clarity, and shake my head. "No way. We'd be closed in."

"It's not normal of them to come into forests," he says. "Honest. It's better than being exposed out here."

He's right, of course. So we veer off the path and into the woods. Trees drape a blanket of leaves over our heads, and the rustling noises of small creatures in the bushes startles me more than once. It never fails to amaze me that life goes on somehow, in places like this, even with the outside world falling apart.

"Leah." Nolan points to a clearing ahead. The stars are just visible through gaps in the canopy above. "We could build a fire here. No one would see."

"Fire." I almost laugh. "We don't actually need to build one, do we?" If we can shoot fire from our hands, surely making a campfire can't be impossible.

Nolan shakes his head at me. "You've never tried to light a fire using your powers, have you?"

"What? Of course not. I haven't had chance. I survived two years out here without knowing about it, anyway."

"Of course you did," says Nolan. "But I... you know what, try it." Strangely, his mouth's quirked up in a smile.

"Try what?"

"Lighting a fire." He starts collecting branches and throws them in a heap in the middle of the clearing.

I approach the heap, frowning. He's bluffing. I can blow

fiends up, for crying out loud—why should lighting a fire be any different?

Still, trying to access my powers without the imminent attack of a fiend proves difficult. I can't get in the mindset. I pull out my dagger, like that'd help, and picture flames running across the edge of the blaze. Doesn't happen. I try again. Again.

A couple of minutes later, I'm rewarded by a sudden burst of flame, as the entire heap of brambles lights up in a flare. I drop the branches I'm holding and scoot backwards, looking up at Nolan in triumph—only to see him smirking at me. I turn my gaze back to the fire to find it's burned itself out, and the branches are nothing more than little piles of ashes.

So much for that idea.

"Sorry. Had to see your face."

"Quit that," I say. Why's he being nice to me now? Does he have to make it so difficult for me to hate him?

I head over to another tree at the other end of the clearing and sit down. I'm not particularly bothered about not having a fire. I'd rather not do anything that might draw the fiends to us. Sighing, I lean back against the tree trunk, peering up through the branches at the stars winking in the tainted sky.

"Sorry," says Nolan, who's come over to join me. "Guess that wasn't the right time to make fun of you, right? I thought it'd distract you."

"Never mind." It was an honest effort, I guess. Plus it stopped me thinking about Cas for about five minutes, which is something.

"I started a real fire," he adds.

The smallest flicker of flames dances in the centre of the clearing.

"Thanks."

"And I set up some traps. We could catch a bird or two. I know you Transcendents probably don't need to eat, but..."

"Thanks," I say, again. *You Transcendents?*

"Unless you have any tips? You survived out here for two years after all." His expression is open. Not quite a smile, but curious.

"Yeah," I say, slowly. He's right, of course. I'm out of practise, but I get to my feet anyway. Maybe my extra-sensitive sight could be an advantage in stalking down prey. "You have traps? What did you even bring with you, anyway?"

He digs his hands into the pockets of his coat and pulls out coils of rope, a water-flask, even a hunk of bread. Slightly mouldy. He breaks off the greenish parts as I stare at him.

"Where did you get that?"

"I picked it up from headquarters."

"Practical," I comment, and he shushes me, indicating the bushes a few feet away. A small animal's wandered into one of his rope traps—a rabbit.

Its feet are already ensnared, and Nolan steals towards it with his knife. I turn away, hating to see him kill it—stupid, really. The number of days I had to help Randy set traps in the wilderness should have numbed me to this, but two years ago, rabbits were common domestic pets. Lissa wanted one.

I shake the thought away, annoyed with myself.

Nolan shows more of the practical streak I never even knew about, cooking strips of rabbit meat over the fire. It tastes pretty nice, especially seasoned with herbs. Which he also stashed in his pockets.

I'm painfully aware that I'm under-prepared for this.

Not that it matters. I never intended to spend too long out here anyway. Tomorrow, I'll find Jared and get Cas back. Tomorrow.

But I can't help relaxing into the moment all the same,

sitting beside the fire with Nolan opposite me, watching the embers of the fire.

It's so peaceful here, you could forget what's happening out there. And, just for tonight, lying under a safe leafy canopy, I do.

5

The shrieks of birds in the trees wakes me. I jolt out of a jumbled dream involving my sister being chased by one of Jared's fiends. Her terrified face flashes before me, and I press the heels of my palms into my eyes, like I can push the image away. It as though my mind's still berating me for failing to save her. But that doesn't mean I can't save Cas. It's not too late for him.

Nolan's already awake. He kicks out the remains of the fire and tosses me a dry strip of rabbit meat. I catch it in one hand, with a nod of thanks. Maybe I can get used to us being allies. For now.

We stay inside the forest but keep moving towards the divide. The forest comes to an end soon enough, and we head back to the coastline. Without the trees for cover, I feel exposed, and the sight of the divide on the horizon doesn't help. It's like an ugly scar, cutting so deep into the earth that the sea's turned into a waterfall, the water running towards it. Unnatural.

I know we won't find anything at the site of the ruined lab, but I can't help wanting to look. Even though I destroyed it myself, the first time I accidentally unleashed my powers. Thanks to that fiend.

My sharp eyesight picks out the Burned Spot where the laboratory used to stand—a mile-wide stretch of ground bare of grass. Where no life will ever grow again. Slowly, one piece at a time, the fiends are turning our world into a mirror of their own.

I wonder if grass ever grew in their world, if it was ever any different. When I never knew if I'd survive to see another day, there was no time for questions, even about the strange red-cloaked people we sometimes saw around towns when we stopped by for supplies. They were rumoured to be in league with the fiends, but Jared said that was because people tend to mistake us for the fiends' shape-shifting leaders. Those fiends didn't look like the brutal but brainless killers, but apparently, like *us.* The idea seemed ridiculous to me, at least until I met one.

And killed him. It.

It's easier to think of them as *it, them, other.* Not human. Even though fiend's blood is what makes me Transcendent.

No way am I ever telling Nolan *that.*

There's nothing to see at the end of the road except the divide, and picking a fight with fiends isn't the plan. So we veer off to the right. I can vaguely remember walking this way with Cas. Talking. Closest to friendly we ever were.

Just before Jared took us, before the earthquakes hit and everything fell into chaos.

Would things have been different if we'd refused to leave? If we'd stayed with the Pyros? Murray could have found his cure and saved us if we'd waited. If only we hadn't tried to be heroes.

But there's no escape. As long as the fiends are here, this world isn't ours. As long as we fight, there's hope. Even if it costs us everything.

I just have to hang onto that as we walk into the tiger's lair.

I can trace our path by the cracks in the earth showing where the earthquakes rippled out from the divide. Nolan and I have to cross them like stepping stones, skirting around as best we can, always alert for fiends. The ground isn't even moving now, but seems to shift with the echo of the tremors from before. We come up to the place where we hid, and Jared ambushed us and the fiends carried us to headquarters. I've never walked all the way there before, and I'm not positive Jared will even be there now. But it's the one place I know. Nolan doesn't have any better ideas, and he at least knows where he's going, so I let him take the lead.

It's too quiet. Not so much as a faint birdsong. No signs of life but tree stumps, and those come to an abrupt halt when we cross into another Burned Spot. The smell of burning is intense—this one must have struck recently. Very recently.

The hairs stand up on my arms, and I feel like we're being watched.

"It's close," I whisper. "So much closer than I thought."

Because this Burned Spot used to be a forest. The same forest Cas and I fled through, right on the edge of the divide.

The memories threaten to overwhelm me along with the thick smell of smoke and burning. Running from the monster. Jared cornering us. Me stabbing him. Running, running for our lives...

It's unrecognisable now, but I've already passed the place I last saw Cas. I pivot around on the spot all the same, looking for—what? Bloodstains? A sign? I left him writhing in pain from the tattoo, powerless against fiends and Jared alike. God knows what hell he's been through in the past few days.

It feels longer than that.

"Leah?" Nolan gives me a quizzical look, noticing I've stopped.

"It was here," I say, my voice rusty from lack of use and the smoke in the air. "Here's where Jared…"

Which means…

I'm sprinting across the cracked, barren ground, but I already know the old headquarters will be gone. An energy blast must have struck, maybe when the Fiordan came through the divide. Did Jared lose all his warriors? He's alive somewhere. If the visions were showing me what Cas is experiencing right now. But what if it was all a lie? What if Jared wanted to lure me back? He knows more about the bond between Cas and me than I do…

"Wait!"

Nolan catches up to me as I skid to a halt in the middle of the Burned Spot. *Nothing…*

There's nothing left at all. What did I expect to find? Rubble? Bodies? A farewell note? *Don't be such an idiot.*

The flat, lifeless ground stretches into the distance. A hundred metres to my left, the divide carves a sharp line in the earth. Before, it shimmered, transparent flames covering a view of the fiends' world. Now, it's blank as the empty ground.

"Dammit," I mutter. "I could have sworn… I thought there'd be a sign."

"Well, there isn't," says Nolan, kicking at the torn-up ground. "Great. We walked all the way out here for nothing?"

"Any other places Jared liked to hang about?"

"You think we stopped for a friendly chat?" Nolan raises an eyebrow. "We should leave."

"Leave." I let out a humourless laugh. "I'm Transcendent. Wherever I go, they'd find me."

He chews his lip, thoughtfully.

"What, you want to go?" I curse the smallest pang of

betrayal I feel at the thought. What does it matter to me what Nolan does? "Not much around here, but there was a town a mile or so back. If the energy blasts didn't take it out."

Nolan turns away, but not before I see a flash of guilt in his eyes. Wait, he's really considering ditching me?

"Go right ahead," I say, turning my own head towards the divide.

One of Jared's fiends hovers above the trench in the ground, silently watching us.

"Crap." I step back, pulling out my dagger. I nudge Nolan, but he's already seen it. He curses under his breath, drawing his own weapon—no, Cas's.

How long has it been there? Fiends aren't usually that quiet.

A warning bristles along my spine. The word *trap* travels through my mind, but the fiend's already spotted us, and there's nowhere to run.

With a screech like car tyres on tarmac, the fiend flaps its wings and launches itself towards us. I stand at the ready, my anger at Nolan turning to rage at the monsters who caused this mess. The fire returns like an old friend, wrapping around my blade.

But the fiend flies over our heads, too high to reach. I duck as its clawed feet snatch at my head, and pinwheel around to face it again.

Nolan swings his sword wildly, trying to reach it, but misses. It's toying with us.

Anger buzzes, a rhythm beating beneath my skin.

Come on.

Another screech rips through the air. *Crap.* Of course there's more than one of them. I look wildly around, while keeping the fiend above within my gaze. It continues to circle us like a bird of prey.

I can do this. I reach for the fire, but the fiend moves in a blur. It dive-bombs us again and I stab upwards, but once again, its claws barely clip my head.

"Get down here and face me," I snarl.

"Leah!" Nolan grabs my arm. In the brief second I was distracted, no fewer than *five* fiends have appeared above the divide.

Stupid. Of course they were inside there the whole time.

The fiends' cries echo around us. Instinctively, I brace myself. One fist clenched, the other holding my weapon. Out the corner of my eye I watch the fiend above, while waiting for the others to strike.

They take flight in unison like a flock of geese, even forming a V-shape as they soar over our heads. What're they playing at? I refuse to give into the impulse to jump, trying to reach them, because it's impossible even for me to jump that high. I imagine Jared laughing at me somewhere and feel another surge of anger.

The six fiends circle, one slightly ahead, followed by two, then three at the back. Like gigantic, ugly vultures, except packed with so much muscle it should be impossible for them to fly. How Jared created them, I have no idea.

"Get down here!" I shout, exasperated.

"Leah!" Nolan hisses, moving in a way that suggests he's going to make a run for it. But he wouldn't do something that stupid. Right?

I'm wrong. Without warning, he legs it across the Burned Spot, away from the divide and towards the unknown. Cursing, I follow him, but it's hard to keep up speed and watch the fiends at the same time.

"What are you doing?"' I demand.

"It's harder to hit a moving target," he gasps out between breaths.

I open my mouth to argue, and something strikes me between the shoulder blades, sending me sprawling. I skid forward on my knees, but the sturdy Pyros uniform doesn't rip. Cursing, I spin around—not for the first time, I'm grateful that my weapon's impossible to drop—but there's no one there. The fiends circle high above.

The smell of smoke is thick in my nostrils, and, now I'm getting my breath back, I feel a stinging sensation on the back of my neck where I got hit. I reach back with my left hand and the bare skin stings at the touch. No, *burns*.

Too late, alarm rings through me.

"They're throwing fire!" I shout at Nolan, who's way ahead of me by now. I sprint to catch up, running in a zigzag pattern to make myself less of a target. A burst of flame drops from the sky, hitting the ground in front of me with the force of a small bomb. I'm thrown backwards, my ears ringing, my vision clouding over...

No!

"Nolan!" I choke out, willing the stinging to stop. The ground's rocking under my feet, and my legs won't stand up. I use both hands to push myself upright again. *Come on! You're Transcendent, for God's sake.* I stagger through the fog, coughing at every breath, the pain in my neck getting worse with every step. *Nolan...*

He lies very still. Unnaturally. Limbs splayed at odd angles. Blood under his head. Did he hit it? Get knocked unconscious? Or... dead?

A screech reminds me of the fiends' presence. I'm too slow to back away when one dives at me. Feebly, I raise my dagger, but it easily pushes me back, claws leaving bloody grooves in my arms.

Flashes of another scene break across my vision. A room underground. Same room as last time. Lines dug into the walls as though a human fingernail had scraped at them—

No! Not now!

I scream, more in anger than pain, and lunge at the

fleeing fiend. My feet leave the ground, and for a split-second I'm airborne, sailing far further than any human could jump. I slam my dagger into the fiend's leg, pulling it down. The dagger slides free, and I stab it again, this time in the back. It has a thick layer of scales all over, unlike any of the other fiends I've seen, but my knife cuts it like paper. It flails, wings splayed, and I duck under one of them, dragging my blade over the fragile membrane. It screeches, blood flying everywhere.

I stab its other leg, and it drops to ground level. I can reach its heart.

"Tran—scen—dent."

I freeze. My hand won't move. The dagger's inches from its heart, but I can't move, can't inflict the final blow.

"What are you doing?" A coughing fit takes over, and through watering eyes, I see the fiend's mouth stretched in horrible smile. Teeth bared.

Kill it!

"You—can't kill us, Transcendent."

The sound of beating wings overhead.

Too slow, I try to dodge, but claws close in either side of my. I close my eyes and brace myself for pain, but it doesn't come. The claws grasp both my arms and I'm lifted into the air, above the dying fiend, above Nolan's body.

I'm fighting, kicking out at the air—falling won't hurt—but the claws are too strong, and I'm limp and fading fast.

One last thought leaves a trail of questions through my mind—*why am I so weak?*

And then, there's darkness.

6

Dreams and reality alternate like a slide show, and I can't tell one from another. A firestorm, pieces of burning metal raining down from the sky. Like the meteor showers that hit during the first attacks—and my mind grabs that train of thought and tugs on it.

I'm back in the classroom at school, the day after we saw the report on the news, the theories about the end of the world. Sitting tensely in class, glancing up at the clock, wishing time would pass so I could go and find my sister and get us both home safely.

Like being at home would create a cocoon of safety around my family, keep away the chaos outside.

The sirens. The fire alarms going off in unison, like a well-timed prank. Screams and cries, the sounds of heavy objects falling outside like cars being thrown about, pieces of the roof falling off.

Running to find my sister. Leaping through the school window, feet hitting the ground, twisting my ankle but running on regardless. Clambering through the rubble which had once been the school's entrance. Pelting down the road, to the primary school. There are kids in the playground, behind the gate, screaming, running in circles. A smoking crater lies where the main building was.

Screaming Lissa's name, clawing at the gates which have turned the playground into a prison.

And she's on the other side, hand grabbing mine through the bars, her nails digging into my hand.

A quake rocks the world.

It feels like the ground is alive, cracks opening in the road to swallow cars, even buildings. The gate buckles and gives way, crushing people underneath it. Lissa's hand's torn from mine. I fall, knees scraping the ground, but stand up immediately. My sister climbs towards me over the twisted remains of the gate—and something's pulling on the end of it.

Fiends crawling out the crater, ugly and twisted like something out of a nightmare. Lissa's screaming and crying, hand reaching for mine. My fingers close around her wrist and I pull her towards me, and we run.

Fiends. Grabbing people, ripping them to pieces before my eyes. I see it all in flashes as my sister and I flee. We're fast, but too late. A fiend lands in front of us, tusks bared. Lissa panics, and her hand breaks free of mine—she runs, and the fiend lashes out and tosses her aside like a limp doll.

I jump over rubble and run to her, heedless of my own safety, but the fiend has already lost interest in me and lumbers over to another poor man fleeing the ruins. Lifting him into the air, the fiend clenches its meaty fist and crushes his skull.

Swallowing back nausea, I concentrate on reaching my sister. The fiend's tooth caught her and tore deep gashes in her arm. She groans, her head flopping back, as I lift her. I'll carry her away from here even if it kills me.

I've run a few metres when a sudden vibration strikes through the air. Everything shimmers before my eyes, and a thick burning smell fills my nostrils. The fiends howl, running away. The ground shifts... Lissa screams my name...

———

I wake, gasping.

Too real. That felt too real.

Shuddering, I let my head fall back. It strikes against metal, alerting me to my surroundings. I'm indoors, as far as I can tell from the lack of lighting. I'm not tied down, and it's a bed I'm lying on, but the walls feel too close. *A cell,* I think, instantly awake. I sit up, bracing myself against the onrush of dizziness. My head swims as I remember. The fiend picked me up and brought me here.

There's one person who would have ordered that. Jared.

I slide from the bed, noting that I'm dressed in nothing but a thin shift, and more to the point, that someone's removed my dagger. *Crap.* I'm defenceless. I feel a slight twinge of pain in my neck where I was burned. Not completely healed, then. I can't have been here long.

I stumble through the dark, hands outstretched. Even Pyros can't see in total blackness. My hands find warm stone, proving that I'm in some kind of cave—or underground. It's stuffy in here, so warm the air appears thick. Deep underground, maybe.

The image of Cas talking to Jared in my visions comes to mind.

Cas. Maybe he's here.

I trace my hands over the wall, mind whirring. There has to be a door somewhere.

A *clang* makes me spin around on the spot, blinking rapidly as light floods the room. A metal door has opened on the other side and the person in the doorway hit a light switch. Sickly-white fluorescent light shines on an all-too-familiar face.

"You," I croak, and before my mind's quite caught up with me, I throw myself at Jared and fasten my hands around his throat.

"Guards!"

Cold stone-like hands grasp my arms, yanking me back and pinning them to my sides. I struggle, glaring daggers at the man who ruined so many lives, who tortured Cas.

Where is he? I have to force the question back. I'm not admitting weakness in front of this man.

"Hold her," he commands, dusting himself off, not looking the worse for wear for my almost throttling him. In fact, he's almost glowing, and not just because of the bright lights. He's practically *beaming* at me.

I spit in his face.

A pause, an endless second stretching out. I brace myself for pain.

None comes. He pulls out a handkerchief and wipes his face calmly, studying me with an almost pitying expression.

"Leah, Leah," he says. "I am sorry for what has happened to you."

Like I believe that for a second. I glare and struggled forward, but the guards' grips are like iron manacles.

"And for your friend," he continues. "It's always tragic to lose another soldier."

Nolan. So he's dead. Anger mixes with an odd sense of regret. *He's dead.* I suppose he did stick around and fight, in the end.

"Were the two of you close?"

So he's trying to gauge my weakness. Like I'd say *yes,* even if it were true.

"Of course not," I say. "He was the only survivor."

A beat. "I beg your pardon?"

As if being overly polite will get him anywhere. I continue with what I've planned to say ever since I got the idea for Nolan accompanying me. Murray has everyone inside the mountain. I don't know how long I can keep up the ruse, but I won't put the others in danger if I can help it.

"They're all dead," I say, tonelessly. "Your fiends killed them. Nolan was our prisoner, and he escaped."

"Really?" Jared's face creases in a frown. "My brother is dead?"

"Yes." I meet his eyes, without flinching. He can't read my mind. And I know how to wear the same deadened expression as the other survivors.

"And you're the only one left," he says, softly. Does he believe me?

"Looks that way." I swallow. "Are you happy now? You've killed him—killed everyone. And now you have me prisoner."

"Prisoner?" Jared shakes his head. "You're not a prisoner, Leah. I want to extend an invitation to you. Join *my* army. We aren't like Murray's. We intend to engage the fiends in battle, and we intend to win."

"You're joking, right?" I shake my head, disgusted. "You think I'd agree to help you?"

"I thought you would want to avenge your friends. The fiends are responsible for their deaths, and for countless others. We need to rid the world of their plague."

"So why'd you try to kill me?"

"Kill you? I have never hurt you, Leah."

A wild laugh escapes me. "You as good as tortured me before."

His placating smile disappears. "I do apologise for that. I overestimated your capabilities." He looks me up and down. "But now... now I think you've advanced a stage. The same weapon would have no effect."

"What the hell does that mean?" I meet his stare defiantly. He *did* hurt me before—just by *touching* me. Now, he has the perfect opportunity to torment me. So why not use it?

"What I did to you before was a modified version of the tattoo-links, if you want to use crude terms."

Like there's nothing crude about *torture.*

"And what?" I challenge. "How am I different now?"

"Your blood has… evolved."

I resist the urge to flinch away. He took my blood while I was unconscious? The sick madman.

"You're no longer susceptible to the method I used to subdue you last time," says Jared. "I'm sure you'll cooperate with me willingly without the need for it."

Wait, what? Does he mean when our weapons touched and I collapsed in pain?

"Yeah, right." I glare at him. "Your fiends killed Nolan and almost killed me, too."

"Leah, any fiend which attacks you is not under my watch. I would never order one to hurt you. The fiends helping me are as much your fellow soldiers as the other Pyros."

"What the hell?" I struggle against the guards' grips, but they hold me still. "I never said I'd help you. You as good as admit you're working with the enemy. I'm not fighting on the same side as *any* of those monsters, whether you think you can control them or not."

We stare each other out. The corner of his mouth lifts in a smile. "I am glad to see you haven't lost your fighting spirit, Leah. Despite your… condition."

I freeze.

"You fought on," he says, softly. "Admirable that you can defeat your enemies when crippled with another person's pain."

Despite my efforts to stay strong, the resolve starts to

seep out of me. He knows about my bond with Cas, knows we feel each other's pain. He saw it affected Cas when I cut my arm.

Damn.

"I'm not fighting for you," I say. "Whatever your purpose."

"I see you're going to take some convincing." He sighs, running a hand through his greying hair. "I don't want to fight with you, Leah. There's been too much fighting—too much loss. My brother..."

Come on. This has to be an act. He almost killed Murray once already.

"There is much I need to tell you, Leah," says Jared. "Time, unfortunately, is not on our side, but I have no doubt that you will be fully recovered in a few hours. Such is your wonderful ability."

His gaze drifts to my left arm. The scar's almost faded already.

"I wonder..." He meets my eyes again. "You came back from near-death recently, didn't you, Leah?"

What does he mean? When I returned from the fiends' world? He can't know about that. He was barely alive. I've no idea how he survived. But it was only hours after I supposedly killed him that I fought one of their leaders. Turned them to ashes.

And I've no idea how I did that. But maybe Jared knows. He survived the first war, too, though everyone thought he was dead. Perhaps I can get information from him. Seeing as he's apparently in a generous mood.

Don't be stupid. He's tricking you.

But it's not like I can go back. And I already told him the others were dead.

He's still waiting for an answer.

"I've been near death ever since I found out I was one of the Pyros," I say, determined not to give anything away.

"That is true." He regards me, thoughtfully. "You're unusual, Leah."

I give a forced laugh. "Yeah, maybe because I'm the freaking Transcendent? In case you've forgotten that?"

"I don't think any of us have forgotten, Leah," he says softly. "Would you like to come with me? I have a much more comfortable room reserved for you."

"So you expect me to stay?"

"You're a fighter, Leah. You do what's necessary for your own survival. And wouldn't you like to see Cas again?"

He gives me an expectant look. *Like I'm going to fall on my knees and beg you.*

"Where are we?" I ask, instead.

"At my new base." He taps the stone wall. "Underground. You almost made it, you know, but it's well-hidden, and close to the divide. No one would dare come near here."

I blink. "You mean we're right next to… them?"

"In a manner of speaking. The divide is closed, as I'm sure you're already aware."

"And you're planning to open it." The words spill out before I can stop them. "You're planning to pit Cas and me against them, aren't you?"

He frowns. "I won't force you to do anything you don't want to, Leah. But the fact remains that the Fiordans are relentless. They *will* find a way to break through again, and this time, we have to be ready to face them. If not, I don't need to tell you what the consequences will be. You've seen it already."

The world burning. Death. Hideous monsters. Like my last dream.

I grit my teeth and glare at him. "Yeah. I seem to remember *you* were the one who caused some of it yourself."

"You weren't there, Leah," Jared says. "Why don't you let me show you my side of the story?"

I want to shake my head, want to run, but the two guards holding me make that impossible. "*Show* me?"

"You'll see, Leah, if you let me. Guards, bring her to my quarters."

"Are you sure?"

It's the first time one of the guards has spoken, and something about his voice doesn't sound right. It's too low-pitched and growl-like to be a regular person's, and images of the experiments from Cas's visions come flashing back.

"Leah, give me the chance to show you what we fight for."

In spite of everything, I can't help feeling a twinge of curiosity about what *he* thinks happened. He might be a crazy psychopath, but he and Murray were on the same side, once. Maybe I can get clues about what happened two years ago that Murray didn't tell me. There was an awful lot he didn't want me to know, that much is obvious.

The guards frog-march me through the corridor. Definitely like a cave, even with the tiled floors and painted stone walls. Fluorescent lights on the ceiling illuminate every corner. I try to get a good look at the guards. They're dressed in black, and their hoods are pulled up so it's hard to make out their faces, at least without not looking where I'm walking. Soon enough, we come to another corridor lined with doors, and I'm strongly reminded of the old Pyro headquarters, except underground.

Several more corridors later, we enter an area where the walls are painted white and the floor's roughly tiled in an approximation of the Pyro HQ. Jared leads the way through a metal door and into a dimly lit room with actual furniture —a plush black sofa, several chairs, a bookshelf in the corner —and a television on a wooden table. An old, blocky TV with a VCR.

I don't know what I expected the quarters of a madman to look like—severed heads mounted on the walls, maybe?—

but it's so plain and ordinary. I stare, especially at the television set and the low table in front of the sofa, littered with car magazines, and even a remote control. I don't realise my mouth's slightly open until Jared turns and gives me a smile.

"Not what you expected, hmm?"

"You—you live *here?*"

"Where did you expect me to live? Inside a volcano?" He laughs, a touch too loud to be entirely comfortable. I want to back away, but my arms are pinned to my sides.

Apparently realising this, he says, "Guards, you can go."

And they let go. My upper arms are slightly numb, and I turn quickly to get a proper look at them. One's hood's fallen back slightly and what I see underneath makes my stomach turn. His skin's been sewn together, but there are different patches of slightly different colours, some pale, some dark, others red.

They're experiments. That explains their unnatural strength.

"Leah?" Jared beckons to me. I tense up, less-than-eager to follow him into his supervillain lair.

"I promised not to hurt you," he says. "See? You're not restrained. You're free to walk around as you like."

Not if you're planning to cut me up. But he needs the Transcendent in one piece, right? I can't trust him for a heartbeat, but I need to be here. Cas needs me to be here.

"You said *show* me," I say, gesturing at the room. "Show me what?"

"This." He walks over to the television, leaving me hovering in the doorway, and holds up an old video tape. "I think this is the one."

I raise my eyebrows.

"This is an instructive video we used to show to recruits."

"And it still works?"

"My colleagues and I appropriated fiend technology," he

says. "Believe it or not, they were as advanced a race as we once were, the Fiordans. Too bad it turned out like this for both of us, but we've adapted with the times." He inserts the tape into the VCR.

Despite the warning nagging at the back of my mind, I walk over to the TV as the screen lights up. Holy crap. It's working. Then again, I suppose Murray did have a working PC in his office.

"Come and sit down, Leah. I promise you it's comfortable."

I walk forward a few more steps, but don't sit. Jared hits a button and fast-forwards the video. The screen shows an all-too familiar sight.

7

A burning red sky. Ground, cracked open by a rift wider than a house. And monsters crawling out of the gap. My nails bite into my palms.

The fiends are crawling out, knocking people aside—yes, there are people everywhere.

But something about them doesn't look right. The way they move—fiends don't move like that. And, now I see close up, the people don't look right either.

"That's CGI," I say. An idea long-forgotten, in this world. "You made that using a computer, right?"

"My brother did. It was exceedingly difficult to capture live footage, before... recent events." He skips the video forward, then hits the play button. Now, the screen shows an above-shot of the Earth. Our planet.

An overhead voice comes on. "This is our world, as it is now. The only world most people know about." The camera zooms in, the scene changing to the image of a field. Grass, blowing in the wind under an honest-to-God *blue* sky.

"But there are others who wish to take it from us. Others

who cloak themselves in our skin, but are no more human than an alien life form."

I stifle the urge to laugh. This is bizarrely like a movie voice-over.

"Aliens," the voice repeats. "Walking amongst us, seemingly harmless. You might have known one once. Talked to one. Made friends with one."

Now, the video is showing a busy shopping centre, packed out with people. All kinds of people, carrying shopping, small children. Images as alien as the fiends.

"But they are not like us. And they are dangerous."

Despite the eye-rolling dramatics, a shiver runs down my spine as the scene darkens, and a figure dressed in a red coat passes in front of the camera.

"Our job is to find them, hunt them down, before they can cause harm. You may wonder what aliens want with humans, why they would hide themselves rather than revealing themselves outright. Some might say they want to escape persecution. Humans, as a whole, are not accepting of those they deem to be outsiders. But these particular outsiders are waging a war against us even as we speak."

Now, the camera's showing what looks like actual video footage, the poor-quality black-and-white images of a CCTV camera. It shows a road between fields and a ramshackle hut sitting at the roadside. A car drives past, and comes to a stop. Someone gets out. The camera's too distant to see anything distinct about them. But even I can't miss the moment when they vanish into thin air.

"They have unnatural powers," says the voice. "For a hundred years, our organisation has struggled to pull together information on our uninvited guests. But through rumours and eyewitnesses, we learned that they are, indeed, not from here."

On cue, three figures appear where the first one vanished.

Again, I can't make out anything about them, but they leave an odd ripple effect behind them, barely visible on the poor-quality video. The three of them get into the car, and drive away.

The air shimmers, the ground shifting, grass blowing in an invisible breeze. Without warning, all the grass in the field vanishes as though sucked into a void. The small hut moves, walls falling apart either side, quivering, coming apart molecule by molecule. The sound's gone, but I've seen enough buildings collapse to be able to fill in the gaps. Within a few seconds, nothing remains.

"They leave a trail of destruction wherever they walk, and it's getting harder to hide their traces." The voice drops dramatically. "This must end. They have waged a secret war against us for more than a century. Our realities are close to colliding."

The planet Earth fills the screen again.

"Every day we hear more rumours. People with unnatural powers. Strange sightings. It's our job to follow these rumours, and eliminate them. We can't allow them to expose us. Because if you're watching this video, you have some power of your own. Maybe you've always been aware of it. Maybe you're confused, or frightened. There is no reason to be afraid, because we are here to help you."

An image of a red coat, with a familiar symbol embossed over the heart.

A flame. Jared's tattoo symbol.

"We are the Pyros. You have been invited to join us. We will train you in the arts of combat, teach you to unlock your powers." A video image of a hall, like a school gym, full of teenagers engaged in the same training exercises we did back at the base. A sudden, unexpected jolt of homesickness goes through me.

"You will learn to fight them. Because we may have only

seen a glimpse of the horrors on the other side, our ancestors have seen it first-hand."

The scene changes to an old piece of parchment, faded and yellowing. A drawing of a twisted monster is scrawled in black ink. Even though it's rough and faded, it can only be one of the fiends.

"Most of the evidence is with us. Why? We don't want regular people to know about us. Our powers are not so different from our enemies'. We would be shunned, forced into hiding. Already, we live in secret communities. There is no place for us in regular life. If you are here to join, you will have experienced some of this already. You will be unnaturally strong and fast, and be able to endure more damage than any regular human. This is not anything to be ashamed of. Now you know our place in the scheme of things. Our organisation was formed to learn more about them, but when they turned hostile, we had no choice but to intervene. Through this, we have learned much about them."

Now, the scene shows a laboratory, through a grainy camera lens. I recognise it from my visions of Cas's past—and from when we actually went there. The old lab.

"Thousands of years ago, a rift was opened between our worlds. The Fiordans decimated their own world, and ever since, these smaller rifts have been enabling them to get through into our world, to invade us. We are gifted with fire for a reason. We are humanity's avenging angels. Time and again, we have protected humans from the Fiordans, and so it continues, and will always continue, until our enemies are vanquished."

The video cuts out. Jared looks at me expectantly.

"Well?"

"Well what?" I say, folding my arms. "That was a propaganda video for your group, right? Not like it told me anything. Avenging angels?"

I admit, it's odd that Jared's symbol once belonged to the group as a whole. But he could have told me that already.

"We were once united," says Jared. "All of us. Pyros against the Fiordans. Why can it not be the same again?"

"Because of what you did." The experiments. The tattoos. Cas. Does he really think a stupid propaganda video will change my mind?

"I see you're going to take some convincing." Jared sighs and pauses the video. "I will take you to him."

My heart flips, and I have to force my expression to remain neutral. *It must be a trick. He wouldn't...* but I can't help thinking of Cas in my last vision. *He's alive. He's really alive.*

"Nothing to say?"

He's searching for weakness again. I meet his stare evenly, though my mind's racing. What has he done to Cas? What state is he in after being stuck here for days, with a madman who can torture him on a whim?

"Cas is in training with the others at the moment, I believe, but if you like, I can show you to the room you'll be staying in, as my guest. You can shower and change, and I'll send someone to call you when the others come back, okay?"

Yeah, like he's offering me a choice. But I can't turn down the offer of a shower and change of clothes, as much as it makes my skin crawl to be dependent on him in any way. Perhaps if I go along with it, I'll have the chance to talk to Cas alone. Tell him I know how to remove the tattoo. Then we can get out of here.

I just nod, and he directs me out of the room and into the corridor again. Two guards have appeared outside the door as if he somehow called them without making a noise. *Probably did,* I think, remembering how the tattoos can affect people from a distance.

I half-expect Jared's assigned me the crappiest room, but it turns out to be pretty nice, as far as underground bunkers go. Small, but cosy. A single bed and table are the only furniture, but there's an en-suite bathroom at the back with a real working shower.

Jared leaves me in peace, but the guards remain outside the door, probably to stop me running off. I might as well make the most of this. A clean, plain black outfit lies across the bed, along with a couple of towels. I take my time showering, but never quite relax, knowing the guards are waiting outside—and, of course, I'm in enemy territory. Still, I feel slightly clearer-headed, and warm, clean clothes are a blessing I'm not quite used to after two years living on the road.

Strange how time passes. Two years after civilisation ended and it's like it's always been this way. Seeing that video... I can't wrap my head around it. Murray *told* me the Pyros had been fighting the fiends for longer than most people knew, but I never really thought about it before. The first fifteen years of my life were about as ordinary as you can get. School. Friends. Dating—well, okay, I didn't have too much luck with that. But I had a life. I had a future which didn't revolve around survival, or fighting monsters. I sure as hell didn't believe in aliens or anything like that. They walked among us. I laugh, shaking my head at the absurdity of all this. Then I stop, peering through the gap in the door. Guards outside. They haven't responded. Probably programmed by Jared. Like robots.

My flesh creeps at the thought. I see a black coat like Jared's hanging on a hook behind the door. I think I'd rather freeze than wear the same uniform as his minions.

After a couple of minutes, the door opens. One of the guards beckons to me, and I know he's going to take me to Cas. My heart starts beating faster. *I have to see him. I have to know he's all right.*

The two guards flank me, walking slightly ahead to lead

the way. I wish I had a better memory. I've already forgotten the way back to Jared's room, which might have come in handy if I decided to murder him during the night. I haven't seen any sign of a way out, either. Worrying. Still, Cas's been here longer. Maybe he can tell me. No way would he take Jared's dominance lying down, even under threat.

Finally, we round the corner and come to another corridor with two doors at the end, flung open wide. A training hall, filled with... Pyros.

I stare, open-mouthed. I hadn't imagined there would be so many of them. Possibly even as many as Murray's group. The guards lead me right up to the door, standing either side like bodyguards. I turn from one Pyro to the next. None are familiar, except...

There he is. At the back of the room, facing a row of dummies. Though he's facing the other way, no one else moves quite like that, decapitating the dummies as though they mortally offended him. His dark hair gleams like a polished black stone under the bright lights, and he's dressed in the same black outfit as everyone here.

Suddenly, I'm mute. It's stupid. I have the chance to go and talk to him and yet I can't even call out his name. It'd sound idiotic, anyway, and I'm sure Jared's watching from somewhere. The guards are bad enough.

I step forward, pushing my embarrassment aside. *Pull yourself together.* A few of the other Pyros glance up curiously as I walk between them, keeping at enough distance to not get in the way of their sparring matches. When I'm a metre away from Cas, he turns around. Like he can sense I'm there.

And he gives me his most unfriendly, antisocial look. "You," he says, without emotion.

What? My jaw drops as my heart plunges in my chest. He's looking at me like I'm a stranger.

"Excuse me?"

"What do you want?" he says, swapping his weapon hand. There's a flash of black on his wrist. The new mark Jared put on him.

A horrible suspicion rears its head. Is Jared controlling him? Is that why he let me come and talk to Cas, knowing it wouldn't do any good anyway?

But he seemed in his own mind in my visions...

I swallow. "I came to find you," I say, conscious of the others listening in. "Guess I'm a new recruit."

"Good for you."

A pause. "Not got anything to say?"

"Guess not," says Cas, turning back to the dummies.

I expect to hear someone laugh, but there's silence. The others continue to practise fighting. Cold fear washes over me. They could be spies. We can't talk here. Cas doesn't look at me, giving no clues about whether he's thinking the same. *He's not Jared's. He can't be.*

"Have fun, then," I say, and turn my back, leaving the hall with as much dignity as I can muster.

8

I spend the rest of the day in my room, thinking hard. Every time to leave, my path's blocked by a guard, and I honestly can't find the energy to fight. I came here to find Cas. I never should have walked right up to him in front of everyone. I need to get him alone. *Idiot.* I was so relieved to find him alive, but with Jared's spies on every corner, we'll be lucky to have a conversation without being caught.

Guilt over Nolan stabs at me, and I can't help thinking of the rest of the group, vulnerable to Jared's manipulations. Even if Jared leaves them alone, the regular fiends apparently aren't scared to go near headquarters anymore. It's not like I have a way to contact them from here. Murray never had a phone, even if Jared does.

I let everyone down.

Moping won't do any good, so I start running through training exercises, always keeping an eye on the door. A guard brings me food at one point, a sloppy kind of stew which has nothing on the food at headquarters. It's probably all I'm getting. I'm good at imagining I'm eating delicious home cooking instead of road kill, anyway.

Time passes.

It's starting to drive me mad not knowing what time of day it is. Obviously, there's no sunlight, and no clocks, either. I'm not tired, but I rarely have been recently, certainly not since finding out I was Transcendent. Sleep is an option. And I want to be on my guard.

I miss my dagger. Not just because it'd offer me some kind of defence, but the weapon was bonded to me. I feel its absence in a way I never expected. I pretend it's in my hand, mime fighting a fiend. An engineered one, with wings. I can't believe I let those get the best of me like that.

If I'm to take down Jared, I'll have to learn to fight them.

But is it what I want? To fight him *and* the fiends? It's too much for one person to cope with. Especially as I didn't know I was anything special until a few weeks ago. Fighting for humanity is one thing, but fighting another human isn't something I ever expected to do. The other Pyros are essentially human compared to me. People who chose his side.

He didn't even mention that I stabbed him before. Like I could ever not be suspicious of this situation.

But Cas is here. He's the reason I left headquarters, and the reason Nolan died. There's no way he's under Jared's spell. He must have been putting on an act.

I have to get him alone.

———

Another day passes before Jared comes to see me again. The guards bring me food at intervals and occasionally swap places with others. Guess they can't stand out there indefinitely. The real question is, what *are* they? Human, or fiend, or lab-grown monstrosities? Is there no depth to which Jared won't sink?

Stupid question.

I nearly jump out my skin when I glance up from contemplating a crack in the wall and see Jared standing beside the door. He gives me his usual insincere smile, and walks in, handing me something. My dagger. He's giving me my weapon back?

"Don't give me that look," he says. "I'm not tricking you, Leah. You're a Pyro. You and your weapon are bonded. You're only half a person without it."

What's he saying? I turn the dagger over, somewhat comforted by its familiar weight, but the memory of sticking it in Jared's chest rushes back without warning. I meet his eyes then turn away, convinced he's thinking the same.

"Well? Are you ready to come to the training hall?"

"You're going to train me?"

Jared laughs. "You won't be much use sitting in your room, will you? Come and meet the other novices. You might even make a friend."

I don't want to make friends with Jared's minions. Where'd he even recruit them from? Are they all traitors, or has he been seeking out new Pyros, like Murray was, and brainwashing them?

Cas isn't in the training hall. Undaunted, I take my dagger and practise a few moves on the dummies. I sever imaginary heads and deal fatal blows, the dagger whistling through the air, and it's some minutes before I notice several people are watching me.

A rush of deja-vu laced with unexpected homesickness hits me. I hadn't realised I was quite so attached to the Pyros, but I guess living with them was the closest thing to stability I had in two years.

I leave the training hall without talking to anyone, ignoring their stares. This is a waste of time. I could be fighting the fiends for real. I haven't thought this through at all. Why did I let myself fall onto Jared's mercy? I almost want to attack him again, just to get a reaction. He's been entirely too calm and rational lately for an evil psychopath.

Preoccupied with my own thoughts, I walk through the corridor, deliberately getting myself lost. Maybe I'll run into something interesting. A clue. I absently spin the dagger in my hand, admiring the way it gleams bronze-red under the lights.

"You could take someone's eye out with that, you know."

I stop. "Cas."

He's hovering outside a door, in the kind of semi-casual way that suggests he's not supposed to be here.

"What's in there?" I ask, indicating the door.

"Memories," he says, cryptically. "What are you doing down here? Does Jared know you gave him the slip?"

"He left me in the training hall," I say, with a shrug. "I figured that gave me licence to go wherever I wanted to."

"He left you," Cas repeats, frowning.

"Yes," I say, slowly, glancing at the other doors to make sure we're definitely alone. "Apparently he's not concerned I might make a run for it. Any reason that might be? I mean, does he have fiends guarding the way out?"

"You've not seen?" Cas lifts an eyebrow. "Damn. You really don't know what you've wandered into, do you?"

A time warp, I want to say. *Or an alternative dimension.* Something. Cas is acting like he did when we first met, and I'm not exactly keen on being alone down here with him. Especially when I catch sight of the red-black mark peeking from his left sleeve. But he's not under Jared's control. He can't be.

"Come on," I say. "We don't need to put on this stupid act. He's not here."

"Act?"

'Oh, don't be an idiot, Cas," I snap at him. "What, you expect me to believe you're Jared's lapdog now?" Catch me letting on that I almost did believe it for a minute back there.

"I could say the same to you," he says. "I can't believe you'd wander in here of your own accord. No one would be that stupid."

My jaw drops. "What the hell? I came to get you out, you ungrateful asshat."

There—I said it.

Cas blinks at me. No longer sardonic, no longer casual. Stunned? Confused? Angry?

"You came to get me out," he repeats.

"Yes, and I know how to stop that tattoo of yours from working." I press on. "Murray figured it out while we were gone. My blood counters it. If I use it on yours…"

"It won't work," he says.

"Not on the new one?"

Something flashes in his eyes. "Who said something about a new one?"

"I… saw it," I say, biting my lip. *Damn.* The visions—how much does he know about them?

"You saw it." He looks away, and I see a flash of something very different in his eyes this time.

Pain.

"Sorry," I say. "It's the best chance we've got. Can I at least try? My blood stopped Elle's mark from Nolan working."

"Thought Murray would have killed him."

Oh, crap.

"No. Um, he's dead, though." I don't meet his eyes. The lie, that Nolan and I were allies, hangs between us. Does Cas have any idea? How much do *his* visions show him? Damn connection.

"Anyway," I say, "Murray can stop it. *I* can stop it."

"How do you know it's the same for me? You know what I am."

"I'm sure," I say, more confidently than I actually feel. "You're a Pyro. Same as me."

"Not like you," he corrects me, and suddenly, he's turning away.

"Wait!" I say. "At least tell me where you're staying!"

"Two corridors from your room on the left, if you can find it," he tells me. "Not that Murray's guards would let us within ten feet of each other."

"Then talk to me now," I say. "Tell me what he's doing here. And what did you mean about something I've not seen? He's using the fiends again, right?"

"Using them... cloning them. Making hybrids." Cas shakes his head, disgusted. "Anyway, that's not why he thinks you'll agree to stay. This place—" He taps the wall—"it's literally next door to the divide. Next to them."

My blood runs cold. The divide, where the bridge opened. Exactly where I wanted to avoid. Crap.

"Jared built this place right next to them?" I whisper.

"It was built long before that. But we're near the original battlefield where the first breach opened. Jared stopped using this place when the divide appeared, but I guess there wasn't much choice after the other place was destroyed."

"An energy blast," I say. "It got hit by an energy blast."

"Did it? I haven't been back." He frowns. "That explains all the new recruits."

"Huh?"

"A bunch of new people signed up in the last few days. Some of them used to be scientists at the old place."

"So... they're new Pyros?" *That happened fast.* But of course, that's exactly how it happened for me, too. Normal one second, different the next.

Cas's raised eyebrow tells me he's thinking the exact same.

"All right," I say. "So how big is this army of his?"

"Not big enough to win," he says. "At least, not against one of their leaders."

"Leaders." God, I have to tell him. "I think I killed one of them already. Over the divide."

Cas starts to speak, then stops, gaping at me. For the second time ever, I have rendered Cas speechless.

"That's what happened after—after I left." I swallow, the word *you* hanging unsaid between us. "I got attacked by that giant fiend again, and there was another one. On the bridge. And—"

"Jared was there," Cas says, quietly. "But it wasn't really him."

My heart skips a beat. "You saw it?"

He bows his head. "I didn't know if it was real. I was half-conscious, totally out of it, and I thought I was hallucinating. Never seen one of their shape-shifters before. Plus, no one's survived crossing over the divide—except I guess Jared did."

"Yeah, about that," I say. "He should be dead. I stabbed him."

His face twists. "Yeah. He used fiend DNA, the sneaky bastard. I almost hoped he'd used *my* blood…" He breaks off, looking away from me as if ashamed.

"Damn," I say, shaking off the implication—that both of us know I'm doomed, thanks to his blood running in my veins. "So he's unkillable?"

"No, just hard to kill as the fiends."

"So I could do it with my powers," I say, thinking of the way I controlled the waves of the energy blast and destroyed the fiends' leader—obliterated him. Like I could do to anyone. Human or fiend. But *how* I did it… I still need to know. Damn. I called the fire when I fought Jared's fiends the last time, but that had nothing on the frisson of energy that exploded through me when I beat the Fiordan. I can't begin to think of how I accessed that. But it'd sure come in handy right now.

You're willing to risk everyone else's lives? a voice in my head asks. Because the others won't be spared, either. Am I heartless enough to kill everyone else to be rid of Jared, even if they've been brainwashed?

"You've used them?"

I glance over my shoulder. "You didn't see me kill the Fiordan?"

Cas's eyes widen. "No. The vision cut out. I didn't think anyone *could.*"

"Except the Transcendent?"

Cas doesn't respond, and the silence feels oddly cold. Of course. He knew the last Transcendent. He was supposed to protect her, but Jared betrayed everyone. I still don't know what exactly happened, but right now isn't the time for a discussion. I can't read his expression. Would *he* sacrifice everyone else? He saw the rest of Murray's group as expendable, after all. The only time I've ever seen him express any kind of feeling for someone else...

Is with me.

I push the thought aside. Like it'll help us now.

I shake my head violently. "I can't use the power here," I say. "We can't guarantee everyone else was brainwashed, right? Some might be clueless as I was when I first joined Murray."

"Well, not quite that clueless."

I gawp, until I realise he's attempting to defuse the tension thick in the air.

"Ha ha," I say. "So, mass homicide aside, I don't suppose you know any other sure-fire way to get rid of the bastard? Short of throwing him in the divide?"

"Never thought of that one,' he says. 'But you'd have to get him aboveground first, and that's not happening anytime soon. The energy blasts," he adds in explanation. "The fiends' last attack triggered a bunch of them over the divide. They're drawing the regular fiends like flies. Even Jared doesn't have a big enough army to fight all of them."

The sheer enormity of the task weighs down on me. "Does Jared really think we can win? Against the fiends?"

"He's close," says Cas. "Closer than Murray was, even, seeing as he has all these engineered monsters at the ready. But it doesn't mean he's ready to face their leaders."

"There's more than one," I whisper. "How—how many?"

Cas shrugs. "He doesn't tell me that much, believe it or not—despite my supposedly being his most *valuable* soldier. I'd say at least three or four. And they'll be seriously pissed you killed one of them."

"Great, another enemy." I shake my head. "I just want to know what Jared's planning to do with me. It feels *wrong*. He's acting like I'm his honoured guest or something."

The tension inside me eases slightly as I voice my thoughts aloud.

"You *are* his honoured guest," Cas points out. "You're the Transcendent."

"So everyone keeps telling me." A shiver dances down my spine. "That doesn't mean I can win the war for him." Of course, there's no other reason he'd treat me as a guest after I stuck my dagger in his chest.

Though… speaking of which. "He's letting me walk around with a weapon," I say, holding it up. "Has he booby-trapped it or something?"

"Let me see." Cas takes the knife from me. "No. Doesn't look damaged to me. So he really thinks you won't turn on him. That, or he's planning to use another incentive."

"He showed me this old propaganda video," I say. "He seemed convinced it'd make me want to stay, but I don't see it. Might have worked on recruits a few years ago, but after what he did? How can he expect me to trust him?"

"I've no idea." He hands me the dagger again. Our hands brush against each other for a brief second, but there's nothing. No pain.

Come to think of it... I haven't had any visions since coming here. Is it because we're in the same place now?

I can't help my gaze drifting to the livid mark on his hand. "Let me help," I say. "At least give me a chance to stop it."

I take his hand in mine, raising my dagger to cut my own skin. *My blood can stop it...*

Without warning, he jerks his hand away. "You're awfully keen to mutilate yourself, aren't you?" The words come out from between clenched teeth.

My heart drops a notch. "What?" *Oh, God, the vision.* "That was an accident. A fiend attacked me on the way out. I didn't realise it'd affect you."

His eyes harden. "I cut myself on my own blade."

"That's not what you told Jared."

"How much did you see?" he demands, hands curling into fists. "Have you been watching me this whole time? And you only show up now?"

"What the hell are you talking about?" I retaliate—then lower my voice, realising we're both shouting. "I thought you'd given yourself up for dead. You won't even let me *try* to save you! It's not like I want to spy on you all the time. Bloody inconvenient, actually."

"Yeah, you could say that," says Cas, and without warning, he punches the wall, leaving a fist-sized hole. "Inconvenient enough to die for."

I feel hollow, like a gaping pit is opening inside me. To die for. He's not referring to me risking my life, but to what Jared said the last time. After the visions started for the other people Cas was forced to heal, they died within weeks. This connection is killing me. Literally. "Then let me help." My voice comes out in a croak. "There must be a lab down here, right? Jared will have research on this kind of thing. He doesn't want to lose his Transcendent, right? I'll figure it out."

"You don't know the first thing about it." Cas stares into the hole in the wall. "Neither of us do. He got the technology from the fiends. You know that little propaganda piece of his, about how the fiends stealing our technology? He used to do the same thing, sending people over to steal fiend technology and blood samples. Half of them never came back, of course. The other half brought him what he needed."

What? It shouldn't surprise me. Nothing about Jared should surprise me anymore.

"So you did watch it," I say.

"I've seen that crap before," he says. "There are dozens of them. How he persuaded eager young people to sign up to be his soldiers. Most didn't have the privilege of being born into it, after all."

"That's not…" I wish I knew what to say, wish I could somehow make it better. But all I can do is listen.

"Whatever," he says. "There's no point to the video now, I don't know why he bothered showing you. He has more efficient ways to get people to obey him, and it's too late for him to brainwash you."

I rub my arms as a chill rises. What *is* Jared planning? "Has he said anything about what happened to him after the battle last time? Has he been hiding the whole time?" Even though I wasn't there, I can't get it out of my head. Jared disappeared, over the divide. Yet he came back. Survived. Made himself indestructible, even.

"You might have better luck getting answers out of him than me," says Cas. "No, he hasn't talked about it. I'm guessing he slunk away to hide out here for a bit. Touched in the head after losing the Transcendent. Not that he wasn't a twisted bastard before anyway..."

"I just wondered about the fiends. Why the divide opened again. Did Jared provoke them?"

"Got it in one," says Cas. "He had his engineered fiends running around the divide, and I guess it was too much for them."

"But... that makes no sense. I thought they'd been coming here for years." The video. The figures stepping out of thin air. Through a gateway? Or something else?

"Yeah, there's the little white lie Murray told us," he says. "The Fiordans were always able to cross over. They never managed it en masse until they set up the bridge."

My gaze snaps onto him. "No way."

The image of the battlefield I saw in my vision, through Cas's eyes, fills my head. The army gathering at the edge of the divide...

"Yeah," says Cas. "He may have omitted that little piece of information."

"*Why?*" I say. "What harm is there in telling the truth? What if it happened again?"

"It is," says Cas. "Jared was the one who kept provoking them, but Murray covered for him every time. Until it was too late."

I shake my head. "How did they open the door, then?"

"Amassed energy," said Cas. "Don't ask me. Did you pay any attention in classes?"

"I never went to class," I mutter, leaning my head against the wall. I feel so misguidedly angry, even though only I'm to blame for wanting to jump straight into the fight, without finding out *what* exactly I was fighting first.

"It means if they opened a bridge, they're probably preparing to open another," says Cas. "Maybe more. See why we need to kill their leaders? They'll do it again. Whether it takes a day or a year."

A year. The idea of spending any longer down here, even a day... *No. I won't do it. I'll get answers one way or another.*

"Tell me where the labs are," I say.

"Huh?"

"I'm serious. Tell me where I can find Jared's research."

"What's the point? You know what he's researching."

"Er, no, I don't," I say. "Fiend experiments, yeah, but not what he did to me."

"If you value your own life," says Cas. "You won't go poking around. Jared doesn't forgive, but he let you in here even though you tried to kill him. He thinks you can defeat the Fiordans."

No way. That can't be it. Jared knows the link between Cas and I will kill me eventually. He *must* have another plan. If he thought I'd willingly cooperate, surely he'd at least do his best to make sure I won't keel over and die on the battlefield. He wouldn't put faith in me, and he can't control me. So what's his game?

"I'm not fighting for *him*," I say. "Did Cas die and leave a cowardly replacement behind? You're seriously letting him take control? Or is it just your lab-soldier issues talking?"

Cas's fist rises, and I brace myself for pain. But he lets it fall to his side. No fight.

I brush past him, my heart sinking as I realise Cas has no intention of being rescued, and now we're in an even worse bind than we already were. Forget Cas. I have to get out of here.

9

I've stormed through five corridors before I admit to myself that I'm lost. There's no one around, making me wonder if I've trespassed somewhere out of bounds. Or maybe gone somewhere that's no longer in use. The few doors I come across lead into bare, empty rooms, more cave-like than anything. Nothing sinister or even remotely interesting. Some contain beds, furniture, like my room. Maybe there were once hundreds of people living here. That idea makes more sense than these rooms being abandoned.

Or perhaps it was intended to be a shelter, in case the fiends invaded. Before Murray found out how twisted his brother was, and took the rest of the Pyros to the mountain.

God, I wish I was back there now. I'd rather have Cas act like he did back then than act like he's given up. My chest aches as if his words physically hurt me. *Inconvenient enough to die for.*

I never asked how many other Pyros died after being healed with his blood, too. I'm just another one. But he's made the mistake of getting to know me. Maybe that's why he can hardly bear to look me in the eyes now.

I walk, wishing I could shut off my thoughts. Cas isn't Jared's, but he may as well be. There's no one else here I can trust. I'll have to find a way out myself.

I don't have time for this.

Frustrated, I break into a run, my feet slapping the earthen floor. I want to breathe the air again, even if it's tainted with the smell of burning, even though the sky is horribly, horribly wrong.

The fiends ruined our world.

Like my thoughts are a trigger, the cry of a fiend echoes from up ahead, raising the hairs on my arms. I grip my dagger tightly, feeling the same odd tugging sensation under my skin as before. I'm more than ready for a fight.

I walk stealthily towards the corridor's end and around a corner, mentally bracing myself. One step after another. Turn the corner.

Barred doors greet my eyes, lining the corridor on both sides. It doesn't take a genius to figure out what's behind them.

It's so quiet, but I can hear living things shuffling about behind the doors. I walk right up to the nearest, a reckless-ness springing to the surface. I could break the door down, throw myself into a real battle. I could even set them free. Flush Jared and his minions out into the open. Force Cas to come with me and re-join the Pyros so we can take Jared down.

A scraping, like something being dragged across the ground. A low-pitched growl. I imagine hot breath on my hands, claws scratching at the door.

"Come on," I mutter through the door. "Come and get me."

A faint growl. *Did it hear?* I wonder, and then laugh at myself. "Of course you can hear," I say. "But you don't care, do you? You don't understand human speech. You're a thick-skulled, empty-headed monster. You don't know about a thing except killing, and killing some more. And crushing everything in your path."

A faint cough.

"What's Jared doing to you in there, I wonder? Taking your DNA? Bleeding you dry, to make more monsters?"

My dagger goes hot. I lift the blade up and see that it's glowing slightly, like burning coals.

Like it's reacting to something.

A faint noise on the other side of the door. I pull away, remembering the time a fiend touched me, awakening me as a Transcendent. *Idiot.* Like freeing them would do anything other than cost lives. Jared wouldn't die. The bastard would sacrifice anyone to spare his own life.

"Tran—scen—dent."

I freeze. The voice is garbled, barely recognisable as English—but it came from the other side of the door.

I've heard Jared's fiends speak before. But how can it know who I am, if it can't even see me?

This is beyond creepy.

I hesitate, torn between caution and curiosity.

"Tran—scen—dent."

A thudding noise like something heavy hitting a wall.

Oh, hell. Is it trying to break out?

Thud.

I back away from the door. The fiend must be restrained somehow, or it'd have smashed through the wall already. I don't want to stick around and find out if that's true.

The desire to fight has gone. Now I'm creeped out. I take a few steps down the corridor, past more doors, and stop as I see one that's open.

It's a laboratory. The glass cases speak for themselves. Despite the prickling at the back of my neck, I lean my head around the door. No one's in there, but it's clearly in use.

There are weapons in some of the cases, racks of test tubes full of blood, and…

I recoil, hand over my mouth. A fiend's *arm* is in one of the cases, hooked up to some kind of machine. The skin gleams dark red, and the fingers twitch slightly.

More evidence of Jared's depravity. Feeling sick, I back away towards the door.

And slam right into Jared.

"Dear me, Leah, I thought you weren't going to cause me trouble."

Heart beating fast, I turn to face him. The corners of his mouth are turned down in disappointment. My nerves shake with adrenaline.

"What were you hoping to find?" he inquires. Hand resting on my shoulder.

"I don't know."

'Perhaps the means of freeing your friend?'

My heart beats loudly, and I'm sure he can hear it, too. I don't answer, though.

"I'm afraid I must disappoint you, Leah," he says. "There is no escape for him. He has belonged to me since I gave him life."

"He's a person," I say, hardly believing what I'm hearing. "He doesn't belong to you, or anyone else. You've no right to do that to him."

"No right? Rights don't exist. Which side are you on, Leah? Those who killed your family and destroyed our world —or those who would win this war?"

"That has nothing to do with it!" I say. "Nothing. You don't have to mark Cas to make him fight the fiends. This is about you wanting control over everything that crosses your path."

"When the time is right, you will both lead my army to war," Jared tells me, no longer wearing the expression of false kindness. "I offered you the chance to walk away, Leah. Now it's time for you, too, to bear my mark."

"Oh no." I back away. "No freaking way am I letting you tattoo me."

Jared sighs, and reaches for something lying on the desk. A needle gun.

Horror uncoils inside me.

"It'll be quick, Leah. That, I can promise."

I raise my dagger, heat rushing through me. *Kill him.* This time, I'm going to make damn well sure he doesn't come back to life.

"Leah, I wouldn't do anything you'll regret. If you use your Transcendent powers, Cas will die, and so will two hundred innocents."

He's trying to put me off. And it's working.

"One last chance for a peaceful surrender?"

"Hell no." Fire ignites around me.

Jared lunges forward, quick as a flash. I dodge to the right and stab wildly with the dagger, but he's too fast. The tattoo gun grazes my arm, but not enough to draw blood.

The enclosed space doesn't make it easy to move around, and I'm backed against a wall. But I'm fast, too. I strike first, leaping at him with a cry that hardly sounds like me. He moves to the right, stabbing with the tattoo gun, but I've already moved out of the way. A spray of blood tells me I caught his wrist with the dagger's edge.

Cursing, he grabs at me, his other hand closing around my left wrist and forcing it upwards. *No. Stop. No.* The tattoo gun moves towards my exposed skin. I kick at his right leg, and he misses. Too close.

I jerk back, but his grip is like iron. I counter the tattoo gun, striking it with the side of my blade, and his eyes widen.

Part of the gun falls away, cut cleanly in two. Fire

consumes it and he lets the other half fall to the ground, eyes narrowing.

"Ha." I kick at him again, and he drops my wrist, knocking me off-balance.

He moves back and grabs a syringe. He's planning to sedate me? He goes for my arm again, and I duck, holding my left arm close to my chest and stabbing at him with the dagger. Fiery light flares, and a sheaf of papers on the desk ignites.

I kick him towards the flames. My feet are like solid concrete, but he's a Pyro, too. Without my Transcendent power, we're evenly matched.

"You shouldn't have lied to me, Leah," he says softly. "I admire your nerve, but my brother is alive, and so are your friends. Don't think I've forgotten about them."

He stabs at me with the syringe. Too slow. I catch his arm in my left hand and force it away, giving it everything I have. *I won't let him hurt the others, not again.*

This time, I won't hold back.

My wrist screams. I move the dagger and aim for his heart.

Jared dodges, and I catch him in the arm instead. My dagger digs through skin and flesh and bone, and his body goes slack when my blade comes out the other side.

I've stabbed him right through the arm, which lights up along with the blade, incandescent, golden-red.

Then the dagger comes away in my hand, and I fall back, gasping.

Jared's severed hand lies a few feet away from his body.

He falls back, mouth open in a silent scream.

I don't move for a good minute. Then I drop alongside him. He's still. Completely still.

No heartbeat.

I back away, thinking of the guards. And Cas. I need to find him...

Dizziness rises within me and I stagger against the wall, the world tipping sideways. Light flashes across my vision, and white-hot pain pierces every part of my body. I'm barely aware that I'm falling before the darkness claims me.

———

I'm crying out in pain, but I'm not me. My left arm burns, and the agony radiates throughout my body. Like a branding iron has been placed on my arm, turning me into a creature incapable of sense, of reason, only pain and the desperation for it to end. I can't see or hear anything. I'm reduced to the barest minimum.

Piece by piece, the world comes back, remaking itself, like a jigsaw of sensations and noises and impressions. Images come into my mind, separate from the pain. Jared falling to the ground, cradling his stump of a wrist. Cas falling, screaming in pain.

A metallic taste in my mouth. Something wet and sticky dripping onto my leg. My eyes flicker open a fraction. I'm still holding the dagger, and I'm covered in Jared's blood. I'm still in the lab. But Jared isn't here anymore.

A choked cry escapes me and I scramble backwards, away from the blood soaking the floor. Did his guards take him away? *That can't be right. They'd have killed me.* Surely. But wait— Jared had them under his control. Does that mean they're free?

I can't have killed him that easily. He survived me stabbing him once before. And what about that vision? Cas, in agony again. Not the past, but right now. I think. In the vision, he stood in the corridor by the fiend cages. Where I was, only a few minutes ago. Did he follow me?

A sob rattles my chest like a monster trying to escape. *Pull yourself together! You can't stay here.*

Slowly, too, slowly, I push myself to my feet. I feel like Cas's pain sucked the energy out of me, and the world's barely staying the right way up. I'm shivering, too, even though my skin—not to mention the dagger—is burning hot.

Certainty grips me with every step. Cas is being tortured right now. I need to find him.

I stumble from the lab to find the corridor empty. No trace of blood. No sign Jared's been here.

Where is he?

I walk. My head throbs with each step, greeting me with another flash of pain. Every muscle screams at me to get a move on. But I've no idea where I'm going.

Without warning, the corridor darkens, and the sound of dripping water reaches me from the head. The ground grows softer under my feet, like I'm walking on earth, not stone. When the wall's suddenly not there anymore, and I'm standing in the middle of the unknown with nothing to support myself.

Arms wrapped around my chest, the dagger cold and damp with blood. Dried tears on my face. The walls here are stone, not plaster, and there are no more doors. Maybe I've reached the end of Jared's place. Maybe this is just regular caves.

Pain splinters through me again. I'm hardly aware that I've fallen to the chilled earth, that my head's dropped to my knees. I'm done fighting. The fire is out, and there's no light in this darkness.

10

I'm trapped behind glass. The room is bright, unbearably so; the world on the other side of the glass made of gleaming pieces. None of it makes any sense. I'm propped up on my feet, knees bent, arms dangling at my side but hooked up to some kind of machine. A machine made of metal and glass.

I feel like I'm drowning, like the water's surface is above my head but something holds me down, keeping me from a life-giving breath. I make a feeble movement of my arm. Nothing happens. Everything's blurred—I can't even recognise the person on the other side of the glass.

I can't even tell who *I* am. Not Leah. Leah's in the darkness, alone.

Cas is trapped with Jared. I have to wake up. I have to go back and save him. *Wake up!*

But the vivid, too-bright room becomes clearer, not fading away like my other visions.

The face on the other side of the glass comes into focus. It's not Jared. It's Cas. And he looks livid. Which means… I'm not seeing through Cas's eyes.

I'm me. A prisoner. Again.

But why's Cas here? I'd have thought Jared would have taken it out on him. Inflicted more horrible pain on him. Even killed him. I'm the indispensable one.

Which I'd guess is the only reason I'm alive.

I try to speak, but there's no air. A thousand questions scramble for attention, and from the expression on Cas's face, he can at least guess some of them. Even though he can't read my mind.

What the hell is he doing? I twist my head to see the machine beside me, though God only knows what it actually is. What it's pumping into my body. I feebly move my arm, but it barely shifts an inch. Damn. I'm stuck.

Cas glances over his shoulder, at a door in the periphery of my vision, walks right up to the glass. A quiver of betrayal goes through me, though I can't know for sure what the hell's even going on. Is Jared manipulating him? Seems likely.

Cas fiddles with something on my right, and the front wall of the glass springs open. I startle as oxygen floods my lungs. I hadn't realised Pyros don't even need to breathe, apparently. Or maybe it only applies to people like Cas and me.

I take a couple of breaths before I remember, again, that I *can't* die from asphyxiation. I choke and end up in a coughing spiral of hysterical laughter. Cas watches, one eyebrow slightly raised.

"What…" I try to say between coughs. "How—how did I get here?"

"I brought you here." His tone is flat. Emotionless. That mind connection would come in handy right about now.

"What… about Jared?" He can't be dead. If Cas is under his control or even putting on a show, it must mean he survived what I did to him.

"He wants you compliant." He indicates the machine.

"This is a combination of fiend's blood and Jared's own. The same thing he uses in the tattoos. It'll make you obey his every request. Fight at the head of his army. And, even if he killed me right in front of your eyes, you could never harm him again."

I lunge forward, trying to pull the tubes from my arms, but I'm still weak. Cas grabs my arm and pushes me back into the case, and my legs all but give out from under me.

What have they drugged me with?

"You can't. A hundred guards are on both sides of the corridor outside. You've no chance of getting out unharmed, and Jared will make things even harder on you."

"Jared." I cough, again. "That guy just won't die, huh?"

The slightest flicker of a smile. "Apparently not."

What's his game?

"So, that's it? I'm his everlasting servant, now? Same as you?"

"If you want things to be easier..." His voice drops to a whisper. "You'll need to be as convincing as possible. Act like he owns the earth. Like you're really, truly sorry for defying him. Like there's not a chance you'll avoid fighting his war for him."

My heart lifts slightly. "And he wants me to declare my undying love?" Cas is on my side, after all. Whatever's in the machine is harmless. He's working against Jared.

"Stay there," he says. "When he comes back, he'll question you. Answer like you've had a complete change of heart —if you do, things'll go the better for both of us. If we're lucky, he'll put you in training right away. I'll talk to you then."

He turns to go.

"Wait!" I say. "How did I get in here so fast?"

"Fast? It's been a day," he says. "He used our... connection to subdue you. Then he sent me to find you. You won't remember a thing, but the drug's wearing off if you can speak."

I shake my head, but it hurts. "I can't believe he wants me to fight for him after that."

"He can only fight one-handed now." His eyes gleam, almost amused. "Pity for him. Stay there, and be prepared to put on your best performance when he comes back."

He closes the glass case and disappears.

I stare after him. Nothing should surprise me by now, and I suppose Jared does need me for his army. Even if I did cut off his hand. He forgave me for stabbing him before, but this might be a step too far. Now he's decided to really bring out the guns. Or, the instant-obedience injection.

Good job I've got Cas on my side. The idea of bowing down to Jared makes me feel sick. His heart stopped beating, so how can he still be alive?

Damn. I really should have made a plan. If I can't kill Jared, the only option is for Cas and I to leave and find the other Pyros. The war's the important part.

But where did I end up? That dark tunnel wasn't part of Jared's hideout.

I make a mental note to ask Cas the way out, next time I see him. I hope he knows what he's doing.

Then Jared walks into view and makes all other thoughts seem insignificant.

My heart contracts, and I almost shrink back. I'm not ready. I let my head fall to my chest, so I don't have to look him in the eyes. So he doesn't see the lies lurking in there.

At least his having Cas's blood doesn't give *him* any insight into my mind.

I let my arms lie limp; my chin falls to my chest. The soft thud of each of his footsteps is distinct even from behind the glass case as he gets closer. An unmistakeable clicking sound as he unlocks the door.

Nowhere to hide.

"Are you awake, Leah?" Jared's voice is soft.

I give the faintest nod.

"Good. You might feel a little strange at first, but you'll be fine. I think you'll prefer it this way, Leah. A life without anger or frustration. You'll be free to fulfil your purpose without emotion holding you back."

As he speaks, he's pulling the wires from my arms. I barely feel them. Head down, I step out of the glass case, shakily. But I'm in my own mind. A cold breeze from somewhere makes me shiver.

"Leah, how are you feeling?"

I can't get away with staying silent this time. I can sense his eyes boring into me, and lift my head slightly. A mistake —now I can see the stump of his arm, wrapped in a bandage, and above that, his oh-so-deceptively calm face. My throat closes up, and sweat breaks out on my forehead. Any second now, I'm going to lose it and attack him again—or worse, panic and run.

But I hold myself together. Somehow.

"I'm fine" I say, slurring the words, like I'm drugged-up.

"Good. I worry about you, Leah."

Now he sounds like some demented parody of a father-figure. Ugh.

I don't say anything to that. I might have to put on an act, but over my dead body am I kneeling down and licking his shoes.

My skin crawls when he takes me by the hand like a child and leads me from the room. I have to clench my other fist to keep from letting fire flare from my arm and sever his other hand. I don't know what he's done with my dagger, but I have a feeling I won't be getting it back any time soon.

Soon enough, I start to recognise that he's leading me back to my room. Strange. Like nothing's happened. Nothing

—and everything. *Act stupid. Act like you need instructions from him before you do anything.*

"Your lessons will begin tomorrow, Leah," says Jared. "Go and clean yourself up, and I will have a guard bring you food later. Rest up and be ready for a full day's training tomorrow. I have something to show you. I think you'll be interested to see."

The slight edge to the word *interested* makes the hairs on my arms stand up. Has he seen through me that easily? Is there something I'm supposed to have done, or something else that's given the game away? But I can't look up and check.

A pause, then he says, "I worry about *all* my Pyros."

I hear a hidden emphasis on *my*, and suddenly, it feels like I'm about to walk into a trap. I'm certain, absolutely certain, he knows the other Pyros are still alive. And some of them are bound to him by the tattoos.

Silently, ignoring the implied threat, I walk into my room. It's the same as before. Clean clothes laid out on the bed. No booby-traps. The door shuts behind me with a *snick*.

Get cleaned up. Right. My clothes are torn all over and I'm covered in some sort of slimy substance from inside the glass case. I shudder, and glance at the door to make sure no one's going to come barging in.

I take my time showering and eating, later, when a hooded guard brings me another bland meal. I don't know what I'm expecting—poison, maybe. Some kind of sign Jared's watching me. Other than the obvious presence of the guards. But I suppose I'm meant to be his obedient servant now. No room for insubordinate thoughts.

Right.

I practise in front of the mirror in the bathroom, making my face go carefully blank. I don't like looking in mirrors much these days, because the changes remind me of time passing, of things that can't be undone. Every scar, every inch of sunburn. But now, there's not a blemish on my face. Even childhood scars from silly accidents have vanished. Even more serious cuts from the few times I narrowly escaped the fiends. My skin's as smooth as though I've never stepped a foot out of doors.

It's not Jared's doing.

Transcendent. But what's the use in being Transcendent if I can't get out of here, with Cas?

Maybe that's not what I should be doing. Maybe I need to get Jared alone instead, so I can use my Transcendent powers to finish him off.

Even if Cas doesn't want to be rescued, Jared's too unstable to leave alone to carry on with his crazy experiments. If I leave now, assuming I even find the way out, I'd be drawing attention to my friends, and the other Pyros linked to Jared via the blood tattoos. Maybe I imagined his implied threat, but I can't afford to risk it.

I drift off to sleep with unease brewing within me, and wake to the sound of my door unlocking. It takes everything I have to appear politely puzzled at the intrusion and not leap to my feet and attack, but when Jared himself comes in, I know I made the right choice. He nods, as though pleased with something, while I give him a bland, bleary-eyed look.

"Meet me outside in five minutes."

I nod. I seem to be doing that a lot lately.

Fully dressed, I meet him outside and walk through the corridor in silence. Head down. Meek. Obedient. Through corridor after corridor, in the opposite direction to the way I went yesterday. Past Jared's rooms, and down a set of stairs.

I'm buzzing with curiosity. What does he want to show me? A new weapon, maybe? We're now walking through a weapon's room, walls covered in axes and swords and daggers. On the other side, there's a door, and he takes out a key and unlocks it.

"Hello?" he says, startling me.

I squint into darkness, but my sight rapidly adjusts. Dim lights come on over glass cases, lying on the ground like coffins, containing...

People.

And they're sitting up. In unison, a dozen people or more —men and women, blank-faced and dressed in identical uniforms—sit up. Even though they don't *look* alike, they move in exactly the same way. There's absolutely nothing remarkable about any of them. Except that they majorly creep me out.

Black uniforms, short sleeves, and on each of their hands, a tattoo like Cas's new one.

"This is Leah," Jared says, into the silence. "She shares your blood."

My insides turn to ice. I shift my head to face him, a fraction too fast. "My blood?"

"Yes. These are your siblings." He pauses, as though to let the words sink in. They reverberate around my head.

I can't say a word. I can't meet their blank eyes, either. *No. I... he can't have.*

"I'm sad it's come to this," he says. "But we're approaching the final stage of our war. The Fiordans will soon be making another attack. We need to be ready."

"How do you know that?" I bite my lip. Too curious. But how can I keep my mouth shut when he says something like that? I keep my gaze down, sure he'll see the anger in my eyes. Sure he'll see that I wish I'd cut off his head, not his hand.

This is deliberate. Calculated. He must have known I wouldn't be able to hold my tongue when confronted with *this*. He used my blood to make more Transcendents. Even though he knows what that means. He knows what happens to the others. He orchestrated it.

He tilts his head. "I have spies within the enemy territory, Leah. They keep me updated. I wish I could say we have longer to prepare... but it's not to be."

At a gesture from Jared, the twelve Transcendents climb out of their respective glass prisons. I tense inside—is he going to set them on me? Can I beat twelve of them? But no, he won't want to waste his army on the likes of me.

I'm not the only Transcendent anymore. The truth sinks in, sharp and absolute: I'm not the Pyros' saviour. I'm just one of thirteen. And we're *all* at Jared's mercy.

"It was you who gave me the idea, Leah," he says softly. "You and Cas. And Murray, of course. The original experiments were horribly inefficient. Cas's powers were taxed to their limit, yet none of the subjects survived. We'd almost given up hope when the Transcendent came along—an ordinary Pyro, who ran into trouble in a mission and was close to death." He pauses. "That was the key. To make a true Transcendent, the subject must be seconds from death."

I don't say anything. I'm sure he can hear my heart racing. *It can't be true.* But it fits the facts.

"Such a small distinction, Leah," says Jared. "But it makes the world of difference." He pats one of the Transcendents on the arm. "These won't break so easily. They are combat-ready, naturally, but it won't hurt to put them through their paces. As the only Transcendent to have been in battle, you will be the standard against which I measure the others."

So that's the plan. Of course he couldn't kill me without making sure my replacements were ready to fight.

I can't tell whether he's fooled by my act, but I bite down on all the other questions clamouring for attention and resolve to find out as much as I can by observing. I'm an idiot for not considering the possibility that Jared would use my blood to make more Transcendents. Perhaps using *mine* and not Cas's will mean they don't suffer the same connection Cas and I do. God, I hope so—it's not something I'd wish on anyone, even these creepy half-alive people. Obviously, Jared's drugged them with the same stuff Cas was supposed to give to me.

But he didn't. The new tattoo can't control his mind, even if it's apparently impossible to remove. Cas is in his own mind, and he saved me. Again.

I concentrate on that, not the creepy new Transcendents or the sickening implications. If Jared created them... I have a sneaking suspicion it isn't because he thought I wanted friends.

Jared gestures for me to walk beside him as he leads the twelve Transcendents from the room. They follow us in eerie silence. I don't say a word either, though I can sense him looking at me, and occasionally catch a glimpse of the bandage encasing his right arm. His heart stopped when I cut him. Why? What did he do to himself?

Corridor after corridor. A maze. I occupy my thoughts with the new information I've learned. Jared has spies amongst the fiends. I guess it makes sense. This is the man everyone thought was dead for two years, after all.

I'm not ready. Not just for the invasion, though I should have seen it coming. It's what I'm supposed to have been preparing for the whole time. But to sacrifice my life? To watch Cas die, to lose every last person in the world I care about?

I'll never be ready for that. I'll never be ready to watch the others die. I have to fight this war, not play games with Jared.

We reach the training hall. Each of the twelve pulls a weapon from a sheath at their waist—short daggers with engraved hilts, like mine. They line up, like robots, before the target range. Jared gestures for me to stand beside him.

"This works best with two pairs of eyes watching," he says. "Tell me if anyone steps out of line or makes an error. We have to be absolutely perfect. Every one of them."

Again, like robots, the twelve hit the centre of their targets with their weapons. One after another in turn. And again. Next, Jared moves them on to dummies. I keep an eye out for anything odd, but other than their creepy perfection, there's nothing.

Jared gives a pleased nod when the final Transcendent decapitates the last dummy, and gestures for us to follow him out of the hall.

My nerves are on end. Tension lingers in the air, like that was some kind of test for me, too. Something's going on that I don't know about.

But by the time we reach the end of the corridor, I know what it is.

Another door is open wide on a spacious, high-ceilinged room with a large chunk of the back wall missing, replaced by a barred gate. On the other side, there's movement. Familiar movement.

Fiends.

My throat closes up, and every nerve in my body stands on end, telling me to flee. The twelve Transcendents, however, stand at attention. Expressionless.

No one's going to help me.

Jared beckons me to follow as he approaches the metal gate, indicating to the Transcendents to stay put. He withdraws a bundle of keys, moving awkwardly with just one arm, but too quickly, he's bending down to unlock the tangle of padlocks at the door's edge. Click. Click. One by one, they fall. Until the gate's free.

He grips a dagger in his teeth, scoring a line across his hand. Blood drips onto the remaining lock, which undoes with a clicking motion. I've never seen a lock move like that.

But that's the last thing on my mind right now. I'm thinking about Jared's foot on the gate, pushing it open, inch by inch.

The shuffling sounds on the other side of the door. Jared letting blood drip onto his fingers, reaching for a metal box. He presses a button.

The fiend within the room roars.

Grasping my back with bloodied fingers, he shoves me through the gap between the gate and the wall. The gate slams shut, and I'm alone with the monster.

11

It's hunched over in the corner of the room. Scaly arms wrapped around itself. Muscled legs bent under the weight of iron chains. Bat-like wings ragged as though slashed through with a sword. It shakes its head groggily, but whatever Jared did with that control woke it up. A voice in my head whispers that that must be how he affects people with the tattoos over distance—but that voice is silenced by the very obvious problem facing me right now.

The fiend shakes its head again, the chains rattling as it straightens up. It's a hideous specimen, all rock-like muscle, and long tusks. One reaches its knees, but the other's been chipped short, perhaps broken in a fight.

I breathe in, breathe out. Glance over my shoulder—Jared's watching me through the bars, face twisted into a cruel smile. If I break out, I give the game away. If I don't, the fiend pounds me to a pulp.

It's not a great choice.

Before I can move, the fiend swipes with one clawed hand and I have to jump back to avoid being knocked off my feet.

Even with the chains around its legs, it moves frighteningly fast.

And I don't have my weapon. I have no idea what Jared did with it. But it's just me and the monster.

The fiend's groggy, but recovering fast. Its ragged wings extend out, one of them clipping the top of my head. It stoops under the low ceiling, chains dragging on the ground.

I have about three seconds to break down the gate before it gets to me.

The fiend cries out, an ear-splitting, horrible noise, like it's in pain. I can almost see Jared's smirk. He's torturing it. My own nerves ignite in response, and I panic, running for the door.

The claw lashes out, and I duck and roll. The fiend stamps down with its boat-sized foot, inches from my head. Its other fist comes up, this one claw-less but twice the size of the other hand, swollen unnaturally large even for a fiend. It drags the chain behind it as it prepares to deal me a death blow.

Or it would, if I hadn't kicked it in the shin.

Without my weapon, I can improvise. Punch, duck, roll, and avoid its clumsy feet. I get a few good hits in before I realise, with a sinking in my chest, that I've let it get between me and the door.

Crap.

The chain drags as the beast reaches for me—the chains mean it can't reach the walls. There's one thing it can hit. Me. And I'm a moving target. I crouch down low and strike upwards with my fist, catching it on the arm. The blow reverberates through me, but doesn't hurt. I pretend I'm not in a cave, not deep, deep underground, far from anyone who can help me. I pretend I'm under the open sky, and the fire's waiting for my call.

There. Sparks fly from my fist, a flame curling to life. Heat rushes through me, kicking off the last of the groggy sleep-walking-type feeling that's been hounding me ever since I stepped out of that glass case. I strike the fiend with a right uppercut, and leave a smoking mark on its arm. Another strike, and it takes a step back. The exhilaration of the fight almost makes me forget I'm trapped, at Jared's mercy, and he's planning to leave me in here until I've reached my limit. That's what the test is about.

I have to break out. I can't stay in Jared's games forever, but I can't take my eyes off the target. The cave rings with the fiend's frustrated cries as I dodge each strike. I'm not stupid enough to underestimate it even though it's in chains. It's as brutal and angry as any of the monsters outside. But all it can do is paw at me with meaty fists.

I dodge a particularly ferocious swipe and find it's pushed me back against the wall, right beside the gate. A couple more steps, a well-placed kick, and I can bring the gate down.

The fiend roars, lumbering towards me. I've been too focused on the door to move quickly enough to dodge its strike. Pain shoots up my left side. *Damn.*

I'm bleeding, but I'm lucky it's a shallow cut. The fiend hisses at me. I edge around the shadows of the room like a cat, just out of its reach. Brace myself.

Kick at the gate.

Pain explodes from the bottom of my foot, and I overbalance, skinning my knees on the hard floor. My vision goes hazy, and my foot throbs again, pain as intense as experiencing Cas's punishment through our connection.

The door. God, I'm stupid. Of course he's done something to it to stop me breaking out.

I can't put weight on my left foot. The fiend swipes again, scraping my skull. Eyes watering with pain, I try to focus on the fire again, but I can't move my left leg, and I half-stagger against the wall, teeth clenched in an effort not to moan.

The world goes hazy around the edges, but within a few seconds, the pain fades. I move my leg and it doesn't hurt at all. With every second, I feel stronger. Gingerly, I place my foot down. No pain.

Healed.

Which means I'm still in the fight.

The only way out is to beat the fiend to a pulp, before it can do the same to me. No more dodging—this time, I have to aim to kill.

As the thought crosses my mind, the lights go out.

Oh, hell.

Everything—the cave, the walls, the gate, and the monstrosity in front of me—is smothered in darkness. The fiend goes silent, though the clanking of the metal dragging on the floor continues. This is just another obstacle of Jared's. Possibly, he's bored watching me constantly dodging the fiend by now.

Or it's part of another game.

Fire springs to life on my skin, lighting the way in front of me, but not enough. Another swipe from the fiend grazes my knees. Apparently, the dark doesn't bother it. Of course, it's been shut in the darkness here for ages. I'm at a disadvantage. Damn.

I let the fire go out.

It's hopeless. I'll have to fight it eventually. But now, I take myself back to the days of living out in the countryside, moving silently as possible to avoid drawing the attention of the monsters. I'm well practised. It's how I lasted two years. How we all did. We were lucky, true, but not everyone has the natural ability to move around quietly.

My feet barely whisper on the ground, but the fiend's shuffling movement gives me no clue as to whether it hears me or not. One careful step after another. Closer. Close enough to feel the warm, fetid breath on my face. Raw terror washes over me. I can't die now. Not here in the dark. Not without saving the others.

The others. I was an idiot. I never should have come. I let my guilt over leaving Cas cloud my judgement, and my error might cost us the war.

The fiend breathes slowly. It hasn't noticed me yet. I have only one chance to strike it, but I can't seem to move. Sweat covers my body. I have to win this. *Have to get out.*

I call the fire. Leap forward. But the fire doesn't come, and the fiend's heavy body smacks into me like a falling boulder, sending me flying. Air rushes past, and I hit the wall with a crash that shakes the whole room. My ears ring, and I can't get breath into my lungs. Pain blossoms from my chest. Cracked ribs.

Thud. The fiend stamps down, shaking the walls, and I slide to the ground, gasping in pain.

I inch sideways, along the wall, fast as I can. Each step sends shooting pain through my ribs, and my legs are wobbly. I curse the darkness. I curse Jared. Anything to distract from the pain, and, worse, the panic clawing at me. The claustrophobic sensation of being trapped in darkness.

Something leathery scrapes my legs. The fiend's wing. It's close. I've not moved far enough away. Pushing aside the pain, I force my legs into motion.

A fist comes out of the darkness and knocks the breath from my lungs. I slam into the wall again, feeling the bones shake in my body.

I'm reminded of a battle with two fiends in an abandoned house. But this time, Cas won't come in to save me. Not with that gate between me and escape.

I can't breathe.

I thought you said you weren't going to give up. That you'd fight back. Whatever the case.

But I never planned for this. Never planned to be in a sick game, pitted against a monster for sport at the whims of a madman.

Smack. Blood fills my mouth as it hits my nose, breaking it. I strike back, feebly, but miss. Growing weaker. A red haze covers my vision. The claws swipe again, catching my face and my left arm.

Fire. FIRE!

Why can't I do it?

What did he do to me?

Or is it me? Am I losing my powers?

The cold from the wall soaks into my skin. I barely feel the next punch. My legs give out, and a ringing sounds in my ears. Hazy images play before my eyes. Cas, as a child, chained in a cage with a monster and made to fight to the death.

I can't feel anything but my own pain. It's all I am.

I scream. A hoarse, ragged scream, like I'm being torn apart inside, to match the outside. I wish I could fade away to darkness, away from the pain. But I can't. I'm still here, and every second stretches into agony.

Then the fist connects with my skull. I hear something vital crack, and finally, blessed numbness takes me away.

———

Not for long enough. Bright lights collide with my face, and I whimper, trying to raise my arm to shield myself. But I can't move.

It feels like there's a clawed beast inside me, shredding me from the inside out, but I know it's by body trying to repair itself, pulling itself back past the point of death. I'm broken, but mending, and the mending hurts more than the breaking. Nothing outside exists. Only the pain. Pain and bright lights.

Time drifts by in waves. Every breath comes a little easier, every movement is less painful. Why is life so addictive, every breath like a drug, when the flipside is pain beyond pain? I wish I could have one without the other. But the same breath that hurt so much now is like blissful oblivion.

I'm lying on a soft bed. The lights above my head are garishly bright after the darkness.

No one's holding me. I'm alone.

Sometime later, I manage to sit up. It's true. I'm back in my bedroom. Did Jared get me out of the room? It couldn't have been anyone else, unless Cas—but Jared would have punished him for interfering if he'd dared. I didn't detect any pain from him, but then, I was too wrapped up in my own.

I shudder, wrapping my arms around myself. It's only then that I notice the clean clothes lying out on the bed. The ones I'm wearing are half-shredded, soaked in blood. My blood.

Was that the plan? To see how far he could push me? So what was the deal with shutting off the lights? Maybe to intimidate me, make me lose confidence in my own power.

I have to find Cas.

It's not the first time I've nearly died at the hands of the fiends. But the helplessness of being shut in the dark clings to me like slime.

How did Cas grow up like that without going mad?

I sure as hell don't feel Transcendent now.

———

It's about an hour before Jared shows up. He smiles at me, as though this is a friendly social call. Not a sadist visiting his victim.

"Glad to see you're recovering, Leah."

It takes every ounce of restraint I have not to throw myself at him and gouge his eyes out. I settle for looking down at myself, like I'm also surprised to see I'm in one piece. Again.

"You're an admirable fighter, as always, and you've given the other Transcendents something wonderful to aspire to."

If they could even see me in the dark.

"Of course, it's a pity about the power cut, but it worked out conveniently for all of us. Time is of the essence, after all."

Liar!

"You almost beat Cas's lifetime record, Leah. Your regenerative powers are astonishing."

He pulls a chart from inside his coat with his one working hand. "Bone regrowth. Time taken: an hour. Remarkable. Beyond even the artificial Pyros. Beyond even Cas. You're unique, Leah." He puts the papers away. "I've yet to see conclusive results with the other Transcendents, but I'm hopeful. Very hopeful. Thank you."

Go burn in hell.

I don't say anything aloud. I can't even look at the man who chillingly let me be beaten to death.

"I won't trouble you any further, Leah. I'll let you get some rest."

And he leaves. Just like that.

I wait, listening to his footsteps outside, clacking on the stone floor. Heading back to torment someone else.

I wait ten minutes, until I'm absolutely certain he's gone, before I scream. I throw myself forward and pummel the wall, hard, so hard my fist leaves a deep dent in it. I barely draw breath, my scream turning into something wild, animal, inhuman. I hit the wall again, even though the damage shows, he's sure to notice, and yet I don't care.

I give myself over to rage and fury.

A guard peers through the door, snapping me back to reality. Hell. Will he—it, whatever—tell Jared? I'm not sure the guards can even speak. Or the Transcendents, actually. Like Jared's stolen their voices away. Maybe it's the blood-manipulation, maybe it's the drugs. Does he still think he has *my* life in his hands? I suppose he does, considering what he just did.

And that was my punishment. I'm pretty sure of it.

But it's far from over. He's still running tests on the other Transcendents. It's part of a long process.

One that can only end in our deaths.

12

The next morning, I'm still intact, and I'm not set for punishment today. Jared gives me free rein, with the understanding that I don't stray more than two corridors past the training hall. I guess he doesn't want me wandering too far off again.

I wonder how he even knew where I was last time. Though it was Cas who brought me back.

Speak of the devil...

He's *here.* In the training hall. Throwing knives at a target, not looking at me. Not that I'm about to let that put me off. Ignoring all the other Pyros training in pairs throughout the hall, I march over to him and say, without preamble, "We need to talk."

"Not now," he says, out of the corner of his mouth. "Did I not tell you to wait?"

A sour taste fills my mouth. "How long? Until he has me beaten again?"

The words are too quiet for anyone else to hear. But Cas's spine stiffens. He turns his back on the dummies, and strides from the hall. I have to hurry to keep up. He doesn't slow until we're two corridors away, with blank stretches of wall either side.

"I thought he threatened you. I didn't think…" He shakes his head, his face a mirror of my own anger and pain. It doesn't look right on him.

"Oh, he did more than threaten me." The anger returns, blazing hot, and Cas is right in the firing line. "I couldn't use my powers. Didn't have to do with what he had you inject me with, did it?"

His brow furrows in confusion. "I didn't. That was your own blood I put in the formula. I didn't know what else to do. It was that or use mine, and I didn't want to give him any more leverage." He moves his hand slightly, and I glimpse the new mark on his wrist.

Why else did my powers stop working? "I was trapped," I say. "With one of the fiends."

I have to lean on the wall to steady myself. The thick, urgent panic claws at my throat again. No, maybe he didn't control me. It was my own fear that broke my powers. Fear of dying without saving the others. Fear of what my blood created. The Transcendents.

Cas's expression shifts from confusion to shock. He shakes his head. "He didn't—"

"Yeah, he did. I think he was measuring me up against the other Transcendents. Or the other way around. But he got a kick out of watching me suffer. Not that I'm surprised."

Cas's eyes go wide. "Other Transcendents? What?"

He doesn't know. Of course not. Jared only showed me, because he wanted to prove a point. Or because he wanted to shock Cas later. I've no idea how his mind works.

"Yeah, other Transcendents. Twelve of them."

Cas's gaze darts about, refusing to look me in the eyes. "He didn't."

My throat's dry. "Don't worry, he used my blood, not yours." The words are drenched in bitterness.

"I don't—you think I feel guilty about *that*? Leah, he tortured you."

A lump rises in my throat as he speaks my name, and I feel like I'm about to unravel, like the healing my body's undergone might come undone.

I meet his eyes. "I know what he did to me. But he also used my blood to make himself twelve slaves. He's torturing them right now, doing the same thing he did to me yesterday. The same he did to you."

His eyes blaze. "So he did decide it was worth the risk." His breath catches on the last word. "That means one thing: he thinks we'll make an attack. Soon. He wouldn't risk using your blood to make an army unless he was certain we'd be marching against an invasion anyway."

"How soon?" My heart sinks. I never thought I'd ever be ready, but how could I ever lead an army like this? Unless he doesn't expect me to. Unless…

"No idea. I can't imagine he'd see an advantage in keeping quiet, considering we're supposed to lead the army. That is, unless he sees us as expendable now."

Is Cas reading my thoughts? With those other Transcendents, I technically *am* expendable. All he needs is my blood. Or theirs. Does it have the same effect? Can he keep multiplying his army forever? *What have I done?* I brought my cursed blood right here, and let Jared use it for himself.

I shake my head. "No…"

"Well, what, then? Running away didn't work out for you, did it?" Cas presses a hand to his forehead, like it hurts him. The mark stands out, red as blood. "That was downright *stupid* of you. I can't always be around to watch your back."

"I never asked you to!" I say, bristling. "In case you've

forgotten, I came to save your damn neck from Jared. I didn't need anyone to protect me then, and I don't now."

"Yeah, that worked out great," he shoots back. We're back to trading insults. But part of me knows he's right. I messed this up. Massively. "Lucky we *are* preparing for the invasion, and that you're so valuable to him. You don't even want to know what he did to one of the other Pyros who attacked him."

I swallow. "Someone really did that?" And am I valuable to him now I'm just one of thirteen?

"He's a psychopath. Of course someone would object. Pity it didn't work." He moves his hand down, gripping the tattooed palm.

"Why didn't he mark me like that?" I ask, calming. I don't want to fight. Not now.

"No clue. After I brought you back from the caves, he told me to hook you up to the IV, said he wanted to keep a special eye on you. But he never touched you. Granted, he was bleeding all over the place at the time, but still."

"He's done the same thing to the others," I say. "It's like mind control." I shiver at the memory, and knowing what he's doing to them now. Just because they're under his control doesn't mean they don't feel pain.

"Blood control," he says. "Impulse control, and total domination. The guards are under it, too. They can't even speak without his permission."

"So this is how he's running his army."

"Yeah, but I don't know how those twelve fit into it. I wonder if he's training them as assassins. What did they look like?"

"I couldn't say. Normal. Why?"

"Because he hand-picked those people to give your blood to. There has to have been a reason for it. Jared doesn't do anything at random."

"Yeah, that's what worries me," I mutter. "So I'm guessing they can heal, like us. But they don't look like the fiends."

"You're forgetting the Fiordans can shapeshift," he said.

"And those Transcendents? Can they?"

"I have no idea."

"Well, how d'you know so much?" I challenge him.

I expect him to give me a sarcastic response belittling me for asking stupid questions, but instead he says, simply, "I grew up around scientists."

"Yeah. But I thought my blood's basically like the fiends'. Jared said I had... Fiordan blood." The part I've still not accepted. How can I? Being a Pyro, being Transcendent is one thing, but a monster—no.

You are part of the monsters you so despise, Leah.

Cas's eyes narrow. *He has it, too.* "You said yourself you don't understand what you can do."

"No, but I'd guess it's linked to the Fiordans. Right? That energy blast thing."

"You regenerate in the same way the fiends' leaders do. As Transcendent, you have that power. But even Jared doesn't know everything about them. He was attempting to create something he doesn't understand himself. There's no way he *can* understand. He has twelve new invincible soldiers at his disposal. Like we don't have enough Fiordans to deal with."

"But I killed one of them," I point out. "The Fiordans can die. So does that mean...one of them could do the same to me? Use the energy blast, I mean?"

"I don't know. I'm not the one who fought one."

"Maybe that's how they... opened the breach." Hell. The end of the world started with an energy blast. And I'm right next to the divide, with twelve mind-controlled Transcendents. Even if I can control my own powers, can the Transcendents?

We *have* to take Jared down somehow, before he does something else that dooms what's left of humanity.

"Look," says Cas. "I don't know all that much about them, really. They didn't exactly parade their secrets about, which is more than I can say for Jared. But they did experiments themselves, that's where Jared got the idea. They engineered themselves. Jared decided he didn't want to leave them to have all the fun." He spits the words out, and his eyes flash. I can see the fury waiting beneath the surface, and I feel a kind of savage pleasure at the idea of Jared at the mercy of that anger. Not that I don't want to finish Jared off myself, after what he did to me. I'm not about to let him make me feel that helpless again.

I can't. I won't.

"Right," I say. "I'm just wondering how Jared expects me to win this war. Is it literally a matter of pitting me against the fiends' leaders head-on and seeing who comes out in one piece?" And does it matter, now there are twelve other sacrifices lined up?

Cas's face twists. "I don't know."

So that's it. No one knows. And we're on a time limit. No way out for either of us.

"Cas," I say. "Please—let me try removing the tattoo. If it doesn't work, at least we've tried everything."

"I don't..." But he holds out his hand, palm up, the ugly red mark gleaming. Fury at Jared rises once again. He did this. Drove us to this. And yet part of me feels a flicker of triumph: I'm taking back control of my own blood. I might be expendable, but I'm still alive. And Jared will regret letting me walk around free.

And then I realise. "Crap, I don't have my dagger."

"He took your weapon away? He'll have put it somewhere —dammit, I don't know. He might have it with him. You don't mind...?" He goes for his own blade.

I nod. "Sure. It's hardly going to be as painful as what I just went through, right?"

I think I see Cas's hands shake slightly as he pulls the blade out, but I might have imagined it. Quickly, he runs the sword's point over my outstretched hand. Blood blossoms to the surface, but it barely stings. Then he does the same to his own marked hand.

I turn my palm over, and our hands touch as the blood runs onto his mark. I draw back, heart pounding in my ears.

"It didn't work," he says, dully. "I still feel it. It's like a slow poison or something."

"You can't know that yet," I say. "Wait a minute."

A cry rings out, an ear-splitting screech. Fiends?

Cas's head jerks up. "What the hell?"

"Are we being attacked from outside?" I ask stupidly—of course, he has no more idea than I do.

"I don't know." But he keeps his blade at the ready. "Crap. I wonder if one of his Transcendents turned on him."

The possibility never crossed my mind. "But I thought they couldn't."

"Never assume anything when it comes to Transcendents. Or Jared. He doesn't have a clue what he's messing with."

Another cry rings out from somewhere up ahead. Louder.

"Someone's coming." He pulls me into an alcove off the corridor. I can't see anything, but this is the way that leads to the labs where I cut off Jared's hand. What else could be hiding down here? Does he even have defences up against the fiends outside? Of course, he has guards...

Someone runs around the corner. We both freeze, watching out.

The figure pauses in front of the wall. They're wearing red uniform.

It's not an enemy. It's Val.

13

"Stop." Cas's hand catches my arm before I can move out into the corridor. "It might be a trap."

"It's definitely her," I hiss back. "I'll bet Murray sent her after us." But I quieten, all the same, when she scans the corridor again. Where's Jared? If this really is a rescue, I'd expect to hear fighting. I haven't seen all Jared's people yet, but our two groups are probably evenly matched... except for the Transcendents.

And Cas. I look at him. The corners of his mouth are turned down, and he appears to be thinking hard.

Before I can make up my mind, Val continues down the corridor and out of sight.

I make to follow her, but Cas grabs my arm again.

"What?" I hiss. "If there's any chance of getting out of here, I'm taking it." I'll figure out how to take Jared down later. Stopping him using me to create more monsters is more important.

"She has his mark," Cas whispers, stopping me in my tracks.

"What?" I stare at him. But he, of all people, would know. I'd forgotten to look for the sign. *Stupid, Leah.*

"Like Nolan."

My fists clench. Then I shake my head. "Murray knew how to stop them." No way would he have left the others to suffer if there was any way he could have helped them. And he could. My blood samples were in the lab.

I turn back to face the direction Val walked in.

"You trust him?"

Cas's words cut through me, like he read my thoughts, saw my doubts. I glare at him. "If you mean I trust him not to let his own team die, then yes, I do."

"You don't know his reasons," he says. "He'd sacrifice us if it meant saving the others from Jared."

"Don't be ridiculous." Of all the times to start attacking my faith in Murray, why now? "I'm going to figure out what's happening. You can stay down here if you like."

And I take off before he can reply.

Val's not in the next corridor, but a door lies open on the left. A lab, of course. I hesitate a moment, then step inside.

And freeze. Val stands beside a desk, holding Jared's tattoo gun.

It's too late to move. She's spotted me, though there's no gleam of recognition in her eyes. A chill breaks out across my back. Now I can see one of her sleeves is shredded, and blood streaks the skin between the gaps. Though I can't see it clearly, the sharp lines of the new tattoo peek out. *Did he ambush and mark her on the way here?*

"Val." My voice is a croak. "What are you doing with that?"

For a heartbeat, I think she won't respond. Either she's not capable of speaking under her own power… or like Nolan, she's chosen this.

Val was one of the first people to welcome me to the base.

To make me feel included amongst the group. She trained me. It's thanks to her I understood how to use my weapon. I last saw her less than two days ago. How can Jared have done this in such a short time?

"Val," I say again.

She steps towards me. Her eyes are glassy and unfocused, her steps hesitant, unsteady. Her sleeve is soaked in blood. What did he do, make her re-cut the tattoo?

"What are you doing?" I ask, again, not taking my gaze away from that tattoo gun. "Did Murray send you here?"

No answer, confirming my guess. She's Jared's. Which means I have to run. Now.

I about-turn, head out the room, and almost walk smack into a guy I don't recognise. The glassy expression in his eyes gives it away. He's one of the other Transcendents. But how the hell did he move so fast? And where's Cas?

"Move," I say. I'm out of patience. Anger stirs beneath the surface. I've been trapped in this cave long enough.

The Transcendent catches my arm, and I recoil. His grip is inhumanly strong. If I wasn't Transcendent, he'd have snapped my arm. As it is, my wrist protests at the strain, and I can't pull myself free.

"What the hell do you want?" I gasp. "I get that Jared has his stupid spell over you, but I refuse to believe he's totally obliterated all your free will. You have to *know* what you're doing. You have to be able to see and hear me."

The Transcendent says nothing. His hand squeezes my wrist, and I notice his sleeve's rolled up, showing the livid red-black mark of his own tattoo running down to his palm.

In one swift motion, he drags me away from the door as Val steps out, holding the gun.

"No you don't," I snarl. "I'm not turning into one of you creepy puppets."

I pull away, gritting my teeth. I'm Transcendent, and no matter how much it'll hurt, I can get away.

I yank my arm out of his grip, hard. Pain shoots up my arm, but I'm already running.

My vision blurs, but I press on. *Dammit. You'll heal in a minute.* But the pain's making it hard to think clearly.

Wait. That's not my pain.

As the thought crosses my mind, a spasm shoots across my back, and my knees give out. Agony shoots up my arms and legs, like I've fallen into a furnace. I groan, and my head cracks against the corridor floor.

Oh. Hell. He's torturing Cas.

Or is it a memory?

It's not mine. I'm not in pain. Except my wrist. I try to focus on the splintering pain from my arm, and that miraculously keeps me anchored in the present long enough to drag myself a few metres down the corridor. I'm near the training room, I remember belatedly. I've no idea where Cas went. But if Val's here, Murray must know. She wouldn't have left without clearing it with him, would she?

Unless Jared used the tattoo to bring her here?

I don't know the way out. And this way will doubtless lead me right into…

A fiend. I stop dead. The creature's hunched up, its muscled form wedged into the corridor. It's completely blocking the path, its batlike wings curled inwards.

Crap.

Cas's hand grabs my jacket sleeve and pulls me back into the alcove. I almost yelp in pain as the movement jars my wrist.

"What the hell?" I hiss. "You were hiding here the whole time?"

"Not a whole lot of options," he says in a low voice. "In case you haven't noticed, someone breached security."

"What's that, a security fiend?"

"You finally get it?"

I breathe out, my wrist throbbing painfully. "A fiend on one side, creepy Val and a Transcendent on the other. Just brilliant."

"Transcendent?"

"If you hadn't been hiding back here, you'd have seen it," I say.

Cas shakes his head. "I didn't hear anyone. Apart from that fiend, and it's making enough of a racket to drown out anything else."

"Great," I say. "So we're stuck behind the wall, or else get our heads bashed in or double-tattooed by…"

I trail off at the sound of footsteps. Human ones. Two sets.

"See?" I mouth. Not that it's easy to see anything from behind the wall. And it's beyond me to figure out why there's a fiend blocking the corridor. Unless Jared knows we're here.

A stinging discomfort in my wrist tells me it's healed, for all the good that does. I grip my weapon. I don't want to attack Val if I can help it, but that Transcendent and the fiend have us boxed in, and I've no intention of being Jared's plaything again.

Screeches echo, close enough for me to know the fiend's speaking. Who to, I have no idea. It doesn't sound like English. But a quieter voice replies in the same shrieking language. The hairs rise on my arms, because I almost… understand. Almost, but not quite.

I peer around the wall and gasp aloud. The Transcendent's talking to the fiend. The man's mouth moves, and those inhuman shrieking noises answer the fiend's own.

Crap. Looks like Jared gave his Transcendents another advantage. But why? Why give them the ability to communicate with the enemy?

The shrieking's loud enough to drown out my pounding heart. I hiss at Cas, "Any plans, genius?"

"Don't die," he says, helpfully.

Seriously? I'm regretting even trying to rescue him. Does he just want me to leave him here? Or does he have a plan? I don't know, and it's not like I can read his thoughts. Just memories.

The shrieking stops. A fluttering like beating wings. I peer around the corner. The fiend's still there, but the Transcendent has gone.

A horrible suspicion grips me. The corridor's narrow here, but the ceiling's higher. Heart in my throat, I tilt my head up.

Cas's hand over my mouth cuts off my scream. Three other Transcendents are on the *ceiling*, clinging to the gaps in the tiles with claw-like hands. And they have the same batlike wings. They've been able to see us the whole time. But they can't speak without Jared's permission, I guess.

"What the hell are you doing?" Cas hisses at me.

"He knows we're here. No way they didn't see me walking into the lab." Whatever his game is, I'm done with it. If Cas wants to stick around, that's his problem, but I'm not going to leave without trying to save Val.

From what I can figure out, Jared's sent her after me. Considering I'm already supposed to be under his spell, I'm not sure why. Of course I knew I wouldn't fool him, but if he was that desperate to enslave me, he's already proven he can overpower me. It's not like I have a crack team of my own mind-controlled Transcendents hanging from the ceiling like overgrown bats.

If I run, I'll wind up near the fiends' cages. The other way leads to my room, and further along, to Jared's. But to get through, I'll have to attack that security fiend. I'm guessing Jared's on the other side. *What kind of game is this?* Of course, there's the strong possibility that he's lost his mind and planned to have Cas and me both killed.

One way to find out.

"Go," says Cas, startling me.

"What?" That's exactly what I was about to do, but why does he want me to leave him here?

"Get out while you can. Leave me here."

"Nice try," I hiss at him. "If you're trying to guilt-trip me—"

"Did it ever occur to you I might have a plan?"

Silence. I stare at him, head tilted. He had a plan all along? Really?

"I'm not an idiot," he says, as though reading my thoughts. "Believe it or not. You go. Get Val out. I'll take care of things here."

"What does *that* mean?"

"Just trust me," he says.

Trust him? Can I do that? Then again, it was my charging in without a plan that got us into this mess in the first place.

"All right," I whisper.

Then I slip out from behind the wall and approach the lab. The Transcendents on the ceiling don't move. He must have given them orders.

Val's already there with the tattoo gun. My insides twist as I catch sight of her palm, a mess of lines and twisting patterns I can't make sense of. She looks up at me, blank-eyed.

"Put it down," I say. I'm not entirely sure I trust my aim, but I have to do something.

Fire leaps along my dagger, which I point at her throat.

"Put down the gun, Val," I say. "I know you're in there somewhere. You'd die rather than letting Jared take over you, right?"

No answer. I swear under my breath. Take another step, readying my dagger.

I move without warning, using the side of my hand to strike the end of the gun as soon as Val moves her arm. She's grabbed for her own weapon, but is slowed by the wounds on her arms. The gun clatters to the floor.

A screech behind me. I whirl around to face… the same Transcendent as before.

"So you talk like one of them now?" I say, spinning my blade to point at him. "Guess Jared overdid it on the fiend blood."

Honestly, I'm guessing. But maybe that's what happened. This isn't an exact science, by the sound of it, and Jared's batshit crazy. Then again, I've done a nice job of getting myself boxed in between two of his minions. There's no question, though. I'd rather hurt his Transcendent than hit Val if I can help it.

"Where is he, then?" I challenge. "He's awfully lenient, considering I'm supposed to be so important. And you, too. Why's he got you all swooping around?"

I don't even know why I expect an answer. I'm out of patience. I take a step towards the Transcendent, and another, and I shove him with my non-dagger hand. Fire flares around both hands, a warning against him grabbing me again. I'd punch him in the face to relieve some of the tension, but I'm pretty sure these creepy servants are programmed to keep walking even if kicked to pieces. Your standard zombies.

A reckless anger surges within me. I swing my knife to cut his moving hand, slicing into the wrist. Like I did to Jared. He makes no noise, but can't prevent himself from faltering. I draw a line of fire up his arm, right through the tattoo mark.

The effect is instant. The Transcendent screams and

drops to his knees, eyes glazing over. I jump back, horrified. I only wanted to see if it was really the tattoo that had the power over Jared's servants. But is that the same justification Jared used for the experiments in the first place?

I stumble into the corridor, and find myself facing two of the others.

Crap.

The only way to run is towards the fiends' cages, which, as far as I know, is a dead end. If Cas is still hiding down the other corridor, I can't see him.

Dammit.

Val steps out of the lab behind me, climbing right over the screaming Transcendent as though he isn't there. The tattoo gleams on her wrist and hand, ugly and painful. I draw in a breath. I'm going to have to move *fast.* But if I free Val, I'll have an ally, even if not a Transcendent.

"Ah, Leah," says a voice.

My heart sinks like a stone.

"Jared."

He steps out from behind the Transcendents, shaking his head sadly. "Disappointed?"

A whimpering draws his attention to the collapsed Transcendent. He sighs. "There's always a weak link. Go." He gestures to the other two Transcendents, and they push past me, grabbing the fallen man by the shoulders and dragging him down the corridor.

Probably to the monstrous fiends trapped at the other end.

I glare. "What the hell is your game?"

"Game? I'm afraid I don't understand your meaning. If you meant why I barred you from the west part of the base, it's because I was in the middle of a precarious experiment and would rather you not jeopardise the operation."

"Operation?" I echo. My heart beats like a trapped bird. The last 'experiment' involved me. And my blood.

"I told you, Leah. Time is running out for all of us. The fiends will make another attack on Earth, and I intend to win. We can't rely on blind faith. Luckily, our knowledge is much more complete this time."

"What are you saying?"

Jared smiles and reaches out with a hand. The hand I cut off. It's grown back... except it's no human hand. Claws extend, curved and burned red. Fiend claws. Jared's smile widens as black wings uncurl from his shoulder blades, filling the corridor. He looks like a demented fallen angel, crawling out of the mouth of hell itself.

And in his hand is a blade, blood-red and gleaming.

I gape at him. "What the hell did you do?"

"What I always planned to," says Jared. "You helped by delivering yourself over to me, but I needed scientists to pull off the experiment. I trusted few, and Murray's meddling didn't help. But his people will be the next to die, and the first at my... hands." He flexes the clawed hand, his smile becoming ever-more inhuman. If that's even possible.

"So you turned yourself into a monster," I say. "I suppose you were halfway there anyway."

Rather than reacting to my accusation, Jared laughs. "I always did intend to use this weapon." He swings the blade, dangerously close to my neck. It's all I can do not to flinch.

Especially as I recognise the weapon as one of ours. He must have stolen it from our base, back when he attacked us the first time.

A weapon made for the Transcendent.

"I'm surprised you don't have more questions."

"Oh, I do." But I can't threaten him now we're equals. I can't accept the possibility he might be stronger than I am.

Not now. "I don't give a crap what you do to yourself, but what did you do to Val?"

"Oh, her?" He turns to her like he's just noticed she's there. "She's the perfect obedient soldier you never were, Leah. She came when I called her."

"And the others? You called her using the tattoo, right?"

"Naturally. I had a tip-off your Pyro friends found some success neutralising one of my tattoo-marks, so I was forced to act to ensure the others obeyed me."

My heart dips, sickeningly. "No. You made them cut their tattoos again. Didn't you?" Like Val. He knew Murray figured out my blood countered it. So he forced them to hurt themselves. *Bastard.*

"I had little choice, Leah."

"That's total bullshit," I snap. "You could choose *not* to be a sadist and hurt innocent people." Like Elle. And Cas. But Jared hasn't mentioned him yet, and I'm not about to draw attention to his absence when Jared has even more of an edge over us than before. Of course he knew the others were alive. Of course he planned to use them against me.

And of course he planned to turn himself into one of the super-soldiers. I should have guessed he wouldn't stop at whatever he did to heal himself from my stabbing him.

Which means... the Transcendents *are* expendable. He can create any number of them now. An army of disposable warriors. Like me. *Oh, God.* How can I stop him now?

"I think," he says softly, "it's time you accepted you're in over your head, Leah. I have all the army I need to take the war into my own hands." His claw moves again, melded perfectly to his arm. A sick feeling rises in my throat. If I'd tried harder to get Cas out of here... if I hadn't been too scared of the damage to use my own powers in here... I might have been able to stop this. Or if I hadn't blindly run after him without considering the damage my own blood can do.

"So, why'd you shut me out here?" I ask. "You must have been pretty confident I wouldn't destroy your labs."

"My Transcendents were ordered to challenge you if you made trouble," says Jared dismissively. "I couldn't have you snooping around and disturbing my work. I'm sure you can understand my dilemma. If I am to command the army, I must be on the same level as they are. As a Pyro, I am more than human. As Transcendent... I will be a god."

"Will be?"

Jared gives a slow shake of the head. "The process is complicated. Almost all those who transformed into Transcendents perished before the second stage. I need to complete my transformation first, before trying for immortality."

Immortality? "So you're not invincible."

"I might as well be." And his hand swipes out, sending a wave of energy rippling through the room. I'm slammed into the wall before I can blink. Although I barely feel the impact, panic washes over me. Now he has the means to obliterate me with a flick of his finger.

And I gave him that.

"Your blood," says Jared. "It's the key to all of this."

Now I know why he didn't punish me for cutting off his arm. He always planned to turn himself into a Transcendent.

My breath catches. How much blood did he take from me when I was unconscious? Not that it matters, because I'm assuming if he wants to create more Transcendents, he can just use their own blood. An army with literally no limits... aside from the number of people he can get to.

I stare him out. I can't manage confidence, especially when I'm pinned by the wave he sent from his hand. Especially when his Transcendents wait outside the door.

But if it's really so easy to create a Transcendent, why keep me alive?

"Is that it?" I ask.

"What?" Jared's expression doesn't change, but I've confused him with my response.

"Is that really why you've chosen to keep me alive? Or are you afraid of me?"

This time, confusion flits across his face. "Why would I be afraid of you?"

Maybe I'm wrong, but he knows more about my powers than I do. He knows if I use the energy blast, I could bury this place under the earth. Surely he's considered the possibility.

"You kept me alive," I say. "I'm guessing you had a reason, aside from the kick you got out of torturing me. My blood is the key, but if the Transcendents have it, too, there's no reason for me to stick around."

I speak more confidently than I really feel, half expecting him to proclaim I *am* expendable and order his Transcendents to strike me down. But he doesn't say anything.

"So, what is it?"

"Leah, I wish you wouldn't make things so difficult." He makes a flicking motion, and I gasp as the rippling air momentarily presses in on me from both sides. Heat rushes up my arms, but no fire comes to my call.

"That's no answer." My heart races. He's actively trying *not* to kill me. Am I really that valuable an experiment, or… what? "You know what my powers can do. You know I could wipe out everyone in this cave. You think I wouldn't, right?" I take a deep breath. "But I'm not your brother. I'm not Murray. And if you're planning to engage the fiends and lure them to attack Earth again, it would be a small loss. That is, if I even have a choice in the matter. I've lost control of the energy wave before."

My heart's beating fast. The last time I tried to put on an act, it didn't fool him. But this time... I'm voicing my own fears. I can't afford to get beaten down again. I won't acknowledge the fear that choked me when I was locked in with that fiend. Fear stopped my power.

It won't happen again. My power is mine, as is my blood.

Jared lifts an eyebrow. "You'd sacrifice your friends? Even him?"

Cas. No. I'd never sacrifice him, but right now, I need to save Val. Cas can look after himself. He said so himself—he has a plan. And Val's entirely at Jared's mercy. But my blood can save her.

"It's like I said. If I had to choose between saving everyone here and saving the humans left on Earth, I'd choose to wipe you and your Transcendent scum from the face of the planet." My voice gets louder; the words, stronger. I have to convince him.

"Really?" Jared's expression turns to disappointment. Not fear. But he can't deny we're at a stalemate.

He drops his hand, and the energy wave pinning me to the wall abruptly dissipates. I stumble forward.

"Come with me."

14

I follow. It's not like I have a choice. I'm no closer to finding a way out with Cas which won't leave the world to the mercy of Jared's Transcendent slaves. The real question is, why now? If Jared will do anything to win against the fiends, then leaving it this long to turn himself suggests he wasn't sure of his plan working. After the Transcendents, I guess he figured it was worth the risk. That, or the fiends really are on the brink of invading.

I just wish there was a way to get a message to Murray. To warn the others.

Jared leads the way down the corridor towards the fiends' prison. The hairs rise on my arms, and it's all I can do not to run. But the other Transcendents walk behind and to either side of me, blocking all escape.

"Wonderful, aren't they?" he asks. "Total obedience."

"What do you want, a round of applause?" I glare at the Transcendent on my right. His face is as impassive as the others. "Brainwashing isn't exactly a new concept, you know."

"Oh, I know that. It's taken me so long to fine-tune the

process. The problem with the tattoos is that they're dependent on resistance to pain. Cas gave me a lot of trouble, I confess, but that'll all change soon."

My heart sinks, but I've no idea what he means by that. "What, is he resistant to your control? Are you pissed off because you can't mind-control him?"

No answer. *So it's true.* Which means he must have more torture in mind.

My fist clenches. "Where are we going?" I ask, instead of striking him, like I want to.

"A show," says Jared. "I think you'll find it instructive, though you did a great job of disabling one of my Transcendents already."

When I stabbed the tattoo. It caused pain, but didn't release him from Jared's control. If I did that to Val, though... would it work?

And Cas?

"Did you use my blood in the tattoos as well?" I ask. "Seems a bit pointless, if they obey you anyway."

"That's the beauty of it," says Jared. "You've never seen the fiends in action, have you? Their coordination is perfect. I believe the Fiordans use some kind of blood control, though I may be mistaken. When I send my Transcendents further afield, I'll be interested in exploring other options. The Fiordans don't give up their secrets easily, but with their blood, anything is possible."

I gape at him. He can't seriously be implying that he intends to copy the Fiordans? Or—use them in some way? *He's mad.* Worse, could he be right? The Fiordans dominate the fiends through blood control?

Like the tattoos. *Oh, God. He got the idea from them.* How could he have found out something like that? Did the fiends tell him somehow, or...?

"I thought you planned to kill them," I say.

"Certainly, if they pose a threat," says Jared. "But that need not be the case. There is much to learn from the Fiordans, especially with our world in such a sorry state."

He can't mean that. Sure, it's *Jared,* and his lack of respect for the Transcendents' lives comes as no surprise. But the Fiordans? He seriously thinks we can learn from them?

My heart beats fast. "Yeah, and they destroyed their own world and most of ours, too. If you take their technology, or whatever it is you're planning, you'll do even more damage."

But that won't happen. I'll kill him first. No matter what the cost. *The Fiordans are the ones who destroyed our world.*

And we share blood. But so does Jared now.

"I think we're all a little wiser this time around, Leah," says Jared.

I tense as we pass by the fiend's cage to the sound of shuffles and growls, but Jared doesn't stop. Another turn later, and we come to a deserted corridor with one set of double doors at the far end. Jared pushes them open with his clawed hand, the other beckoning us to follow.

Seats form rows at the front of the room but the majority of the space is covered by a cage with rust-red bars, right up to the high ceiling.

It comes as no surprise to me when Jared orders two of the Transcendents to enter the cage, then locks the door and orders them to fight until neither can continue.

So this is my latest punishment: to watch him assess the Transcendents and judge their skills. Sick anger gives way to resignation when it becomes clear neither of them will give ground. He must have ordered them not to use their Transcendent powers. Even those bars won't stand up to an energy blast.

The Transcendents are evenly matched. All are quick, lethal, and emotionless. The perfect soldiers. But I stopped one of them before. If Jared wants me to fight them, he's going to get a show, all right. His words ring in my ears. *Blood control.* But if it's blood that's the key, and they have *my* blood… maybe there's something I *can* do.

It can't be that easy. No way. He wouldn't have told me if he thought I could use the information to my advantage. No way.

The fight's over. Blood streaks the arena floor, and one Transcendent kneels over the other, his face also streaked in blood. Neither makes a sound, but their pained expressions force me to look away. Jared applauds, while the others look on blankly.

At his orders, the other Transcendents drag their fallen comrades out of the arena. Then he points to another pair. So this is how it's going to be. I glare at him, but he's watching the show with rapt attention. I'll bet he doesn't care who the superior fighters are. He just enjoys the violence.

The sick bastard.

Finally, I'm pitted against the remaining Transcendent, as I predicted. Val isn't invited in, presumably because the Transcendents will take her to pieces, and Jared intends to hold her fate over me. Like everyone else's.

"Are you sure?" I ask him. "I'm having doubts about obeying you, Jared. I'm not bound by the same orders as your servants. My powers might escape by accident and destroy this place. What if this fight pushes me over the edge?"

"It won't," he says. "I know what you're capable of, Leah. If the power didn't activate in defence of your life against that fiend, it won't here." He points me towards the cage. "I'll let you keep your weapon."

Not like even he could pry it out of my hand anyway. But it's given me an idea.

The Transcendent attacks the instant the cage door closes. His fist swings, and I duck the blow with the reflexes of a Pyro. I don't know how much fighting training these guys had before Jared took them under his wing, but I'm not about to give ground easily.

I block and dodge a few more blows, trying to get an opening. I've no intention of giving Jared the horror show he's expecting, and even now, the idea of crippling another human being is repellent. But if Jared's putting me under watch, this may be the one chance I'll get to try out my theory.

I catch the Transcendent's fist in my hands with a blast of fire, taking my chance to throw myself at him. The momentum sends him crashing to the ground, where I pin him down and swipe at his tattoo with the dagger. The Transcendent stops mid-strike, making a low noise of pain. I dig the knife in deeper, then yank it free and slash my own palm. Still pinning him with my entire body weight, I press the flat of my palm against his tattoo.

Jared's yelling something, but I concentrate on the rush of adrenaline in my veins, and the beat of blood as it rises to the surface.

"You obey me now," I whisper to the Transcendent. "Get us out of this cage. Attack Jared. He's your enemy."

Nothing happens for a long moment. My heart thuds like a trapped bird against the walls of a cage. If my guess is wrong, there'll be hell to pay.

The Transcendent's head snaps up and locks on Jared.

I quickly jump back before I'm thrown off him, and the Transcendent lunges for the door, hands outstretched.

Everything blurs in confusion. Jared barks orders at the first Transcendents to fight, but they're having difficulty walking after they beat each other up a few minutes ago. The Transcendent I gave the order to easily knocks them down and makes for Jared. He looks more angry than frightened, but the red-tinged knife gleams in his hands. I shove my way out the cage as the Transcendent leaps at Jared.

My target is Val.

Jared hasn't given her an order. She stands as blank-faced as the rest were. As the other Transcendents are caught up in confusion, no one even looks at her. She doesn't react when I grab her tattooed hand and swipe the side of my blade across it.

Unlike the Transcendent, Val doesn't scream. But when I cut the rest of the way around the flame on her wrist, trying my best not to press too hard, she gasps in pain. Whimpers behind me suggest Jared's got the better of the Transcendent, but I can't stop now.

"Sorry," I whisper to Val, and drag her after me out of the room.

Jared's shouts follow me, and there's the sound of a scuffle. The Transcendent's still fighting. *It can't stop obeying your orders.* I'll deal with that thought later. I pull Val alongside me, wishing I'd thought of a plan rather than acting on the spur of the moment.

"Are the others safe?" I ask.

Val's eyes are wide, and confusion crosses her face as her gaze drops to the cut on her arm, but she nods. "How did you do that?"

"Long story," I say. "The others?"

"There's a camp not far from here. We weren't sure of the location. But when I felt the tattoo… he did something to me."

"I know," I say. "But I stopped it."

It worked. It actually worked. And… I can use blood control like Jared. But right now, I can't think about that. We need to run.

"You don't remember the way out, do you?" I ask. "Are the others close by?"

When she nods, my heart can't help but lift. "We have to

move fast." I let Val lead the way, and my heart sinks again when I remember the security fiend.

And Cas. He can't still be hiding behind the wall, can he? To think he didn't even try to intervene. But however much of a coward he's acting now, I came here to rescue him. I can't leave him behind.

We round the corner and I'm forced to shove those thoughts to the back of my head. The fiend's there, all right, blocking the whole corridor with its lava-like form.

I nod to Val, and we sneak up behind it, one of us on each side of the corridor. *Finally* a fight where I have the upper hand.

I take a swing at the fiend's hunched, ugly back. My dagger is melded to my other hand, and ready to intercept as the fiend awkwardly twists its body in an attempt to strike back. Val doesn't have a weapon, I realise belatedly. But we can take the fiend down with our fists, even an engineered one like this.

The beast snarls and lashes out with clawed hands, but the corridor boxes it in. I hit all its vulnerable spots, and the fire finally answers my call. Like it's always been there. A rush of heat flares down my arm to my fist, and my punch blasts the beast into pieces. Val watches, wide-eyed, as rock-like fragments crumble to the ground.

"Wow," she says. I forgot just how much I haven't told the others about what I can do. I'm not even sure how much I *can* tell them, especially about the messed-up connection with Cas. But the others need to know Jared has created more Transcendents. And that he's changed himself, too. With my blood.

I've taken back some control again. I freed Val. Maybe there's more I can do. It's *my* blood. But we're not ready for this fight. Even as Val and I kick the remains of the fiend aside and climb past, I'm torn in two. There's no way Cas could have got past the fiend without fighting it. He *must* be hiding. But Jared and the Transcendents are that way, and they won't be incapacitated for long. I can't risk Val getting captured again.

One thing for it. I have to let her take me to the way out, and then go back for Cas. It's the only way I can think of to get the others out unscathed without Jared getting his hands on anyone else.

Taking a deep breath, I walk alongside Val, swiftly, wondering why it's taking Jared so long to catch up. Maybe the Transcendents really hurt him. He created them to be invincible, after all. But we can't count on anything.

We pass by the training room and pick up the pace as the discordant noises of fighting come from up ahead. Screams and weapons crashing. The training hall is deserted, which means one thing: its occupants are busy fighting somewhere else.

The others really did come back.

I can't help myself. I stop and peer behind the alcove in the wall near the fiend's remains. No sign of Cas. Of course. *Trust me*, he said. Trust him to stay alive while I get the others out? Can I really do that?

"What are you doing?" she hisses.

"Cas and I hid behind here." Not that I think he'd hide from a fight, but it's beyond me to tell where he could have disappeared to. He could have wandered anywhere on this side of the base while I was forced to watch the Transcendents fight. God knows. Surely he guessed I'd be followed? Surely he didn't think Murray would abandon both of us?

"Now what?" she asks, as I push open the door to the training room and scan the floor and walls.

"You can't go out there unarmed," I say. "Not if they're blocking the exit. There's nowhere safe to hide here."

"I got in okay," Val says. "Jared has some nasty booby traps. Three people lost their weapons trying to get in."

"They did?" My heart sinks, and a new suspicion prickles at me. *Too easy*, I think, though I suppose Jared never could have anticipated what I did to the Transcendent. Though he was the one who told me I could use my blood to control it in the first place.

And what does that mean for the war?

Later. I spot a dagger discarded on the floor. I toss it to Val, and we take off down the corridor again. Towards the noise.

Before we reach the end, a deafening boom shakes the walls. I glance at Val, whose eyes are wide. The floor trembles. *Not an energy blast?* But though my ears ring, and particles of dust rain from the ceiling, there's no ripple of energy in the air. No widespread destruction. I shake my head, willing the noise to clear.

Val mouths at me, "It's all right, Leah. Let's move!"

I want to ask what in the world she means, but at that moment, a guard runs into view, pursued by two red-cloaked figures. Flames burst into life, and the guard cries out as his entire body catches fire.

"Enough!" Val shouts at the Pyros, one of whom turns to glare at her. "That's enough. They're brainwashed."

"Thought you ran out on us," says the Pyro, a shaven-headed guy I don't recognise. "You're not on his side, are you?"

"No," says Val. "Long story. We need to move. Did you get the fiends?"

"Garry blew a hole in the wall," says the other guy. "I hoped it'd do more damage."

"What are you talking about?" I ask. "What was that blast?"

"Later," says Val.

The guys have already run off, leaving the guard smoking on the floor. An expression of agony marks his face, and I force myself to look away as we follow.

It's chaos. The corridors aren't anywhere near wide enough to fight in even without the fiends. As it is, two giant monsters block the way, but through gaps between them, I can see red-cloaked figures fighting. And the noise is over-powering. The clang of metal re-ignites the fire in my bones, and I launch myself at the nearest fiend with a hoarse scream.

My dagger easily slices through the fiend's arm in a frenzy of flames. Val kicks at the second giant, while I make easy work of my target, leaving a mess of fragmented rock all over the corridor. But I don't stop. I have to stop Jared's guards hurting the others. If a small group came to find us, they're bound to be outnumbered. Val's dispatched her opponent, and we follow the red-cloaked figures around the corner.

Shoving a guard aside, I run through the newly-cleared corridor. The other Pyros easily took care of the fiends, but if I'm anything to go by, the Transcendents won't be far behind.

"You have to go," I say to the others. "Jared's held back, but he'll come after us. He's pretty pissed at me. I turned his puppets against him. One of them, anyway." I'm rambling. I need them to see they have to get out of here before we're trapped. But Cas… *he told you to leave him.*

I turn to Val. "Can you make sure everyone gets out?"

"This again?" Her mouth turns down. "Look, Leah, I know you came back for Cas, but our priority's getting as far away from this place as possible. He's probably Jared's minion by now."

"Don't say that. He isn't."

But can I risk everything for his sake, knowing it might

do no good anyway? *Trust me.*

"What happened to you?" asks a suspicious-looking guy I don't know. "You and Cas actually worked with Jared? Val, too?"

"Not exactly," says Val. "Well, I can't speak for Cas."

"He's on our side," I say quickly. "What was the plan, then? Because even if you kill the guards, Jared's made himself unkillable now. And he's planning to lure the fiends over here."

"Seriously?" The Pyro curses, kicking pieces of dismembered fiend aside. "Murray never said anything about that. We were just supposed to get you out."

Get me out. The truth clicks into place. *Hell.* Now I know what Jared's plan was. *My blood is the key.* He planned to use me to lure the fiends over to this world. Except because he's changed himself, he doesn't have to use *me* to do that.

So why did he let me stay? Unless he had some other plan for me. I never did find any research on the Transcendent.

A roar behind us. *More fiends.* They can't have escaped the cages, can they? Unless Jared set them on us.

Several Pyros run towards me. Then more—at least twenty, too many for the corridor to hold. "Get out!" one of them yells. "There's a big-ass fiend coming this way."

"Come *on*, Leah," says Val. "Cas can take care of himself, remember?"

Before I can reply, the crowd surrounds us, and I'm pulled along with them. I can't fight my way back without hurting anyone.

The corridor walls and floor tremble. *They're not safe. You have to get them out.*

I picture Cas looking at me with disdain in his expression as if to ask why I'd risk the others' lives for his sake. Cursing him, I follow the others, leaving the noise of the rampaging fiend behind.

15

Guilt trails me as I join the others. *We'll come back,* I think. But I feel like a coward all the same. Either way, Jared won't take this lying down. He'll strike the others.

I have to be there to protect them.

Screaming behind us prompts the leading Pyros to quicken their pace. The hairs stand up on my arms, though the screams don't sound human. *Fiends. They must have escaped.* Surely not the one in the cage, though—that fiend ought to be pissed enough to tear Jared to pieces.

We reach a blank stretch of corridor past Jared's rooms. I'm tempted to backtrack and check if he's hidden anything in there, but if he had anything useful, it'd be in the labs. Hell, my *blood's* probably the most dangerous, volatile thing in here, and thanks to my idiotic decision to go after Cas, twelve brainwashed mutants and Jared himself have it.

There's no time for regret now. The Pyros leading the way take us into another corridor, and Val shoves at a wall panel, revealing a hidden staircase. It's a narrow fit and we have to climb single-file, but I make everyone else go in front of me first. I don't trust Jared not to have a last booby trap. I hang about until the last moment, and a warning shout from Val forces me to follow the others into the stairway.

The space is tight, too tight. My throat closes with each step. We're running away. I'm running away. The thought of using my powers to bring the ceiling down and make sure Jared and the fiends can't get out strikes me, but we'd be condemning Cas to death along with the others. Would Murray allow that? Last time he and his brother spoke, he said he didn't want to kill Jared. But what about now, when Jared's mutilated himself, made himself into one of the fiends?

The questions press on me like the tight walls, but soon, the smell of clean air fills my lungs. We climb fast, and the stairs become a sloping tunnel, then flat ground, then...

I roll out onto burned ground, breathing in sharp gasps. The other Pyros are recovering. Val grabs my hand and pulls me to my feet. "Everyone's out."

"Not everyone," I whisper.

The world goes black, and I fade away.

My back throbs, sharp daggers behind my shoulder blades. I'm lying on a table, Jared bending over me, grinning a manic smile. This Jared has a clawed hand.

But he doesn't see the Transcendent until it's too late.

The figure leaps from the ceiling, wings spread wide, and slams into Jared. I catch a glimpse of the expression of total shock on his face before the scene blurs into agony again and I'm floating.

No, two people are carrying me, my legs draped over someone's arm. I snap to my senses immediately. I'm outside, and we escaped the lab...

"She's awake!" says one of the guys carrying me. Ryan, I think his name was.

"Yeah." There's no dignified way to jump to the ground, but it's better than being carried. My feet slam down onto the cracked soil. "The Transcendents are going crazy back in the lab."

I realise my mistake a second too late.

"Transcendents?"

Now they're staring at me. Twenty or so red-uniformed Pyros in total, all bedraggled-looking but none visibly hurt.

None of whom have a clue what Jared's really doing in there.

"I'll tell you later," I say, lamely. *Oh. God.* Murray didn't tell them about Jared's habit of experimenting on anything that moves.

The lying has to end. Secrets got us into this mess in the first place. I have to tell them the truth. Even if it means they see me as non-human. As like Jared. Now he's one of *them,* even Murray won't be able to deny the others need to know.

We hurry, running uphill. This area's all Burned Spots, not as much as a blade of grass under the red sky. The world didn't change during my time underground, though it feels like I was gone much longer than a few days. Now, it hits me just how much I want to see the others. To know they're all right.

And yet, I can't stop thinking of that last vision. If I take it as true, the scene must have happened right now. One of the Transcendents attacked Jared. What the hell is happening down there?

And what's happening to Cas?

Occasionally, a fiend cries out in the distance, but my ears have become accustomed to picking up which sounds are likely to be a threat, and the noise comes from beyond the divide. We're moving away from that direction. Away from the labs.

Finally, we come to a rise, where a number of tents appear as if from nowhere. This seems too close to Jared's place, but when I turn to look back the way we came, I can't see anything but burned ground. I'd forgotten how quick Pyros move, even carrying me, unconscious.

I never found a way to shut off the visions, and instead of breaking the connection between Cas and me, what if I'm linked up to the Transcendents as well?

The image rises again, accompanied by the coppery taste of blood and the smell of burning. But I blink furiously. I can't lose control again.

Talk to Murray first.

"Murray's not here," I say to Val, glancing around at the red-cloaked shapes walking amongst the tents. "Right?"

"No. He couldn't leave Elle, especially when no one knows where Nolan went."

Something twists inside me. "He's dead," I say, as we start to descend the rise into the camp.

"At least there's some good news."

I swallow hard. I don't think Nolan was a villain, not like Jared, anyway. But that thought's too complicated for now.

"How'd he die?" asks Ryan.

"Jared's fiends," I say. "They took him to pieces, I think. I blacked out then, so I wasn't conscious when Jared took me into the labs. That's why I didn't know whereabouts Jared's place actually was."

"We do now," says Ryan. "We're going to stake it out. I know he has all kinds of batshit-crazy monsters in there, but we can't afford to let him live any longer. If Murray's thing works…"

"Murray's thing?" I ask, but at that moment, a crowd descends on us.

"Leah's alive!"

Poppy and Tyler launch themselves at me and hug me, almost knocking me off my feet. "Whoa," I say. "Calm down."

"We thought you were dead," says Tyler. "Poppy was frantic, she thought Nolan had abducted you in the middle of the night."

Guilt sinks its claws in me. "It's kind of complicated. I'm sorry I left you guys."

"You're back now," says Poppy. "You went into Jared's lair alone?" Poppy exchanges raised eyebrows with Tyler. "Did you really miss Cas that much?"

She gives me a look, like she wants me to start on about what a wonderful person Cas is, underneath all the sarcastic bitterness. Except I can't exactly do that. I have no idea what I think of him, let alone whether he's a good person. I think he is, but how do I know what I think isn't the result of our bizarre connection?

"We couldn't afford to lose another warrior, could we?" I say instead.

"You're hopeless," says Poppy with a slight flicker of a smile.

Tyler grins. "You have to tell us all about Jared's creepy place. Does he really have robot servants?"

I start to speak, but the words won't come. Jared's torturing Cas there right now. And how many brainwashed-but-innocent people died because of us?

"Sorry," he says quickly, his mouth pulling into a frown. "I forgot. It was probably awful for you, wasn't it? I'm sorry."

"It's okay." But it isn't. None of this is fine, not a bit. I've dragged all these people into danger, and it'd be doubly hard to ditch them again if I decide to go after Jared. But I can't beat him alone. Even with Cas.

If he's alive.

Stupid thought. Cas is pretty hard to kill.

The image of him on that table fills my head.

Stop. "Look, I need to talk to whoever's in charge of the camp," I say. "This is important. I hoped Murray might be here, but he's going to be pretty mad at me for telling you all this."

"Telling us what?" asks Poppy.

"Leah?" Val's back, and she hands me a flask of water. "Come over here."

They've made a campfire, and it startles me to see the sun sinking. The red of the sky never changes. I lost all sense of time underground, and the memory of the fiends stalking me in the cold night rises again as it always does when I'm outside.

Two other Pyros, the senior members I vaguely recognise, argue with one another. Now I'm closer, I can pick up the drift. They're talking about the tattoos. And Jared.

"We can't let him live," says one, Peter, with a brief look at Val. "How many more of us has he marked up? What about the others at the base?"

"I think we should be talking about how she didn't *tell* us," adds the other guy. Garry. "How many more of you have those tattoos?" he shouts across the campfire in general.

"Tattoos?" Poppy exchanges glances with Tyler, puzzlement etched on both their faces.

Crap. Did Jared only call Val, or are there others from the base under his control coming this way? He implied as much when he threatened me. *Oh, no.*

"If you'd all *be quiet*," says Val, raising her voice, "I'll explain."

"Explain what?"

"Why you ran out on us?" says a younger guy. "I thought you'd joined Jared's lot."

"Quiet, guys," says Ryan. "Val was under... mind control?"

"Not exactly," says Val. Now everyone's listening. The other Pyros, about twenty-five of them in total, move closer around the campfire. "Look, I'll be honest. I don't think we have a lot of time to debate, but I guess I owe you an explanation. How many of you were mentored by Jared back when he was Murray's equal?"

Two hands go up amongst the senior Pyros.

"He marked some of us as his special favourites… literally." She pushes up the red sleeve of her coat, and peels back a bandage on her forearm. Of course. The cut from my dagger when I broke the mark won't have healed. I instantly feel ashamed for assuming everyone has crazy healing powers. What's the matter with me?

Val raises her arm to reveal the mark, and the cut slicing across it, gleaming in the firelight. "This gives him the power to control me through blood. I don't know everyone he marked, but that's what he did to Nolan. He can inflict horrible pain on us, if he wants. Nolan betrayed us because he was afraid of that."

Silence, aside from the fire's crackling.

"So… yeah. It's messed-up. I thought he was dead, and the whole thing freaked me out, so I never told anyone about it. Even when Jared came back, he didn't use the tattoos, except on Nolan."

"And Cas," I say quickly. "That's why he got caught."

Val catches my gaze, surprise flashing in her eyes. "So that's why…"

"Yeah," I say. "Did he use it on you while you were at camp?"

"Must have done," says Val. "I don't remember most of the past day, up until you cut the mark, Leah." Her voice shakes. "The others back at the base don't know, but some of them will be marked, too." And that's the cue for the silence to end as the air explodes with questions.

"Did he do it to everyone?"

"Mind control's impossible, even for *them*."

"Jared's capable of anything!" Val shouts over the group. "It's more than that. Leah has something to tell you."

My heart sinks. But I have to tell them, now. Even if it kills their faith in Murray.

"All right," I say, once it's quiet. "Murray didn't want anyone to know this, but I expect you've all heard the term *Transcendent*?"

I assume from the silent response that means yes.

"Well, that's me. At least, I'm one of them. It's complicated, but Cas's blood healed me when the fiends attacked me. Just before I came to the base." He'll be pissed at me for sharing his secret, but what does it matter now?

"Healed you?"

Confusion ripples through the group. Val nods, confirming she knew, but it doesn't look like many of the others did. I briefly run through the history of the Transcendents, from my arrival at the group, Murray thinking I might be Transcendent and then realising Cas's healing me must have made it possible. Then I explain about Jared's experiments and how they tie into the whole thing. "I had no idea about any of this until Jared threatened us." I'm trying to get the words out as quickly as possible. "Jared wanted his hands on me *and* Cas, so we went to him to stop him attacking the base. I managed to escape and his lab was destroyed by the fiends, but Jared survived the attack and took Cas. I wanted to stop Jared using his blood to create more Transcendents."

"So that's why?" asks Garry, loudly. "I thought you just went back because of him."

Doesn't take a genius to figure out he means Cas.

I narrow my eyes at him, in a pretty spot-on imitation of Cas himself. "I went in there to kill Jared. It didn't quite work out that way."

"So he doesn't have you under mind control or anything?"

"No. Those tattoos of his control you through blood, but they don't work on Transcendents the same way. He tried to use an injection on me instead, but Cas sabotaged it."

People are muttering to one another, but I raise my voice. "Jared kept me prisoner and tortured me, the same as he's doing to Cas. He's made twelve of his own Transcendents, but he also took my blood and used it on himself. I don't know how, but he made himself into one. Like the engineered fiends. You can still hurt him, but he'll heal himself. The Transcendents are the same."

This time, the shouts drown out my voice. Questions. Accusations. I let them wash over me, then shout, "Listen!"

Amazingly, the noise quietens.

"It's up to you if you want to attack him or not. I don't know how we escaped the lab so easily, but I'm betting he's up to more twisted crap in there, and his insanity's drawn the fiends' attention. He's right by the divide. If they attack us again, they'll wipe us out."

"So will Jared," says a despondent voice. "You're telling us we're doomed either way?"

I can't answer. I don't know myself. Only that we've survived for too long to give up now. *Cas has a plan. He said he did.* "This was always a long shot," I say. "Us against the fiends. But I killed one of their leaders before. They're not invincible. And his Transcendents were in pretty bad shape the last time I saw them. They might not die easily, but they can be injured."

"And that's where our plan comes in," says Val, who's taken this news with surprising calmness. "Our new weapon. Murray's, really. We haven't tested it yet, but we always work on the assumption that our targets are going to be wicked-tough to kill. It's basically an energy blast, but contained."

The dim light of the campfire shines on a shape in her

hands. Looks like some fancy kind of electronic device, but the reddish colour of rock.

"What *is* that?" I ask.

"Murray scraped it together," says Val. "It's… a bomb, I suppose. He used bits of technology scavenged from the old labs. We've been gathering the stuff for months. It's supposed to be fiend technology."

Fiend technology. Their leaders are an intelligent species. A chill runs down my back at the thought of so many enemies waiting out there. What is there to do? Set Jared and the fiends against each other and hope some part of the planet survives another war?

"So you planned to… to blow up the lab, with him inside it?"

"Yes, but we don't know if he's reinforced the place or not. That blast earlier when we were escaping was a smaller version, a test-run, right?" She nods to Ryan. "It took out one of the walls, but not enough. We're not sure how much ground Jared's place covers, but for it to have survived that long, he must have done something to it. If the bigger bomb went off, it'd bring down the ceiling, crushing everyone below. We were going to do it as soon as we got you out. Even a Pyro can't survive it. But that was before you told us…"

"He can't die." Damn. I've killed their hope. "His servants can, but they're not Pyros. If it's like an energy blast, we can't die either, right?"

"No. It'll only take out the enemy. I planted it before we left."

A moment passes. I stare at her. She looks tired, sad, but resolute. Others wear similar expressions, though my ears pick up on a whispered argument about Murray and Jared being in cahoots. The experiments. I don't have time to argue with all the dissenters now. Not with everything depending on us making a decision as quickly as possible.

I let the general noise resume while Val exchanges words with Peter, the senior Pyro. The other, Garry, is arguing with Ryan. Sounds like Garry thinks we shouldn't have bothered coming. It wasn't worth the risk. I don't particularly care what he thinks of me, but it's a reminder that I'm the one who took the risk without thinking half the Pyros would come after me and wind up in danger. We were lucky not to lose anyone. *Too* lucky. The only explanation is the vision, and even that makes no sense. What was Jared doing to Cas that was more important than chasing us off?

I've shared as much as I can with the group, but they're demoralised enough already. Several shout questions at me. I ignore them.

"Val," I say, in an undertone. "Can I talk to you alone? It's urgent."

She glances at another Pyro, who's in the middle of gesturing at the metal contraption at her side. The bomb. None of us can die from a regular, non-Transcendent energy blast, but I eye it warily all the same.

"One minute," says Peter. "You have a *lot* to answer for, Leah, but if it affects our plan…"

"It does," I say.

Once I've checked no one's listening in, I ask, "How do you use the bombs?"

"With Pyro fire," she says, showing me the device. "I planted one in the lab and I was going to activate it as soon as we got out, but I wasn't sure we'd get out of range in time."

"Seriously?"

"I'd do it now, if I could."

"Cas is in there." Sure, he can't die, but burying him under a ton of rock with Jared after everything he's been through already isn't a fate I'd wish on anyone else. Especially after all the trouble I went through to find him.

"If he's the one who can create Transcendents in the first place, then…" She cuts herself off. I stop mid-curse as I see she's struggling not to cry. "What choice do we have? Jared's entire team's in there and it's the one way to take them all out at once. There are innocent people under Jared's spell, but if it wins us some time, Leah, we might have no choice."

I can't fault her for that. I slump to sit on a rock beside her. "Look, this is going to sound weird. But healing me isn't the only thing Cas's blood did to me. It… changed me. I sometimes get these weird flashes, like visions, where I can see what he does. Sometimes it's a memory, sometimes it's not. But they're real. I feel when he gets hurt. It's like we're connected." I'm rambling because her expression is incredulous, and panic threatens to overwhelm my tiredness. "It's got worse lately. That's what happened when we were climbing out of the lab. I saw… him. Cas. Jared was torturing him again." I stop. "It's my blood. The Transcendents are linked through my blood, but they don't get the same visions. It's all connected, though. I can influence them, like… you know how the fiend armies seem to work together? It's the leaders. They use blood control, something similar."

Val shakes her head, her face pale. "What…? Did Murray know *that?*"

"I don't know," I say honestly. "He kept a lot of things from us, but Jared was behind most of the experiments. Anyway, he says my blood works like the Fiordans'. That's what the fiends' leaders are called. I can control the Transcendents. Somehow. But it doesn't work on Jared…" Or does it? My mind spins. I haven't had time to process all this, let alone think of a plan.

"You… you can control the fiends?"

"I don't know," I say. "The Transcendents, definitely. That's why one attacked him when we were escaping."

"Oh." Her eyes widen. "So you… wow. Leah, this could redefine our whole strategy. You said you saw what's happening in the lab?"

"Yeah. But I never know *when* the visions are taking place. I can't see the future, only the present. And memories, sometimes. I have no idea how it works. It's through Cas, and I saw a Transcendent attack him. That's the truth. But I don't know when that was. Or Jared's plan. He said I was expendable now he has his little army, but he didn't expect me to be able to control them." He didn't expect me to take ownership of my own blood. But now I have, I'm using it. No question.

"Damn." Val brushes dust-streaked hair from her forehead. Her hands are shaking. "I don't … it'd be safer to activate the bomb now…" Her gaze passes over the other senior Pyros. "We didn't plan for this. Our strategy was to get you out, and blow up the place with him and his crazy scientists inside it. Minimal damage. He's far too close to the divide."

Yeah. He is. If we use the energy blasts, we could be dooming ourselves… and the rest of the world. Is it worth the risk?

"And the tattoos are another problem," she adds. "We need to make a decision now, but everyone's tired from the trek here. We've been running flat-out. Barely reached here when I blacked out thanks to that tattoo. But he can't have known we're here…"

"He might have. His flying fiends are everywhere," I say. "And I guess I know how he's controlling them now. Blood, again. He's been injecting himself with theirs. Before he decided to *make* himself one of them."

"Transcendents and the fiends," Val says quietly. "They're not the same, though, are they? Fiends can die. Their leaders… you said you killed one?"

"Just about," I say. "I controlled an energy blast, and..." I shake my head, wishing, not for the first time, that I'd tried to find out more from Jared before I struck back at him and forced him to put his plan into motion. "I don't think the fiends are our worst problem now, to be honest."

No sooner do the words leave my mouth than a familiar cry rings out, cutting through the noise of camp.

The sound of fiends on the hunt.

16

O h, God," says Val. "Who's idea was it to camp here?"

"Good question." My heart drops. As if we need to be anyone else's targets. *Too close to the divide...* but it could just as easily be Jared's fiends I heard.

"We're hidden," says Peter. "Ryan, could you check?" he calls across the campfire. Ryan nods and heads up the cliff again.

"There's a small town over the rise, though," says Val. "It's reinforced, but Jared's fiends can fly."

My heart sinks. *Oh, no.* Have we unwittingly put everyone in the area in danger?

"We can't go around saving everyone," says Garry, exasperation clear on his face. "You're telling us our enemy's got mind-control abilities and has turned himself into a freakshow with a bunch of invincible servants, on top of the mad fiends he's already got on his side. We can't protect every human and our own at the same time."

Val says, "This is ridiculous. We need to vote on our plan. It would help if we stopped arguing amongst ourselves. We came here to save Leah and we did it, and the logical plan is to rest here. If the fiends attack, we fight. Then we head back to the base as soon as we're rested up. Tell Murray the latest."

"It'd help if we had mobile phones," says Tyler. "How many fiends are there? We only heard the one cry."

"You're not going," Val says. "I only agreed to let you and Poppy come because you'd have followed to get Leah anyway."

Guilt rises as I look over at them. I'd completely forgotten they're not fully qualified Pyros yet. Neither should I be, technically, but my training was accelerated thanks to my being Transcendent. They're kids, thrown into the middle of a war.

"You two should stay put," I say, standing. "I'm going to look out, see if I can spot where the noise came from."

"Already taken care of," says Ryan, appearing at my side. "Val, there are two of them prowling around up there. Not too close to the town, but the way they're moving... I don't like it. It's like they've picked a target and are stalking them."

"Not us?" Val's on her feet, too.

Ryan shakes his head, the hood of his coat falling forward. "No. They're too far off. I could barely see them."

"Damn," says Val. "Okay. I vote we send a couple of people over there to check it out. Ryan?"

"Leah," he says. "Does being Transcendent give you enhanced eyesight?"

"Uh... not that I know of. But I'll come."

If we're going to fight, I need to be at the front of the action. Better that than being Jared's experiment.

"You're not leaving again?" says Poppy.

"I'm quick," I say. "I won't be long."

"Just don't get caught again." Tyler joins Poppy. "Seeing as we came all the way out here to find you."

"Don't worry." I force a smile. "You forget I'm inde-structible."

"Yeah…" Poppy exchanges an anxious look with Tyler. "Were you ever going to tell us you're Transcendent?"

Oh, crap. "I didn't know for sure until… a few days ago? Cas and I had to leave in a hurry. We didn't want to cause a panic. And then, when I went after him… the same." It's a lame excuse. I should have trusted them.

"Murray kept us in the dark," says Tyler. "I always thought he was a bit distant, but I guess it explains why he never talked about his family. His brother's a giant dick."

I start to laugh, then stop. "He's one of the monsters now. Keep an eye out from here, okay? I'll be back in a minute, but just in case."

Even if his Transcendents turned on him, it's been quiet far too long.

As if on cue, another screech sounds, this one closer. I say goodbye to Poppy and Tyler and run to join Ryan.

"They talked about you nonstop all the way here," he says. "They were worried. Elle was hysterical too."

"I don't understand," I say, in a low voice, as we climb the rise. "Why risk everything to come after me?"

"Why'd you risk everything to go after Cas? It's human nature, Leah."

Human. Pyros never thought of themselves as separate, except Cas. But Transcendents? My blood marks me as different. What happens when the last of my humanity is burned out of me?

The burning sky and the noise of fiend screams are a blazing reminder that *normal* as I knew it will never exist again for anyone. But I can at least keep the people I care about safe from the dark shapes becoming clearer by the minute. On the ground, not flying, though their silhouettes are too hazy to make out whether they have wings or not.

I nod to Ryan. I don't know him, but I'm glad of the company. We walk slowly at first, to get our bearings and figure out where, exactly, the fiends are heading. Not this way, nor towards the distant walled shape of a town. I can't tell if it's the one Nolan and I passed by. I'm struck, for the thousandth time, by the alienness of my own planet.

Our planet. Jared's lost the right to be part of it.

"They aren't Jared's," I say in an undertone to Ryan. "They're not enhanced." But they're definitely moving with purpose. We walk in a curve so we end up behind them, at an angle, a hundred metres away.

And then I see what—*who*—they're stalking, and the blood freezes in my veins.

People. Wearing red coats, except one, a small figure in the middle of the group. All crossing the burned ground in an uneven formation but perfectly in step. Like robots.

Like they're under blood control.

"No," I whisper. "He activated the tattoos."

How could I forget? Val's is deactivated, at least for now—I can't know for sure that I permanently stopped it. With Jared, there's no real way of knowing.

Right now, the important thing is driving off those fiends. Whether Jared sent them or not, the marked Pyros are distracted. I don't know if the tattoos affect their ability to use their powers, but I can't risk it. I draw my weapon, with another nod to Ryan as we get within range of the fiends.

One of them spins around, ugly face twisted, giant hand already clenching. No claws. These bastards aren't going to live.

I launch myself forward in a burst of energy that propels me higher than I intended to jump, and I slam down in front of the fiend, fire bursting from my outstretched hands and sending them both staggering back. Slow. They're too slow.

And they're not going to hurt my friends.

Ryan runs at them from behind, swinging a short sword. The first fiend recovers, but I easily dodge its clumsy fist and stab the point of my blade into its arm, sending a burst of fire alongside it. The fiend screeches as the limb goes up in flames.

As do I. Fire flares up from my hands, catching the other fiend before it can run. The ground starts to shake under my feet.

I falter. *No. You can't lose control.* I won't use the energy blast here.

I don't need to. The fiend collapses in a halo of flames, and Ryan's made short work of the second one. I jump over the monster's crumbled remains and head after the retreating group.

None of them turn around, even though they must be able to hear me. They're too deep under Jared's spell.

"Leah!" Ryan calls a warning, but too late. I sprint across the burned ground, realising in horror that we're closer than I thought to Jared's place. I recognise the dip in the ground where we left, even though I was half-conscious when climbing the ladder and leaving with Val and the others.

I skid to a halt, a couple of metres in front of them, between the Pyros and Jared's lair. Not one of them stops walking. They're so out of it, they might well mow me down.

Yet I can't help it. "Stop," I say loudly. "You don't have to do this."

My heart's beating fast, my eyes scanning for an opening. I have to get Elle out first, but she's right in the middle of the group, and I can't guarantee the others won't turn on her afterwards. Damn. I aim for a guy on the right, one I don't recognise, and grab for his left arm. The one which will bear Jared's mark.

He snaps into action the instant my fingers brush his

hand, drawing his weapon with the other. The others do likewise.

So be it.

I block his strike with the edge of my own blade, wishing I had two. Quickly, I grab the wrist holding the sword with my other hand, drawing on every bit of Transcendent-enhanced tenacity I can, and squeeze as hard as I can possibly manage. His grip falters on his weapon, and in a burst of inspiration, I send a jolt of fire through mine. The flames don't hurt him, but makes his blade tremble and drop a fraction. I wish I knew more about how to disarm a person. We only really covered how to fight the monsters, not each other, and attacks that would disable a normal person have no effect on a Pyro.

The others have backed away from the fire. That makes no sense, but I have to press my advantage. I set my other hand ablaze, the one gripping his arm, and he flinches. Instinct, I'd guess. He can't be a new Pyro. Shame the coat's fireproof, even though I don't want to do any more damage than I have to. These Pyros don't heal, and they're miles from the base here. They must have walked nonstop.

The ground shakes without warning. *I'm not doing that.* No. Something else is brewing, a thickness in the air quite separate from the fire burning around my hands, around me. His weapon drops, and I quickly shift my dagger and slice the skin of his palm. He yelps and lets go, and just like that, he's disarmed. In fact, his eyes are empty. The others have stopped, too.

Something isn't right.

Another tremor. Wait. We're standing directly on top of Jared's headquarters at the moment.

And something's happening underneath. Unless it's coming from the divide.

Blood spurts. I've cut his arm blindly, but not too deep. I

grab his hand, seeing I've nicked the edge of the tattoo, and complete the cut. I do the same to my hand, press it to his…

A quake sends us both flying. He slams into the ground, while I roll over uncontrollably, sudden bursts of pain exploding behind my eyes.

I can't see. It's dark. There's something big moving in the darkness…

Cas. He's with the fiends.

And I'm back in my own body again, coughing on dust, blinking it from my eyes. I've rolled right to the edge of the rise.

Below is the entrance to Jared's place. And a shadow moves down there. Not human-shaped.

Dirt flies everywhere as one of Jared's fiends claws its way out in a snarling, fanged blur. I back up, hand stinging as the healing cut brushes the ground. The fiend launches itself up into the air and dives, claws outstretched like a mutated, demented bird.

I ready my weapon just in time, ducking to avoid the swipe of claws. The group scatters. Apparently, even Jared's influence hasn't obliterated survival instinct. But they aren't prepared to fight. Not like this.

I'll have to draw the fiend away. No doubt that's Jared's plan, to distract me while he calls in his unwilling army. Wherever the hell he is.

Fury surges, and before I have the chance to doubt myself, the fiend descends again. I jump, slashing at its clawed foot. The fiend hisses, circles above, and dives. I've drawn its attention onto me. I need to taunt it some more.

This time, I let fire flow to the edge of my blade and slice the claws of one foot clean off. Blood sprays me, but I don't care. The fiend screams and thrashes, abandoning its diving tactic and trying to take my face off with its remaining claws.

But I'm too fast. And too close to Jared's cave. I walk

backwards, far swifter than I'd ever have been able to as a human, slicing the dagger in a figure-eight motion that keeps its claws getting close to my face. Every step brings me closer to the place the opening to Jared's place lies.

If he thinks I'd hurt my friends to kill his monster, Jared's sorely mistaken. Instead, I'm going to draw him out... and take him down.

Maybe this isn't a wise plan. But right now, I don't have a lot of options. The divide's too close, more than I thought. From here, it's barely a hundred metres away, and the thought of it behind me reawakens an old fear of being hunted, even as I'm the one luring the fiend away from the others.

A shout. Ryan runs towards us, having dispatched the other fiend. I'm right at the edge of the cliff now, above the entrance.

"Come and get me," I mutter. "Or fly back to your shit-hole home."

The fiend's claws miss me by inches, but I successfully sever its wing membranes, sending a burst of fire across its back. Its russet-red skin goes up in flames, and its huge, heavy body slams down as its wings give way.

Ryan assails it from behind with his own blade, but I have the situation in hand. Literally. The point of my dagger pierces the fiend's palm, and with a final burst of flame, the fiend ignites.

Both of us back away as the monster explodes into rock-like pieces. Ryan gapes at me, then turns to the others. The spell seems to have worn off, because they're staring aimlessly into space.

"Dammit. I'll fix those tattoos. You... keep an eye on the entrance?"

"Will do." Ryan shifts to peer inside, down the ladder, I'd guess. "It's dark in there. But I hear something..."

"Don't get too close," I warn, approaching the blank-eyed group of Pyros. "Wouldn't surprise me if he set up a trap."

"We set a trap," he points out, but he backs up slightly. "If it goes off… let's hope Val decides to hold of hitting that switch."

Hell. The bomb's right under our feet. But I can't stop now. I reach the Pyro whose tattoo I cut before, and quickly finish the job. I automatically look for Elle next.

But she's not there.

"Are you sure you want to be doing that, Leah?"

I freeze, knowing before I turn around who's come back. Even clawed, winged and twisted, Jared looks the same: raving mad.

And holding the Transcendent's blade to Elle's throat.

17

R yan swears, but neither of us dares make a move. Not with Elle's life at risk. She doesn't even react when blood wells around the blade.

"This isn't her fight. Let her go."

"I'm afraid I can't do that, Leah." Jared's eyes narrow. Crap, he's seriously pissed off. No wonder his cheerful demeanour is even less convincing than usual. "You've made things unreasonably difficult for me. Your blood was supposed to be the key. Pity…"

I want to ask what the hell he did with Cas, but more urgent is getting Elle away from the madman. Distracting him. But I can only fight close-up, and if I move, he might kill her.

"What do you want me to do?" I let defeat seep into my voice. "We both know I won't let you hurt her. Just because you can't kill me…"

"Oh, I can, Leah."

"Then what? I'm sick of your games. If you're going to make your big play against us, do it already. We're all bored with you, Jared."

The blade slips, and I still my tongue. He's shaking with fury now, his clawed hand trembling. In fact, blood seeps down his arm. And one black wing hangs limp at his side.

"Someone attacked you," I say slowly. "Your experiments turn out to be a little too much to handle?"

"Quiet!" Jared snaps. "You've been nothing but a liability from the start. I want your full cooperation." He drags Elle with him towards... no, not the entrance to the lab.

The divide.

"You sure you want to get so close to the Fiordans?" I shoot at him.

"Afraid?" He laughs coldly. "I've captured enough of their kind for them to be wary of me. If not for your interference, Leah, I would be more than capable of taking the Fiordans down."

"And you're not?" I shoot at him. "Not even as a monster?"

"Monster?" Jared laughs. "This isn't a level playing field any more, even for the Pyros. The Fiordans want this world, and they might as well have it already for all the use most of you are. But *you*, Leah, there's hope for you yet."

"So what, you want me to be your prisoner again? Not sure it'll work out in your favour." I indicate his clawed hand. But from what he said earlier, it sounded like he intended to capture the Fiordans and use their knowledge. For what— domination of both worlds?

He smiles. "I want to control you. Just like her. Just like them."

He points at the huddled group. And the air goes up in flames.

I'm sent flying, dust filling my vision, the ground quaking. My back slams into cracked earth, the red sky spinning around me, my ears ringing. There's blood on my face, though only my hands hurt.

My hands are on fire. Not literally. It's not my power, not mine…

"Your blood, Leah…"

My left arm ignites, and this time, I scream. The flames consume my vision, and I can't see where Jared's voice comes from. Whether Elle's still alive.

For the second time, I tumble head over heels. My hand catches on something. A red coat.

Red, everywhere. The other Pyros lie on the ground, scattered. Unmoving.

Ignoring the pain, I push to my knees, lurch forwards. I don't know the girl, but her arm is a mess of red.

The tattoo. Jared—he—

He killed them. They're dead.

I fall, and the world is swallowed up in black.

———

I almost welcome the vision when it comes. I expect to see the lab, like usual, but instead, red-cloaked figures gather around me. The campsite.

For some reason, Murray's there, in the centre, shouting. My ears ring, making it impossible to hear anything other than the words coming from another mouth than mine.

"Don't hit the switch. She's underground."

Underground? None of this makes sense. If it's a vision, what's Murray doing there? He and Val are arguing… arguing over a piece of metal in Val's hands…

The bomb.

"Don't! She might be alive."

"He killed *all of them*." Murray's voice.

"I didn't see her," says another person. Ryan.

When is this happening? I only fell a second ago. A few seconds. Everything blurs again, as much as I try to hold onto the image. Just to know they're alive. Poppy. Tyler. Val. Murray. And Cas…

———

But I'm pulled back with a sharp jab between my shoulder blades. This time, a familiar room spins around me. The lab. I'm flat on a table, and deja-vu rushes in as I remember seeing the room before, through Cas's eyes. But I've been in here myself, and it looks different. So red…

Bloodstains. The walls and floor are stained red, bright and unnatural. I stare, my head propped up against something hard and metal. I'm still clothed, but my sleeves have been rolled up, wires inserted into both wrists. My dagger is gone, and its absence is like a physical ache.

I twist my head, pulse beating fast. No one's around. *Not again.* What the hell happened this time? This is where the Transcendent attacked Jared when he was doing something to Cas.

I half-sit up, tugging at the wires. Sharp pains sting where they pierce my skin, but it'll heal if I pull them out. So I do, properly sitting to look around me.

The sight turns my blood to water and makes nausea rise in the back of my throat.

A body slumps inside one of the glass cases at the back of the room. Maybe the one Jared trapped me in before. The body's almost unrecognisable, every inch of skin covered in sharp lacerations, as if someone took a knife and deliberately cut, slowly, taking their time with the torture. The slumping angle of its legs suggests bones are broken, but the glass is smeared with blood, making it difficult to tell. Though I can't see the face, I know it's a Transcendent. Probably the one who disobeyed.

So where are the others?

I'm shaking, and barely react when blood spurts from where I pulled out the wires. My dagger's no longer in sight, nor are there any weapons in here that I can see. I stare around at test tubes and odd contraptions. Nothing looks dangerous, either for me or for other people. The Transcendents are resistant to most things, anyway.

If any of them are working for Jared anymore.

I don't dare hope. He somehow got me down here. He killed the others with the tattoos, slaughtered them in a heartbeat.

I put my head in my hands, gritting my teeth. *Elle. God, not her.* I thought my blood made the tattoo stop working. But if it's not true, did Val fall under the spell again, too? *Oh, no. Please no.*

One thing at a time. If Elle's alive, she has to be underground.

I have no intention of spending another second as Jared's plaything. My arms sting, but the cuts will heal within seconds. My feet touch down on the floor. At least I have my shoes on, because the polished linoleum is slippery with blood. I swallow hard and head for the door.

Once again, the corridor's empty. But there's a gaping hole in the wall further down the corridor, at least five metres wide. I head that way, unable to contain my curiosity. This must be where the Pyros set off the test bomb, I realise, eying the smoke rising from the collapsed stone wall. Lucky they didn't bring the whole place down.

Crap. I shouldn't be going this way. I race in the opposite direction instead, recalling the way out from last time. Must have been hidden behind a wall. But I can't leave, not without finding out what happened to Elle.

Footsteps. No time to hide. My fists clench, and it hits me like a wall of falling rock: I'm unarmed.

I'm not defenceless.

But I'm done being ambushed, taken by surprise. I march towards the noise instead of away…

And run smack into Cas.

I gasp, my mouth falling open. "You're alive?" are the first, stupid words to come out.

"Disappointed?" His face is a mask, as impassive as though this is a random encounter on the street.

I stare at him. He looks the same as usual, not at all as if he's been tortured or worse. The only thing out of place is the absence of his usual blade. He has no weapon, either.

Thoughts tangle in my head. "What the hell is going on?" I demand.

"I could ask you the same question. I thought you were aboveground. Then I hear you decided to go chasing after the fiends again."

"Hold up," I say. "That vision was real, right? You talked to Murray? He's out there?"

"He's out there," Cas repeats, and what little light there was in his eyes seems to go out. "He's pissed off. Really pissed off. Val and Ryan had to hold him down to stop him coming back here when I did."

"Yeah, still missing something here," I say. "How long was I out for? Jared has an awful habit of locking me in places and disappearing into thin air. It's almost not a challenge to escape anymore."

"Don't speak too soon." There's an odd expression on Cas's face, like a smirk. "You've been here an hour, I'd guess, but Jared's sadly indisposed at the moment. It looks like he's having trouble adjusting to his new upgraded form."

"He what?" I stare at him again. "It's not working?"

"Oh, it's working." Now he's definitely smirking. "I never thought I'd be glad of Jared's total idiocy as a scientist, but he conveniently forgot I grew up in labs. I thought it might work, after I switched out the fiend blood he tried to inject in you before, so I stole a serum he'd been messing with."

"No way. You... tampered with whatever he's injecting himself with? What did you do?"

"It won't kill him," says Cas, with a disappointed edge to his voice. *"That* part of the experiment worked. But he'll be out cold for a while. I've been searching every lab. Didn't realise he'd put you so close to the unstable area."

"Unstable? You mean the hole in the wall?"

"Yeah. He didn't put anything in you, did he?"

"Wires." I hold up my wrists, but they've healed. "Never mind that. We need to find out if he brought any of the others down here. Elle..."

"They're dead," says Cas. "Ryan said no one survived."

My heart plunges. "No. Jared had her as a specific hostage. He wouldn't do that. She's his niece!"

"He doesn't give a shit, Leah. I'd have thought you'd know that by now."

"I *do* know that," I snap. Unbelievable. We've been reunited all of two minutes and he's already managed to wind me up. "Having Elle as a hostage will make Murray do anything he says. He wouldn't kill her because he's not done screwing with us yet. He might be totally batshit, but for all he knows, he might need Murray's help in the future. Or hers."

A pause, then Cas nods, surprising me. "Good point. Question is whether he's too scared of losing face to admit to his brother he majorly fucked up. He's been claiming to hold the moral high ground as long as the two of them have been at odds. His pride's taken a hit because this whole invincibility thing isn't working out for him. And that makes him even more dangerous. Now he's killed most of the people he marked, after losing most of his guards. They ran for it when the Pyros came to get you out."

So some of them got away. At least not everyone died thanks to Jared's depravity. But... Val was marked, and she wasn't amongst the others when he killed them. I saw her in the vision of Cas at camp...

"Val. She didn't get hit, did she?" I ask, my heart beating faster. *Please not her, too.*

Cas shakes his head. "No. As long as the asshole's sedated, he can't screw with anyone left with the marks. It's a damn good job I knocked him out. Come on."

He indicates the way he came, down the corridor in the direction of the training rooms and beyond that, the other labs.

I hesitate. "Where?"

"I locked him in his own lab," says Cas. "We need to get back to Murray before he does something stupid and reckless."

"No, we need to find *Elle,*" I say. "He won't have put her in..." I swallow. "The labs?"

Cas's eyes narrow. "I didn't see her. But I haven't checked the labs on the other side of the fiend cages. I'm pretty sure you guys killed both of the security fiends, but I don't trust him to lock those cages properly."

My heart plummets. "He can't have put her in a *cage,* can he?"

"Maybe. There's nothing that way, thanks to the people who decided to blow a hole in the wall."

"Fine." I follow him, arms crossed, feeling the absence of my weapon like a nagging voice in the back of my head. "He didn't have my dagger with him, did he?"

"Not that I saw," says Cas. "Was it not in the room with you? I thought he was doing one of his usual mad tests to see if he could hurt you by breaking your weapon."

My insides twist. "Let's hope not."

But it's a reminder that the visions are never far behind.

What I saw when I was unconscious... Murray thinks his daughter is dead. However long has passed since I saw that, the sooner we find Elle, the better.

I can't afford to think about the alternative.

The corridors are eerily quiet, but signs of the damage from the fight earlier remain. Crumbled pieces of rock. Fiends. No bodies. The guards took their chances and ran. No wonder Jared was pissed off enough to kill the others he marked. In one second, he activated that tattoo and...

My hands curl into fists. "Can't I strangle him in his sleep?"

"Wouldn't work," says Cas. "And even Pyro hands can't tear through his enhanced skin. You'd need a blade, but there weren't any weapons in the room with him. Looks like he cleaned out the weapons room, too."

"Then where's yours?"

He doesn't answer.

"This really isn't the time to be all secretive, Cas," I snap. "If you have any idea where my weapon is, tell me."

"I haven't a damn clue," he says, through clenched teeth. "He took mine from me when his Transcendent scum knocked my lights out after you escaped."

I wince inwardly. "What happened then, anyway? You disappeared off the face of the Earth, while Jared took me and his creepy clones to beat the crap out of each other for his amusement."

"He did that? When is he gonna *quit it?*" He slams a fist into the wall, so suddenly I jump. Stone crumbles to the floor, and his hand falls to his side. "I've had about enough of his twisted crap. I'd literally tear him to pieces if I could, but I can't. There's no other way out..."

I draw in a breath. "We're finding Elle. Getting back to the group. Unless you do have a way to kill him. What about that bomb?"

"Yeah, about that. We're probably standing on it."

"Would that kill him?"

"I don't think he'll die. It'll wound him, but once he crawls out of the rubble, he'll be pissed."

"I can't think of a better idea," I say, and start walking again. "Other than at least making sure no one else is stuck down here first. Especially Elle."

Cas makes an impatient noise, but follows me, swiftly catching up. As the shock of waking from the vision wears off, I can push my legs to their limits again, regardless of the slippery blood under my shoes from the lab. I march on, checking behind every single open door. The labs are oddly bare, which strikes me as wrong. As does the absence of weapons.

"What's his game this time?" I mutter. "You were here longer than I was. How many hiding places did he have?"

"I already checked his quarters," says Cas. "Not sure we should be more worried about the missing weapons, or that eight of the Transcendents are unaccounted for."

"Eight?"

"Four were in the room I locked him in."

"And there was another in my room." I shudder. "He was in a pretty bad way."

"Damn. So that leaves seven. More than enough to take out the others, if they get aboveground. I hope Jared being out of it means they'll shut down, but we can't count on that."

"No, but it's a start," I say. "They shut down before. But that was when he told them to, I guess. Last I saw they were in a room just down from the fiends' cages."

"Right," he says. "I've combed the whole east side of this place. Only place I haven't checked is beyond right here. I didn't go near the cages when I was scouting around."

"You mean, when you were hiding," I say. "Seriously. I'm not impressed. You let him play sport with us while you went running around without even trying to get us out. What the hell is this plan of yours?"

Cas stops dead. He turns to face me, his expression a furious mask. "I was trying to save your damn life."

Before I can ask what he means, a deafening crash makes me spin around. Cas swears, and drags me after him by the arm. "Bet the bastard's trying to break down the door."

"I thought you knocked him out!"

"I did. Never knew how long it'd last with his crazy new enhancements."

"Brilliant," I say, savagely. "This is just what we need right now. So, fight or run away?"

The choice is obvious. This might be the most vulnerable position we get him in... but it's also most likely our only chance to find Elle. I can't fight Jared without knowing he can't hurt her anymore.

We don't have time to search every room, so I'd better hope my guess is right. I put every ounce of Pyro-Transcendent super-speed into my stride. In no time at all, I pass by the door to the training room, mentally ticking off a list in my head. If I'm assuming this room, where I met Val under the tattoo's control, is the one I saw in my vision, there's nothing in there but a mess. The door's wide open, and a glance tells me the Transcendents aren't in there. I check the other rooms, then turn a corner at the corridor's end. This way leads to the cages. A faint shuffling raises the hairs on my arms.

Footsteps sound behind me, and I tense before realising it's Cas. "I reckon she's in one of these cages," I whisper. "Are there empty ones?"

"That way."

We edge past the one where the fiend almost took me to pieces. I hear shuffling on the other side. Jared's pet's still in its prison.

A growling noise follows me, and a faint sob comes from my left. From the cage with the fiend. Every drop of blood freezes in my veins. *No way.* It's dark in the cage. Too dark even for the fiend to see.

Jared locked Elle in with the monster.

18

F or an instant, I stare, suspended in horror. Cas grabs my arm and drags me away from the door.

"We can't do anything."

"The hell we can't. You can't seriously want to leave her here?"

"I don't *want* to do any of this," Cas says quietly, through clenched teeth. "But opening that door will set that monster on her instantly."

Damn. He might be right. The only way she could have survived so long is if she kept really, really quiet. It's so dark in there, and I must have done some damage to the fiend when I fought it.

A rattling crash echoes from back the way we came. *Jared*, I think immediately, and Cas tenses again.

"It's us or her," he says.

"We have to try."

"No, we don't." His voice is a whisper. "You really want to set that thing loose in here? She'll die, you'll be Jared's plaything again, and that'll be the end of the others. There's no way around this, Leah. We're not meant to save everyone."

I can't speak. A lump blocks my throat, and my hand clenches so tight I can envision the lock splintering under my touch, the bars giving way as I pull Elle to safety.

"Get out of here." I force the words out. "Go warn the others, just in case this goes wrong."

"You're shitting me." Cas doesn't move.

Fire flares around my fist, which pretty much speaks for itself.

Another crash.

"Fine." My heart beats wildly. I know Cas is right, deep down, but I can't seem to accept it. Not now. Elle never should have been dragged into this, and I'll never forgive myself if I let her die. I reach for the cage's bars, squinting into the dark. I can make out a small, human-shaped huddle a metre away from the bars. She hasn't seen us yet. From what I remember, the fiend's chained up ten metres away... which gives us about three seconds.

Lucky we Transcendents move fast.

I take in the challenge, examining the cage bars from all angles. Examine the lock. I take a deep breath.

"Don't you dare," says Cas, leaning over my shoulder.

I say nothing, and as carefully as I can, I reach for the lock and snap it off.

A shuffling sounds, alerting me to the danger. The fiend already knows someone's outside, and Elle's right in its path. I throw caution aside and yank the bars out from the roots with a wrenching noise loud enough to wake the dead. In another second I've darted to Elle's huddled shape and pulled her aside. She lets out a squeak of surprise and then a scream, but I can't see to cover her mouth in time.

The fiend's massive paw misses us by a hair's breadth. I jump back several feet, knocking the twisted remains of the door aside. The fiend bellows and Elle screams again. Her round, terrified eyes meet mine.

"Leah," she whispers.

I manage a half-smile and back away a few steps, colliding with Cas. He swears. "It'll have those chains off within a minute," he says.

"Good. The fiend can slow Jared down."

On cue, a deafening crash carries down the corridor.

A sinking feeling tells me Jared beat down the door of the room Cas imprisoned him in. Which means…

I set Elle down on her feet, but she slumps against my side. Cas makes an impatient noise and lifts her over his shoulder before I can move.

"Come on," he says, his expression hard.

I have no idea what to make of that, but getting out of here as fast as possible is the best move right now. Except we're on the opposite side from the exit, and Jared's seriously pissed off.

Cas's already hurrying the other way. I run to keep pace, and we clear three corridors before I remember running this way before and ending up in the dark. I don't know what he's thinking, but I have to run to keep up. More corridors fly past. The place is like a giant rabbit warren.

"Wait," I hiss. "Seriously, Cas, do you even know where you're going?"

"Out," he says.

"There's another exit?"

"I haven't seen one, but there must be. Jared brought in the fiends this way."

My heart sinks. I should have considered those monsters never would have fit down the stairs I escaped through last time. Another way out… but last time I ran in this direction, I ended up lost in darkness. *Wish being Transcendent meant I could see in the dark,* I think, as we run through another corridor. Doors are open on either side. Labs. I risk a quick glance in either direction, and can't see any weapons. But there's no

181

time to search. A shattering roar strikes, accompanied by the screech of metal.

I shoot Cas an alarmed look. Elle's curled up in his arms, whimpering. Blood soaks her left arm. The tattooed one. *Oh, God.* I have to get that marking off, but we can't stop.

And then we're in darkness so absolute, it's as though a hand drops from the sky to block out the light. The chill of recognition settles on my shoulders. This is where I collapsed and had the vision of Cas in pain.

Flickers at the corners of my eyes tell me I'm in danger of the same thing happening again.

"Where the hell are we?" I ask loudly. At least I'm not alone this time.

Never thought I'd be glad of Cas's grumpy reply, "I haven't a damn clue, but at least even that bastard can't see in here."

"He can't?"

"Not unless he gave himself enhanced sight, and he won't have got that from the fiends." I move closer to where his voice comes from, so I don't lose him in the dark. I assume we're in a corridor, but it's impossible to tell. The smooth floor turns to spongy earth. I'm guessing this is a newer tunnel he never bothered to decorate and add lights to, but that doesn't explain what it's for.

"Well, that's something," I say. The easiest way not to lose each other is to keep talking. But at the same time, we can't risk walking at top-speed without knowing what's ahead. One wrong step and Elle could get hurt. I brace my hand against the nearest wall and feel my way along. The soft pad of footsteps beside me tells me Cas's doing the same.

"Have you been up here before?" I ask.

"Yes," he says.

"Helpful," I say, when he doesn't qualify that with an explanation. "I ran this way after I cut Jared's arm off, but I got lost somewhere and… I have no idea how far it goes. There must be an exit somewhere, right?"

"It's the only way," says Cas. "I've searched every inch of the place, and this has to be it. Question is why he left it dark. He must *really* want to keep this place clear. Even fiends don't have a tendency to wander into dark places. Especially enclosed ones."

That detail gives me pause. They always hunt at night, but on open ground. Not in forests, or near similar places. Except that one time I was attacked in a forest… wait a minute. The winged fiends are Jared's. Did he do something to kill their natural instincts?

"They must have been pissed when he brought them this way. How's he controlling them, anyway? Same tattoos?"

"Blood control," says Cas's voice, from my left side. "Same as the tattoos, except he didn't inject himself… though now I think about it, he probably did."

"He said *my* blood made him Transcendent," I say. "But he's mutating, turning into a monster. So are the others…"

"Because he gave them fiend blood," says Cas. "He said he wanted to give them a boost, the moron. You're not the same, you had *my* blood."

Is he trying to reassure me I won't mutate into a winged, clawed monstrosity like the fiends? Before I can wrap my head around it, my left foot reaches out and meets nothing but darkness. No ground. "Stop!" I say quickly. "There's a drop here."

"Damn," says Cas. "We can't turn back. Is there nothing on your side?"

"No…"

I squint ahead into the darkness, where shuffling noises make the hairs stand up on my arms and my heart quake in my chest. This is it. We're trapped at a dead end with monsters on one side and the unknown on the other.

The shuffling continues. I freeze, and Cas swears under his breath. There's no doubt the noise comes from behind us, and it's either stick around and get caught, or…

Cas's hand grabs my wrist and drags me to the left. "There's a path. Don't step to your right, or you'll fall."

Encouraging. Cas holds onto my wrist, pulls me to the left again, and lets go. From the way he brushes past me, I can tell he's directly in front of me, leading the way.

I'd better hope I don't lose him in the dark.

The path is soft underfoot, but after a few slow, tense minutes, it turns to rock, and slopes upwards. *Aboveground,* I think, with a barely-suppressed flicker of hope. A faint breeze comes from the right, and my skin crawls for some reason. There's no noise close behind, and we're moving further from Jared's trap by the second. So why do I feel like claws are about to close around my throat?

Yet, I can definitely feel something I couldn't before—the faintest breeze, not air con, but the suggestion of fresh air.

And the smell of burning on the breeze, accompanied by a tugging under my skin, a pull in this direction.

My heart beats frantically, like it might leap from my chest. My vision turns to red spots, the darkness dissolving into a blur of colour. *No.* I grip the wall on my left with my hand, fingers digging in, trying to steady myself in the present. If I black out, I'll fall.

Focus, Leah.

One foot in front of the other. Only the faint sound of Cas's breathing, and Elle's, stops me losing the plot completely. The breeze grows stronger by the second. There *must* be an opening soon.

As the thought crosses my mind, Cas stops so suddenly I walk into him.

"What's going on?" I hiss.

"Dead end."

"You're joking." My heart sinks like a stone.

"You think?"

I jerk back as a thud comes from ahead.

"What in the world was that?"

Elle moans. "Put me down. I can stand."

I jump, having forgotten she's there. "Elle, are you okay? I'm sorry. I should have asked."

"No, you shouldn't have," Cas snaps. "If you're absolutely sure, I can put you down here. Leah, back up a bit. I'm gonna break the wall open."

"Is that really the only way? What if there's another drop?"

A noise, which makes me think Cas's ironically laughing at me. "We're screwed either way. Back up."

So I do. Seconds later, arms wrap around my waist. Elle.

A thud shakes the ground we stand on.

"You might have asked if *I* wanted to break down the walls," I say, but my words are lost in an avalanche of falling rock. I stand stock-still, not daring to lean on the wall in case it gives way. I damn well hope Cas knows what he's doing. For all I know, I can bore straight through the wall like a human drill, but there's no realistic way to take Elle along for the ride without her getting hurt or killed in the process.

My vision flickers. I grit my teeth and dig my heels into the ground, but quickly realise this isn't a vision. Light streams through gaps in the collapsed rock wall. Even as I watch, the lights turn into orange-red beams, like the sun.

Except this isn't ground level.

Crash.

Elle and I cling onto each other tightly as a final tremor rocks the earth, and bright lights explode before my eyes. And then it stops.

The smell of burning takes over, so strong it becomes

difficult to breathe. Like standing close to an energy blast. But there can't have been one down here. Which means…

The light dims enough to see. Cas brought down a wall at least a metre thick, but it looks as though he uncovered part of a hidden set of stairs, leading up to a platform. Caution disappears and I walk ahead, climbing the short way up to the platform, which ends on the edge of a cliff. The beams of light *are* sunlight, shining directly down onto the platform. A cliff faces us, like the one we stand on.

We're inside the divide.

For a moment, I stare, convinced I've walked into one of my visions. Jared's tunnel comes out partway down the side of the cliff. I step forwards, squinting at the opposite edge.

"Crap," I say. "Well that explains how no one's got out."

The other side of the divide lies several metres away. The air shimmers above the edge, and the ground's scorched red. Not as much as a blade of grass grows on their world anymore.

"There's not a—bridge, is there?" I whisper to Cas. I can't see one like last time. But here, the two cliff sides almost touch.

Cas shakes his head. "No, but his spies fly right into fiend territory. That's why he always knows what they're up to."

My heart sinks like a stone. I can't see any fiends on the other side, but this close to the divide, nothing's certain. A semi-transparent veil hangs over the air, with two scenes transplanted on top of each other. In one, the Burned Spot continues, but in the distance, there's the shape of hills and dark green patches that suggest surviving forests on our side. In the other, the barrenness goes on, and on. And there's another collection of shapes in the distance, gathering on the horizon like storm clouds. *No. Those can't be fiends. There can't be* that *many.*

Cas grabs my arm and pulls me back.

"Get inside. They'll see you."

Mutely, I step back, into the darkness. The red sky above looms tantalisingly close.

"Did you know about *that?*" I whisper, my voice hoarse. I can hardly believe it. Perhaps it was a trick of the light... But somehow I know. It's an army.

"I guessed, but that explains why Jared made so many new Transcendents."

"Does Murray know they're so close?" And there are so many?

"I have no idea."

A roar thunders through the air.

"Hell," I whisper, again. "We're in trouble."

No sooner have those words left my mouth than a dark shape flies overhead. I duck down, but it's already turned around to come this way.

One of Jared's fiends.

Cas spits out a curse and grabs me around the waist, and jumps down the stairs. We land a few metres down, the impact jolting my legs, but the fiend spots us and dives, clawed feet splayed, ugly face twisted in anger. Claws swipe at us, catching me on the arm.

"Transcendent. You should not be here!"

"Bit late for that, you pathetic excuse for a spy," Cas snarls, and spears the fiend through the neck with his sword. One flick, and the fiend's ugly head goes flying.

"Great," I say. "How the hell do we get to the surface?" I didn't see any stairs from the platform. With his winged fiends, I suppose Jared doesn't need them. I move forward, past Cas, who doesn't appear inclined to respond. The short platform juts out from under the overhang, but even when I walk right to the edge, I can barely make out the top of the cliff above. Up there, somewhere, the others have made camp. But we can't reach them.

A screech rings out. I freeze, glancing behind me in panic. The cry came from above.

Which means Jared's fiends are hunting again.

Just what we need. I glance at Elle, mentally calculating our chances of climbing the cliff unscathed. The odds aren't good.

Pain stabs my left arm, without warning. My legs wobble, and only instinct makes me brace myself against the wall to keep from falling.

I push myself upright, head spinning. But my body doesn't move. My limbs are like water.

I'm not in control of my own body anymore. My left arm pulses with white-hot agony, and out of the corner of my eye, I see Cas fall to his knees. Elle clings to the wall, shouting my name, her voice oddly muffled.

Claws dig into the cliff front, and the monstrous shape of a mutated fiend pulls itself up to our level.

Shit. Shit. I can't move. Cas lies flat on his face, Elle's shaking him, shaking me. I've slumped into a sitting position by the edge, my arm a torrent of agony. My head hits the ground as I fall sideways.

Move. Move, Leah. I'm not going to let the fiend get at the others.

But I'm paralysed, and another image threatens to overwhelm my mind. The clash of weapons fills my head, along with the image of Pyros fighting fiends. A familiar battlefield scene.

Stop!

This time, I think I scream out loud. Talons pierce my shoulders, and my eyes fly open to find the fiend's grabbed me, pulling me towards the cliff's edge.

"Leah!" Elle's shout breaks through the clamour of fighting. But I can't reply. The fiend lifts me from the ground, and, wings spread wide, carries me into the sky.

19

"This is it."

The voice is familiar, but I can't place it. I blink, and the world rearranges itself. I'm crouched behind a rock. The smell of burning hits me, and as I glance up, it's obvious why. The sky is on fire. Not just the burned red colour it is now, but a blazing orange inferno that hurts my eyes to look at. Directly beneath is yet another familiar sight: a jagged rip through the centre of the Earth.

The divide. We're less than a hundred metres away, but I can't make out the other side. There's too much smoke.

Outlined against the fog are images from a nightmare. Giant hunched shapes, far too many to count, form a line along the horizon. An army.

I can't breathe. I look down at myself, and I'm wearing a Pyro's red coat, though there's something different about it—the left side is marked with a badge, shaped like...

Like a flame.

The sky is newly boiling, the divide smoking, growing bigger as I watch. This is the beginning of the war, as Earth knew it.

"You get one chance," says the same voice as before. "Just the *one. You'll have to move* fast, *when I distract them. They won't be fooled for long. But you've seen it, haven't you?"*

"How d'you mean?"

I'm speaking, but the voice coming from me isn't mine. Something about this feels...

Oh God. *The voice speaking to me is Cas. So who am I?*

I turn sideways to him. He's crouched behind the rock next to me, dressed in his red coat. He wears a worried expression, but other than that, he could be the double of the Cas I know.

"They move in unison," he says. "Far too coordinated, considering they're supposed to be brutes. I have a theory..."

"Can't it wait?" I ask. "We're in the middle of a war."

"I know that," he says. "But suppose I don't make it out. I need someone else to know the theory. I reckon Jared knows, but Murray doesn't."

"Knows what?"

"They're using some kind of mind control."

His tone is serious, but I laugh. "Mind control. Right. You know, I could accept all the crazy magical superpower stuff, but that... I don't know. The fiends don't seem capable of intelligent thought."

"Behavioural control, then." The corners of his mouth pull down. "Whatever it is, we're outnumbered by far."

"I can take them," I say, tapping the dagger at my waist. "So, where's this mighty Fiordan?"

"That's just it." He shifts position, and I get the impression we've been crouching here a while. Hours. "He, it, should have appeared by now."

"If it exists."

"You think this happened by accident?" He gestures around, at the blazing sky and the smoking divide. "No, there's an intelligent being behind it. Jared isn't wrong on that one."

"Jared's paranoid," I say. "I'll get over there, lock up the divide, and people will be none the wiser."

My own thoughts intrude. How can she be so casual? If the

war's just started, the fiends are on the brink of invading. The divide cut right through the centre of the world...

I'm missing something here.

"Come on," Cas mutters. "Get it over with already. If I'm gonna die, it better be fast."

"You're not going to die," I say. "You're my lookout, right?"

He nods, and again, my own feelings intrude. It takes a second to place the jealousy, but it vanishes in a second when the person whose eyes I'm seeing through looks up again at the army of fiends.

———

I'm pulled back to my own body for a second, enough to feel a spike of pain in my left hand.

Air rushes past. Claws dig into my shoulders. And I slam back into my own skin with such a jolt, I almost fall out of the air. Only the fiend gripping my back stops me from falling. We're flying above the divide, rising higher by the second. The strip of jagged ground is burned red on one side, but the other is lost in shadow.

"Put me down!" I shout stupidly, which at least has the effect of anchoring me back in the present day. *Shit.* I can't see Elle or Cas down on the cliff. I can't see anyone at all. I'm too high up. This is going to hurt.

I wriggle as hard as I can, and when that doesn't work, I tear at the fiend's claws with my hand. *I can break it,* I think, and amazingly, when I squeeze hard on a claw, the fiend hisses and kicks out. I squeeze harder with every ounce of Transcendent power I possess, and add a burst of fire for good measure.

The fiend's claw breaks off in my hand in a flood of reddish-brown blood. I gag, but immediately shriek as its other claws let go of my shoulders. By instinct, I grab at its other leg, managing to get a grip as it plunges towards...

191

The divide.

I cling to the fiend wildly, clutching its severed claw. I'm bleeding, my other hand slippery with fiend blood mixed with my own, and I let go of the damaged claw to get a better grip.

We're falling fast, spiralling towards the divide.

"You've got wings, use them!" I scream, and part of me wants to laugh at myself for screaming at a monster that can't understand me in the last few seconds before we're plunged into a world of pain.

It doesn't come. The fiend's wings spread wide as we reach ground level, and it flips over, depositing me on the edge of the cliff. My back aches where I hit the ground and the ghost of pain passes over my left arm, but I'm on solid ground at last.

And so is the fiend, but it's not attacking. The monster crouches in front of me, blood streaming from its ruined claw. There's something different in its expression, something odd I can't put my finger on for the life of me. It's not like I can read fiends' facial expressions. I've never had a reason to. But there's something…

Our eyes meet, and I gasp as the truth hits me like a blow. Fiends don't look directly at their prey. They *never* stop if there's a human nearby, even if they're injured. And this one's bleeding where I cut it.

My own blood got in the wound.

No way.

"Move forward," I say, my voice little more than a whisper.

The fiend obligingly shuffles towards me.

Oh my God. It's true. My blood gives me control over the fiend. I almost laugh, but common sense kicks in immediately. "Carry me," I command. "Carry me down to the platform."

I don't know how long I blacked out for. But that was the last time I saw Elle and Cas, with Jared on their heels.

The fiend's non-injured claw shoots out and snatches me up again. A yell escapes as its wings beat and once again, I'm airborne. But this time, I'm the one calling the shots. *Holy crap. Oh God.* Very good job heights don't bother me, but the divide lurching below is almost enough to make me airsick. I look up into the burning sky instead as the fiend drops over the cliff's edge into the divide. Now the platform's in sight. But no one's there.

Oh God. Jared better not have taken Elle again.

"Land," I tell the fiend. "No, on second thoughts, carry me into the tunnel. Don't let go until I say."

I'm pretty sure that platform Cas and I walked up can't support the weight of a fiend. This one doesn't seem at all happy about going into the dark, judging by the snarling noises coming out of its mouth. But it doesn't let go of me even as we're swept into darkness.

This time, the journey takes no time at all. Wings. I have wings. Something like laughter rises inside me. The monster is no longer an opponent, but our weapon. *My* weapon. It's my blood that gives me the power.

Is this the same thought that drove Jared to murder?

The thought stabs into me, erasing any plans I had. What can even one fiend do against eleven, twelve Transcendents? I can't control all of them at once.

The light grows. We're coming up to the corridor again. I couldn't hear the others, so they can't be in the tunnel. Which means…

The fiends' wings scrape either side of the rocky walls. We're near the labs now, and it still hasn't let go of me… but I can hear something.

Crying. Screaming. The clash of swords.

We round the corner, and my mouth falls open.

The door to the room where Jared pitted the Transcendents against one another is open. Two people inside face off inside the cage, with Jared himself looking on from the side… along with the Transcendents. All of them, though one glance isn't enough to count.

Because the two figures in the arena are Elle and Cas.

I struggle to take in the impossible sight before me. Both Cas and Elle are armed, Cas with his usual blade, Elle with a shorter one. My heart sinks in my chest as she advances on him. *Why?* Did Jared threaten them, force them into this? Elle's not a fighter by human standards, let alone…

And then I see her face, and my breath catches. Elle's eyes are blanked-out in a horrifyingly familiar way. Another blow to my heart. *Why the hell didn't I stop that mark?*

With our escape, with everything, I overlooked the obvious. And now, she's…

Elle leaps at Cas with a catlike speed I've never seen her capable of before. Cas's sword blocks her attack, and in that moment, I know what Jared's game is. Cas isn't under the tattoo's control. It's yet another sick game. And when I look closely, all twelve Transcendents are present. They must be back under Jared's control. As if they never turned on him at all. The twisted, evil man.

My fist clenches, and I become aware that I'm still holding onto the fiend's claw. Right now, it's all I have.

I tiptoe as quietly as I can, barely breathing. Three more steps puts me behind Jared. I hesitate, almost letting him have the chance to turn on me and catch me. But he doesn't. Not before I recall the lessons in training on how to stab someone from behind, so it pierces the heart. I don't have a blade. The claw's barely a ruler-length long. But I have the power of a Transcendent behind it, and I'm pissed off enough to make it work.

I lunge forward and bring the fiend's claw in an arc, like a blade, right through Jared's back.

A choked gasp escapes him. My hand shakes wildly and I nearly drop the claw, but I think of *fire* and flames burst into life, sending the nearest Transcendents staggering back.

Cas looks at me, eyes wide.

Elle's knife sinks into his chest.

Panic and fear freeze me to the spot. *That didn't just happen.* My wavering vision seems to confirm it. *I'm dreaming. This is all some sick hallucination. Jared probably drugged me.* It's possible.

More possible than Cas sinking to his knees, blood soaking through his front, Elle standing blank-faced, hands stained red to the elbows. *Oh, God. No.*

It takes a good minute to realise blood soaks my own hands. Jared makes a choked noise, barely audible under the noise of the crackling flames. The fire, coming from me, like in the vision, turning my body into a furnace.

White light bursts before my eyes. The claw slips from my hand, still buried in Jared's back. The fire dies down, and a familiar face smiles at me. One of the Transcendents.

But he, it, has Jared's face.

It's too much. I scream, brandishing the claw, but the weapon disintegrates in my hands as Jared drops to his knees in front of me. Now I have a full-on view of the arena. Of Elle's horror-stricken face as she stares down at Cas's lifeless body.

The Transcendents close in, except for one, whose bat-like wings unfold behind him. Jared's voice says, "I thought you'd come back for your friends, Leah. But you're too late."

"How?" I whisper. The fight's gone, my weapon's broken, and as I spin around with my last burst of strength, the empty corridor behind me tells me the fiend's run away, too. Even the monster has run away.

"I thought you or your friends would come back for me, Leah," says Jared. "Lucky my latest experiments were a success." He gestures at the two Transcendents closest to him, both of whom look up at me.

With Jared's face.

"What… the hell?" I can't help but stare. A voice inside me screams for Cas, for Elle, wishing I could bring the whole building crashing down, that we could get away from this nightmare…

"I'm not that easy to kill, Leah. You can't have forgotten what I told you about the Fiordans, how they shifted form to blend in with humans? I have all their secrets now, Leah."

The Transcendent speaking has to be the real Jared. Not that it does much good now I'm weaponless. But the fire…

I reach inside for every piece of anger, every raging, white-hot particle in my body, and will it all to burn.

And then I'm not me anymore.

———

When I turn to the side, I see flames extending the length of my arms, like wings. When I look down, I see blood spilling across the cracked earth.

Whose blood?

I try to turn my head, but my body's still, lying on a battlefield. I've seen this before. I'm sure of it.

Cas stands over me, clothes ragged and bloodstained…

"It's fading," he says, voice cracking. He holds up his hand, palm out. The ugly scribbled mark stands out, harsh lines bleeding around the edges. "The traitorous bastard."

Now I'm looking through his eyes, at the body. Raging grief chokes me, so intense it takes my breath away.

Blood drips down his—my—hand as I gently run my fingertips over the corpse's arm. Even though it's burned almost beyond recognition, I can make out a familiar shape cut into the skin. Fire. The tattoo.

"The lying son of a bitch," snarls Cas's voice. "It was a trap all along. He meant you to die. I was supposed to die too..." I stare helplessly at the body. "I should have guessed... my blood would be the end of you."

I reach out a blazing hand, and as my fingertips touch the corpse's, it turns to ashes and dust.

20

A slap across the face brings me into my own body with a resounding crash. I taste blood at the back of my throat, my legs ache, and it hits me that there's something restraining them. My arms, too. I'm strapped down to a table. In the lab with the blood-soaked floor. Blood. *My blood will be the end of you.* The words ricochet around my mind as I struggle to lift my head, to see the person standing next to me.

Jared bends over me. I'm not even sure if it's him or not, but he just slapped me. There doesn't appear to be anyone else around.

"You're awake," he says, almost sighs. "I thought it was over, but it looks like I'll have to stay here a little longer."

I try to lift my head again, but even my neck's restrained. "What the hell... what did you do to me?"

"I didn't do anything, Leah. I restrained you because your Transcendent powers were out of control. You were slipping, and I feared you'd cause damage you'd regret."

Everything comes back in a wave, enough to know he's

talking complete bullshit. He'd never worry about me. But—
"Cas," I gasp. "Elle…"

Jared shakes his head. "You should be more concerned with your own life. Every Transcendent in the past was overwhelmed by the memories of their predecessor. They were consumed by madness, and by their own power. I injected you with a suppressant, but it might not be enough. You're living on borrowed time, Leah. Unfortunately, your well-meaning Pyro companions are still out there, and if you try to go back to them, they'll undoubtedly end up as collateral damage."

My heart sinks, bile rising in my throat. "No. It's not true. You're lying."

"You've seen the visions, haven't you? You've felt the sensations, lived the past…"

"Yeah, how you betrayed them," I shoot at him. "You lied to the last Transcendent as well as Cas, didn't you? You're the one who activated the tattoo in the middle of a war. You let the Transcendent die."

The truth is written on his every feature, and I know without a doubt this is the real Jared.

"You bastard," I say, my arms straining against the restraints. I'm Transcendent, and I'm more than strong enough to break them.

But nothing happens, even as the bonds cut into my wrists.

"I told you, I injected you with a suppressant," says Jared, shaking his head pityingly. "To save your life, of course, but it also binds *all* your abilities."

He raps on the bench I'm tied to with his clawed hand, and I recoil. Clenching my teeth together to keep from screaming, I take short quick breaths, determined not to break down in front of him. I've faced death in the face too many times to fall apart now.

I lift my head the best I can and glare at him. "So this is it?" I ask. "I'm tied up, I can't use my powers, and if I do, memories of the last twisted thing you did will take me over and I'll die. And you get to watch the show. Well, I'll give you a show, all right."

I spit at him, but Jared moves back, out of range. He sighs heavily. "I'm here because I wanted to ask your preferences after your demise. Obviously, your blood will be invaluable to either side, and I would prefer the fiends didn't have a chance to get their hands on it."

What? He seriously thinks I'd give up my blood to him? "I'd rather die," I snarl. "I'd rather die than help you in *any* way. You can forget it."

"You *are* going to die," he says, matter-of-factly. "According to my notes, you're at the second stage of Transcendence, which for the last one, meant her regenerative powers came into their own. Unfortunately, for all the other test subjects, this was the stage where they were overwhelmed by Cas's memories and lost all sense of self. Their powers consumed them, one and all, and they died within a week."

My heart drums in my chest, cold sweat beading on the back of my neck. "A *week*? You're lying. I've been having visions longer than that."

"And what of their frequency? Are they not occurring in your waking hours, causing you to lose long stretches of memory?"

I don't answer. He's right: it *does* seem to have been getting worse. The visions are more vivid, more consuming, each time. And what about Cas in the last one? *My blood will be the end of you.* His blood. No, fiend blood. That's what Jared used to kill the last Transcendent.

I'm the same. A bomb. He could activate me at any time, and now he's suppressed my powers, I can't fight back.

So why hasn't he yet?

"Your other Transcendents," I say slowly. "Are they slipping, too? Or are you losing control of them?"

"That's quite enough insolence," Jared says, his expression strained, his claw-hand's grip tightening on the table. His claws make dents in the metal.

He's not even in control of himself.

"You," he snarls, "are notoriously difficult to contain."

"Wonder why?" I retaliate. "You keep sticking me in labs unsupervised. Did you really think I wouldn't get out last time? And did you think for a second I'd let you lock Elle up?"

"I'd have thought what happened to your Pyro friends might have given you an incentive to stay put."

"You mean when you killed them." But the face that comes to mind is... Cas.

"Tattoos aren't a reliable method of control for everyone."

"Is that why you didn't mark me?"

"I don't need to," he says. "You're no threat to me."

Now his claw-hand is shaking. I can feel it through the table, and I can't help but stare at him. His skin is so pale, it's practically see-through. His clawed hand has turned brittle-white, while I'm positive it was the same red colour as the fiends' the last time I saw him.

It's going wrong. His experiment's going wrong.

Not that he's any less dangerous. I'm tied down. And dying, apparently.

He might not even be telling the truth. He's an accomplished liar. In fact... he avoided the question. Why didn't he mark me? His answer makes no sense. I *was* a threat to him, from the start. He couldn't have known I'd cut off his arm, turn the Transcendents against him, set Val free. He's unhinged, yes, but every time he's tried to control me, the effect's only been temporary.

I have Fiordan blood. I'm Transcendent. Somehow, I know there's more to this than what I've been told. That white light when I used my powers, like when I faced the Fiordan...

"Where are Elle and Cas?" I ask.

A heartbeat passes. Then he shakes his head. "I'm sorry, Leah. I did warn you about the consequences of crossing me."

My heart plummets. "You're lying. Cas can't—he can't be killed." I have to say it. It's the truth. It *is.* "Elle. Why would you torment her? She's not even a Pyro. And she's your niece..."

I swallow over the lump in my throat. He *has* to be lying. But he set Elle against Cas using the tattoo. From what I saw, it looked like Cas let her stab him rather than risking her getting hurt. What the hell was the point in that, other than cruelty?

"This link between me and Cas is killing me," I say. "What harm will telling me the truth do?"

Jared's eyes narrow. His face is paler than ever, and the table's shaking under his grip. "Elle's sedated," he says. "The tattoo's effect lifted quicker than I anticipated and she was distraught to wake with Cas's blood on her. I had no choice but to sedate her for her own safety."

"And Cas?" I hardly breathe. "He's... you locked him up? Sedated him?"

Before he can reply, the door crashes open. I twist my head, trying to see who just walked in...

And it's another Jared. This one, without a clawed hand.

"Tell me I'm not seeing things," I say. "Did you screw around with their DNA, or is this hallucination part of the Transcendent thing?"

The Jared at the table sighs. "What is it?"

The other Jared says, breathlessly, "There's a fiend, one of yours, and it's unlocking the cages."

Jared stares at Jared, and the absurdity almost makes me laugh. The Jared beside me says, "Impossible. They were locked up. All of them. No fiend's come in or out since..." His gaze drifts to mine.

No way. That fiend I brought in here. It vanished.

Could it be freeing its brothers?

Not that it helps *me* in any way. I'm still tied down. And dying, apparently. Damn experiments. I wish Val *had* blown this place up. But then Cas would be buried with him.

There's no way out.

"Damn," says Jared, letting go of the table, leaving five claw-shaped dents. "Where are the other Transcendents?"

Wait. They're talking to one another. That didn't happen before. Is whatever control serum he used wearing off? *Can I make the Transcendents turn on him again?*

I squirm against the restraints. The effect's temporary, and the power in my Transcendent blood will win out eventually. It has to.

And speaking of blood... is the fiend I used my power on earlier still under my control?

"They're trying to restrain the fiends, but it's no use; the sedative won't work. One of them already got into the tunnel."

It's beyond weird to hear two Jareds having a conversation. But *what* did he say? The sedative...

Move, dammit! I struggle. Neither of them are looking at me anymore.

"You let it escape?" Real Jared stares at his counterpart. "Send at least three into the tunnels. *Now.*"

The Transcendent-Jared shakes its head. "We can't. That other Pyro experiment of yours collapsed the platform."

Real Jared peers down at me, a perplexed expression on his face.

"Not her. The boy."

"Cas?" I ask, disbelieving. Collapsed the platform? Does he mean the stairs, the other way out? If so… why?

"We can't have those fiends reaching the divide," says Real Jared. "This shouldn't be happening, especially now. *All* the engineered fiends this side of the divide belong to me."

"All except one." There's no emotion in Transcendent-Jared's voice, but the other stands upright, his hands shaking with anger.

"I refuse to believe even you allowed that worthless excuse for a Transcendent damage my property, let alone allow one of my servants to walk away free. It's impossible to break the spell. You of all people know that."

"Yes, master." Is there something mocking in Transcendent-Jared's tone? I have no idea. But suddenly, I want there to be as much chaos as possible. I want all Jared's sick experiments to collapse around his ears.

"Lock down the whole area." Real Jared's face is a furious white. "You know what to do. We can't survive an attack from the other side."

Transcendent-Jared nods, and leaves the room.

Real Jared whirls to face me. "Damn… I hoped it wouldn't come to this."

"What the hell was that about?" I shoot at him. "So your fiends are disobeying you, and it sounds like you're having trouble controlling your Transcendents, too. And did Cas wreck your escape route?"

"It was no escape route, Leah." Jared shakes his head. "It was a direct connection with the other side of the divide. I hoped to wait a little longer… you know the consequences if the breach opens."

"What, you're planning to *open* the bridge to the fiends' world?" I gape at him. "You'll die, and even if you don't, every other human on this planet will."

"I'm no human, Leah, not as long as I share your blood." Jared's mouth twists in a smile. "And you forget the power I have over you."

And he pulls out my weapon. My dagger. I feel the stirring in my blood even though he's holding it far out of reach.

"What...?"

His hand closes over the blade. And pain ignites in my bones. I cry out, my vision instantly flashing to a familiar battlefield...

And then, just as quickly, it disappears. Before I can do more than gasp, my bonds are severed, my hands fall free. I blink several times, convinced I'm seeing things.

Jared lies limp on the floor, a sword through his back. And Elle stands at my side, my own dagger in her hand. She cut my bonds.

So who...?

"No 'thanks for saving my ass'?" asks a familiar voice from behind me.

"Cas," I say, my throat hoarse. "How...?"

He walks into view. It's him, for sure. Blood stains his combat clothes, which are more than a little worse for wear. But it's his sword he pulls out of Jared's back.

"Idiot managed to send all his people after those fiends. He keeps forgetting the Transcendents aren't the only ones who heal damn fast."

"I thought you were dead." My heart races, and I jump as Elle cuts the bonds on my ankles, too.

"I thought *you* were dead," she gasps, hands trembling. "Jared was raving about how you were going to die, and..."

"Come *on*," says Cas impatiently. "He's distracted, but I wouldn't put it past him to try something. We're going to have to break down the barricade."

I sit upright, wincing. "What barricade?"

"To stop anyone using the exit you escaped by. Unfortunately, since I did away with his other escape route, that leaves us no way out. His fiends might be losing control, but they'll get in our way. We need to leave."

"Can you quickly tell me what the hell happened? I collapsed on the platform, and the next thing I see is you two fighting to the death, with his Transcendents watching as though one didn't try to kill him earlier."

Elle winces. "I blacked out just after you did. I woke up when Cas…" She swallows. "I'm sorry."

"Yeah, yeah, you've apologised already," says Cas. "You both passed out on me. I couldn't fight Jared alone without either of you taking the hit, so I pretended to fall under his spell, too. I was watching for an opening, but he'd injected all his Transcendents with more fiend blood for obedience. I figured I'd play along… until he put me up against her." He glances at Elle. I can hardly believe what I'm hearing. That he cared enough about us to stick around and act as Jared's plaything.

"And then?" I prompt.

"She stabbed me, I blacked out. Next thing I know I'm waking up in Jared's cage, and his fiends are rattling the doors. One of them ripped all the cage doors out of the ground. I took my chance and ran for it. Elle had the same idea."

"I thought you'd be here, Leah," says Elle. "He didn't inject you with anything, did he?"

"Some kind of suppressant. But I think it's wearing off." With a sickening jolt, I realise that the vision must have been a sign. I'm going to die, no matter what, if I believe what Jared told me.

"Right." Cas's face is a blank mask. "We're all armed. Don't lose that dagger again. Come on."

Something feels off, but sticking around would be a stupid idea right now. So we run out the door. From the left comes the distant noise of crashing and screeching that can only be the fiends, but we head right, in the direction of the ladder.

Except two corridors later, we reach a dead end. A wall blocks the corridor where there wasn't a wall before. I stop dead, but Cas marches ahead.

The barricade.

"Can't you use your powers at all?" he asks me.

"I can try. I have my weapon now." And I'm damn glad of its reassuring presence in my right hand.

But when I try to call the fire, nothing happens.

"Of all the timing." I kick the wall, furious. But Cas gestures to stay back.

"Leah, you shield Elle."

I start to protest, but Elle nods and places herself behind me, tugging on the back of my top. I back up a few steps, as does Cas.

Then he runs at the wall, so fast he blurs. A deafening *thud* sends brick flying everywhere. Cas falls back, his nose bleeding. The wall isn't damaged at all.

"Damn," he says. "It's blood control, like our place. We need his blood."

Crap. "Jared's. How long will it take him to recover from...?"

"I have no idea." Cas's voice is a sharp blade, and the blood around his nose makes him look even more frightening. "He never let us see the limits of *his* endurance."

This is madness, but what choice do we have? I let Cas take the lead. He doesn't seem overly harmed by the fact that he just ran headlong into a wall.

Before we reach the corridor's end, a scraping noise

behind us makes me spin around. Another noise, like metal scraping on metal. Then a crash.

"I think there's someone on the other side," I say, uncertainly. "You don't think the others…?"

"You two wait there," says Cas. "I'll run back and get some of his blood. Damn. We should have done it from the start."

"I'm not leaving you alone with him," I say evenly.

"And you're willing to put *her* in harm's way?" He indicates Elle. My heart sinks. She's the only one of us without healing powers or immunity, whatever Jared's tattoo did to her.

"Fine."

Elle grabs my arm. "You can't keep sacrificing yourselves for my sake. I'm a liability, Leah, you know it."

"It's not true," I say. "You know that's not true."

"I'm no Pyro." Her eyes are brimming over. "Let alone Transcendent. I don't have a place in this war. I'm as good as dead."

"So am I." The words come out before I can stop them, and her eyes widen. It's too late to take it back now.

"I'm dying," I say quietly. "What happened to make me Transcendent is killing me. That's why I black out. I get visions of what happened in the last war, and I have no control over when it happens. I'm going to die. Soon, Jared said. I wouldn't believe what he says, but none of the other Transcendents have survived it."

Her eyes are huge, tears spilling. "No. You can't die."

My throat closes up. I still haven't accepted it. Not really. But if I'm really living on borrowed time, I'm going to do the best I can with every second of it.

"Murray didn't say anything to you, did he?" I ask. "About the Transcendent? Because if even Jared the mad scientist can't figure it out…"

"He didn't say you were *dying!*" Elle bursts out. "There has to be a mistake. It's not true."

"It's true," says Cas, flatly.

My heart drops, even though I should be glad he's alive. Though, considering his apparent indifference towards my death, maybe not.

"So this is it? Why go to the trouble of rescuing me at all?"

Instead of answering, Cas walks up to the barrier again, this time holding a glass tube of reddish-brown liquid. Jared's blood. And mine, I guess. And fiends. And whatever other crap he put in there. A scraping, and the wall slides into the ground. I stare, unable to help myself, even with the racket of fiends screeching in the background.

On the other side, a row of Pyros waits, led by Val.

"I knew it!" cries Poppy. "I knew they were alive."

"Yeah, attract everyone's attention," Cas mutters. "Where's Murray?"

"Elle!" Murray rushes forward before the wall's fully down, vaulting over it and sweeping his daughter into a hug.

"Can it wait?" demands Cas.

"Yes, yes…" Murray looks at me, his eyes glassy. "Take care of her for me. This can't go on any longer."

I blink at him, confused about his meaning. It sounds like he's planning to stay behind.

"Come on," says Cas. "He's at his weakest. His Transcendents are out of control, and it sounds like his fiends are escaping their cages, too."

"Good," says Murray, moving forward and pulling out the twin blades I once saw him use.

"You're not going after him?" Cas lifts an eyebrow.

"He threatened Elle," says Murray, his face tight. "He killed too many Pyros to count, not to mention ruining lives through his sick experiments. He doesn't deserve to live in this world any longer."

"You can't fight him." Cas bars the way. "I already stabbed him, but he'll heal within minutes. He's Transcendent now. He has enough fiend blood to make him one of the monsters."

Murray looks him in the eyes. "So do I."

21

My heart misses a beat. "You what?"

Murray's gaze drops. "It's my greatest regret... when Jared suggested using fiend blood to combat our obvious disadvantage against the Fiordans, I agreed to be the test subject. It was that or risk him taking one of the other Pyros, or kidnapping a defenceless human. I only knew half of what he was up to in his private labs... we didn't live in the same headquarters, you see." He swallows, turning his left-hand weapon over.

I blink at him. "So what *were* you injected with?"

"Pure Fiordan blood," says Murray. "Not the fiends', but their masters'."

"It's... different?" I always thought all the fiends were the same, even after facing one of their shape-shifters. But—but Cas said the Transcendents are out of control because Jared went over the top with the fiend blood...

"The Fiordans doctored their own blood," Murray says. "It's too complicated to explain now, but it means they never get sick or weak, and injuries tend to heal quickly. Basically, like a Transcendent, except without any drawbacks. I used a small amount, as the Fiordan Jared captured escaped within a day."

"Wait, he captured one of them?" But that's not the important part. "That's how he created the mutant fiends, didn't he? But… he injected himself with *my* blood. Why do that, if he could do better? He's losing control already. Turning into a monster. Is my blood doing that, or…?"

"I have no idea what my brother's thinking," Murray says. "But he only captured a Fiordan before by sheer luck. I'm sure he kept a sample in the old lab."

"And it had no side effects?" I gape at him, unable to believe it. "No… visions?"

Cas twitches out of the corner of my eye. But it's no use expecting to keep this quiet now. *Please. There has to be a way to stop this.*

"None," says Murray. "I wish I'd known Cas's healing ability passed on the Transcendent power sooner. The situation with the last Transcendent was muddled—I didn't know until much later that Cas healed her. I never made the connection, because…"

"You didn't know I had monster blood in my veins," Cas says flatly. "So you assumed she gained the power through chance, or genetics, as you've said all these years. You claimed she was the last. You lied to all of us."

"I had no choice," says Murray, but he doesn't sound like he believes it. As for me, my thoughts are whirling. Despite the common sense voice that kept me alive in the wilderness whispering in my ear that getting my hopes up will only lead to more heartache, I can't help myself.

Murray sighs. "If I'd told everyone, they'd either have cast me out or hunted down the Fiordans themselves. Jared had just betrayed us. I couldn't risk any more chaos. We were devastated, and so was Earth. I didn't display any of the symptoms of the Transcendent for over a year afterwards, and even then, I assumed it was an evolutionary quirk. We'd lost all our research by that point, and most people had given up hope on the possibility of finding another."

"So what about when I showed up?" I stare at him. "You couldn't have—no wonder you were so confident I wouldn't hurt people."

"Leah, I'm sorry I lied, but your powers surfaced at the same time rumours about Jared did. I only realised after you and Cas left to find Jared that you might be in danger of the same symptoms that killed the previous experiments."

"And now?" I ask. "Why aren't *you* at risk?"

"It's a question of balance," says Murray. "Complications result when the blood's passed on second-hand, but not when it's taken from the Fiordans themselves. Too much Fiordan blood and the human part of you can't take it. I hoped after you faced the Fiordan last time it meant... it would stop. I'm sorry, Leah."

I have no idea what to say. "After... after I faced the Fiordan?"

"You awakened as a Transcendent when you encountered Jared's fiend on your first mission," says Murray. "When you faced the Fiordan, that was the second stage. I assumed it meant you wouldn't suffer the same fate as the others. Only the real Transcendent could use an energy wave, and without the visions."

My knees sag underneath me. "You might have told me this before. *Stages* of Transcendence? Jared mentioned something like it... he said because the visions struck me at this stage, I'm a lost cause. What happened to the last Transcendent then?"

Murray shakes his head. "I don't know. She was the only one to survive that long. All the others, including Jared's Transcendents—maybe even Jared himself—have second-hand blood, so they'll suffer the same as the others. Unless

Jared did inject himself with a high amount of pure Fiordan blood, which wouldn't surprise me."

I blink, feeling dazed. The Transcendents are linked to me through blood. And I'm linked to Cas. But if blood was taken directly from a Fiordan... why isn't Cas Transcendent? Because he's artificial? Because it takes a near-death experience to make the blood transfer work?

Cas fidgets again. "Come on. We need to leave now. Don't do anything stupid, Murray."

"Elle needs you," I say quickly, pushing aside the growing anger. "Come on…"

A roar sounds behind us. Several of the other Pyros swear.

"Get Elle out first!" says Murray. Before she can protest, he hands her over to two other Pyros. But the others step forward, not back.

"You can't beat him, Murray," says Val. "I can plant a bomb. I'll activate it at your signal, and this place will blow up. He'll be buried a hundred feet underground, and so will his Transcendents."

As if in response to her words, a bone-shaking tremor goes through the corridor, and most of the Pyros are forced to steady themselves against the walls. Murray swears, and runs down the corridor faster than I've ever seen him move.

"Shit!" Cas draws his weapon, his expression murderous. "He's not going back to fight that madman alone."

"Hold on a second," I say, at the same time as Ryan says, "No way. Cas actually cares about someone?"

Cas shoots him a furious look, turns his back, and heads after Murray. Shouts, crashes and clangs ring through the corridor, and the occasional screech from a fiend. My heart races, as I imagine more of the Pyros, fighting, dying. They need to leave. But now…

Dammit. Murray said something about a cure for the

visions. Might the Fiordan blood be here? The only possible cure for what's happening to me? The old lab went up in smoke. This is our only option to get our hands on his research. Part of me knows this is a stupid idea, but I have to try. I wanted to gain control over my blood. If my blood's the key to the war, it's about more than just my life.

And I'm too good at survival to give up now.

"Leah!" Val grabs my arm. "We can't lose you, too."

"I'm dying," I say, and raise my voice so everyone can hear. "The cure might be here. Jared keeps blood samples in all the labs, and if you blow this place up, we'll lose all of them. It might even stop the tattoos, too. I have to try…"

Val sighs, glances back at the others, then turns back to me. "Then we'll help."

"You can't," I argue. This is an entirely selfish mission, and I'm not putting everyone else in danger for it. "Someone has to take care of everyone else, especially with Murray gone."

"Yeah, but we don't count," says Poppy, pushing forward with Tyler at her side. "We're quick. We can search the labs while you and Cas blow things up. We don't want you to die either, Leah. You don't have to do this alone."

I take a few calming breaths. We're wasting time. Jared will more than have his hands full with Cas and Murray, but what about the other Transcendents?

"Give it up, Leah. You know we'll follow you anyway."

I give Val a desperate look. "You can't be serious about this."

"Leah… I know you're used to working alone, but I think you should let them come with you. You're forgetting they've had more experience in the labs than you have."

"I can tell fiends' blood from humans'," Poppy says. "Can you?"

"Er…" No, I can't. Dammit. "Guys, please be careful. If

you see any of the Transcendents, don't fight. They're pretty much invincible."

"No one's invincible," counters Poppy. "But yeah, fine. I'll take the left labs, you take the right, okay, Tyler?"

"Val, you can't," Ryan says as she makes to join us. "That tattoo might get you again. Besides, someone has to keep everyone else from wandering off."

"All right."

The sounds of fighting ahead grow louder. I walk ahead of the others, hoping I'm not leading them to their deaths.

When we reach another corridor, there's no sign of Murray or Jared, though the noise of swords clashing make standing still almost impossible. But doors lie open to either side, and I'm all too aware this is the last chance we'll have to search the labs.

Damn. I hope Murray knows what he's doing.

Cas grabs me by the sleeve and drags me to the side. "What the hell are you doing?"

"Looking for the Fiordan blood," I hiss. "It has to be here."

Cas swears. "You idiot. Why did you think I came back here? What did you think I've been looking for all this time? You just had to put yourself in danger again."

My eyes go wide. He was trying to find the cure all along? *That* was his plan?

"I've searched all the labs down this end," he says. "The others are past the fiend cages, and the monsters are breaking out. You can't go that way."

"Neither can you," I point out.

"I'll take my chances."

Blood streaks the floor. Jared's blood. This is the room I was imprisoned in. But I already know there's nothing of use in here. Poppy and Tyler are already on the case, searching the other rooms. Cas walks ahead, barely glancing in each room before striding off, before he disappears around a corner.

A tugging sensation grabs at my veins, sharp and unexpected. And that's when two winged Transcendents drop from the ceiling. Before I can register that the ceiling appears to be *moving*, one of them lunges at me with a clawed hand, the mirror of Jared's.

Crap. I'm eternally glad to have my weapon as I swing the dagger in an arc, severing the claw at the wrist. I stab again, fire flowing to my fingertips and along the blade.

Cas runs around the corner, knife at the ready and anger etched on his face. I stab the first fiend in the shoulder, throwing a blast of fire for good measure. The fiend staggers back, the wound already cauterising by itself, but the fire spreads in a haze of light. I stab it again, dodging its every attack, my body moving with barely a conscious thought from me. Finally, I'm at full power again.

Cas has already speared the other through the chest, just as he did to Jared earlier. He yanks the blade free, spattering blood everywhere, as I deal the killing blow to my enemy. Both fiends crumble to the ground. Literally.

"Damn," I say. "If it came from the cages, Murray and Jared must have gone pretty far, unless they're caught up in the middle of it…"

"Hope they break Jared to pieces," says Cas savagely. "Come on."

Tyler and Poppy run out into the corridor, sidestepping the remains of the fiends.

"Be careful, guys," I say. "Jared's experiments are on the prowl."

The corridor's a straight line, which at least makes it hard for anything to sneak up on us. But the rooms appear deserted as ever, as I remember from when I was trying to find my weapon. It's like Jared intentionally hid anything useful. But where, if not here?

"Whereabouts did my weapon come from?" I ask.

"I have no idea." Cas walks swiftly, and I have to hurry to keep pace behind him, while worrying about leaving the others behind.

"And yours? I thought he'd hidden them."

"He did," says Cas. "Locked them in a secret room inside his personal suite, but I've already checked. I'd guess he threw the other weapons away in case any of his Transcendents bonded to them and made his life even more difficult. Pity they didn't."

I open my mouth to respond, and the clash of metal on metal interrupts. We're two corridors away from the fiends' cages, and unless they know the way out, they'll be frantically trying to escape.

We turn the corner, in time to see Murray running at his brother, two swords held high. It's definitely the real Jared, judging by the blood trailing from the wound in his chest. He shouldn't even be standing.

Jared grins at us over Murray's shoulder, where his brother has him backed against the wall with his twin blades. Fire sparks around the two of them.

"Are you sure about this, brother?" asks Jared. "You seemed certain you didn't want to kill me. Don't we have a common enemy?"

"We haven't been allies in a long time, Jared," says Murray. "You know that." He strikes without warning, the left sword coming down at Jared's weak side. His brother dodges the blow, countering with his own blade, not at all deterred by his still-bleeding wound. My heart sinks.

"Relax," says Cas. I look at him, surprised to see his mouth curling into a smile. "Murray has two weapons. And I bet he knows Jared's weakness."

He really believes Murray can win? I turn back to watch the standoff. Jared's blocking Murray's sword, but the other weapon flashes forward.

Blood spurts into the air and two claws drop to the ground. I feel a burst of shame for ever doubting our leader.

"I see your enhancements aren't working out for you," Murray comments.

Dripping blood, Jared pushes harder with his blade against his brother's.

"You're a fool. The Fiordans are on our doorstep, brother."

"Who built this place on top of the divide?" Murray counters. "If I didn't know better I'd take it as an invitation. You don't give a damn about the rest of the world."

"I care about winning this war," says Jared. "And I'll cut you down if I have to."

Murray blocks his strike, raising the twin swords in an X. Blood drips to the ground, but Jared hardly seems to notice. They're evenly matched—but Jared's lazy confidence makes icy fingers trail up my spine.

"So you do mean to kill me?" Jared grins widely. "And there I was, thinking the fiends would finish you before you'd give me a fair fight. What do you say we give these willing spectators a show, hmm?" He looks back at me and the others, eyes lingering on Cas.

"I'm not playing games with you, Jared," says Murray. "This is war."

"Oh, you always were a killjoy."

The two brothers jump, almost at the same time. Next thing I know, Murray has Jared pinned to the wall.

"I knew you wouldn't be able to kill me," Jared whispers.

Murray curses and aims a killing blow at Jared's exposed neck.

Jared jerks his head back and kicks Murray in the shins.

Murray hisses between his teeth, blades spinning. My eyes widen. If Jared wasn't equipped with the speed and power of a Transcendent, those blades might have taken his head off.

Murray's really trying to kill him?

I step forward, though I'm not entirely sure what I'm going to do. Stop the fight? Kill Jared myself? I've no idea.

But before I can move, a tremendous roar echoes through the corridor and a giant muscled fiend rampages through the corridor, one wing dangling uselessly at its side, one hand dragging claws.

It got out, is the first thing I think, stupidly.

"Get back!" Cas pulls me out of the way. Murray ducks down and strikes at the fiend with both swords—but Jared's already taken the opportunity to run.

The fiend shrieks, and rather than running at us, runs headlong into the wall. Its eyes are red and wild, and it doesn't appear aware of its surroundings at all. But it's also barring the way between us and Murray. When the fiend hits the wall again and the path clears, Murray's gone. Must have chased after Jared. *Oh, shit.*

Cas makes an impatient noise and swings his sword close enough to cut into the fiend's arm, before I can warn him he'll set the monster on all of us. Sure enough, the fiend lumbers around, swinging its clawed fists. It's not the fiend I dominated, but the wings mark it as one of Jared's. Which means they're probably all out their cages, beating the walls down to get out of this prison. We haven't a chance of searching the labs without putting the others in the path of the fiends.

When the fiend swipes wildly again, I have no choice but to raise my weapon. I can't give it any more mercy than I would one of the monsters outside, even if I've given one of them *my* blood.

The fiend charges the wall again, this time leaving a dent

half a metre thick. Bits of stone fly everywhere, and I raise an arm to protect my face. Those bat-like wings beat, and it claws at the ceiling, sending rock raining down on all of us.

I gape, the dagger limp in my hand, as the fluorescent lights retract into the ceiling, plunging this section of the corridor into darkness. Then the next. Now we can barely see as the ceiling shifts with a rumble that shakes the earth.

Cas's blade flashes red. Fire. Of course. I let flames flicker along my own blade, too, illuminating the area around us in pure white. Brighter than I intended. The fiend staggers, blinded, and its fist pummels another hole in the wall. Its body follows, breaking into the room on our left. A lab. At least, it was. The fiend staggers over the newly-created threshold, kicking furniture aside, sending test tubes flying and blood spattering the walls. I curse, remembering what we're looking for, but even I could be in trouble if I get too close, and injuries will cost us precious time. I back out, but Murray and Jared are nowhere in sight and the corridor's blocked by rubble.

Before I can move, another resounding crash shakes the tunnel as the fiend throws itself at the wall to the neighbouring lab.

"Dammit," Cas hisses. "It'll bring the place down if this keeps up."

I'm pretty sure we have bigger problems. The others are boxed in behind me, and the ceiling's shifting, the remaining fluorescent light moving further away by the second. Cas's blade glows so bright my own eyes are dazzled, and I have to tighten my grip on my own weapon to anchor myself in the here and now. If another vision hits me, I'm utterly screwed.

"Come on," I say. "We can't stop that thing now. Murray's..."

Crash.

Rubble rains down, bits of rock hitting the floor like

gunfire. Cas swears and runs forward, kicking it out of the way.

"What the hell are you doing?" I call at him—he's running right through the place where the ceiling just collapsed. I pause to check on the others. Luckily, the fiend next door took most of the hit.

"Crap," says Tyler. "Right. Let's check those labs as quick as we can and then get the hell out of here."

"Agreed," I say.

Cas and I clear the rubble out of the way and we run, holding weapons like beacons. Lights flicker ahead, but there's no sign of Murray or Jared. Unease skitters down my spine. We can't afford to waste any more time in here.

Another corridor. Several tense minutes pass while the others search the labs, and I keep an eye out for any trouble. Including the suspiciously-still ceiling. I guess it explains why those winged Transcendents were able to sneak up on us before.

Damn Jared and his games. I lose patience and search a couple of the labs myself, but don't come any closer to finding anything useful. Worse, Cas has decided to run off ahead, and I have to hang back to make sure no fiends appear and attack the others. The crashing and snarling from the fiend trying to claw its way out are driving me mad, and I almost want to put the creature out of its misery.

Another sudden jolt shakes the corridor, knocking me off balance. I stumble to the side, glancing up to check the ceiling isn't falling down. But somehow, part of me senses the vibrations rocking the floor are coming from somewhere on our right.

I don't get time to wonder how in the world I know that, because the wall on the right explodes. Dust clouds rise into the air, once again plunging us into darkness. A chunk of ceiling falls and strikes the floor, shattering into fragments. Shards cut into my arms, but I barely notice.

A scream.

"Tyler!" I yell. "Poppy! Are you guys okay?"

"Yeah, we're fine!" comes the response... from behind a wall of rock.

"Damn. You guys better get back."

"Are you crazy?" Tyler says. "I can break rock open with my fists, you know. Have you forgotten who taught you about wall-punching?"

"This place is gonna collapse," I say. "If it does, Cas and I will survive it, but you..."

"Come on, she's right!" shouts Poppy. "We'll go—"

Another bone-shaking tremor. This time, the remainder of the right wall bursts open, and I'm sent flying into left wall with such force, I feel a cracking sensation in my left arm. I cough, and blood sprays the dust-filled air.

An explosion. An energy blast? I groan, and my vision swims. *Not again. Not now.*

"You know what, we should *all* get out of here," says Poppy's voice from behind a haze of dust.

Ouch. My arm throbs. Self-preservation wars with the reminder that if we leave, I'm forfeiting my chance to ever find a cure for the visions. The pain in my arm is enough of a reminder I'm living on borrowed time. But I can't let the others get killed on my account.

A hiss comes from ahead, through the dust. Cas stumbles towards me, clutching at his own arm.

"Stand back," he says. "The roof's going to come down. Leah, stay where you are."

"Wait, how do you—?"

But Cas has already jumped, knife swinging, severing what's left of the wall in fragments. The remainder of the ceiling collapses on top of it.

"What are you doing?" The words escape in a flurry of coughing, but I already have that stinging pins-and-needles feeling that tells me my body is healing itself. I stagger upright, blinking dust from my eyes.

"The cages are ahead," says Cas. "Running that way brings us right into a trap. But if we knock the walls down, we can search each lab this way without opening the cages. They're only on one side of the corridor."

"If you say so."

I'm more worried for the others, but like hell am I bringing them into danger again. Even as I feel the bones of my arm knotting together, I know I'm lucky to have escaped worse injury.

Crash.

Lucky I moved out the way in time, because the fiend chooses that moment to run through the opposite wall. The same way Cas went.

"Cas!" I yell. Even that direction's blocked by fallen rubble.

"Don't worry about me, idiot!"

I spin wildly around, to find the way back's still blocked, too. "Poppy? Tyler?"

"We're fine!" Poppy yells. "What the hell is happening over there?"

I jump back as a massive chunk of ceiling falls down. "Guys, get back!"

Cas appears in front of me, blade slicing the falling rubble to pieces. The view clears, even as everything shakes again.

I stare. The fiend's left a trail of destruction in its wake, and yet all I can focus on is the beam of sunlight shining down on the wrecked lab. There must have been some kind of hidden exit. In fact, as the dust clears, I can see the outline of stone stairs, which must once have been concealed behind the wall at the back of the room.

"Guys?" I say, and point, though I've no idea if they can see me.

"Damn," says Tyler's voice. "Guess Jared built more ways out than I thought."

"Yeah, but that fiend's out there." I can hear it rampaging away, probably clawing down the walls in a bid for the surface.

"Wait," says Poppy, and there's a shuddering crash as the wall between me and them breaks away. Poppy and Tyler stand on the other side, weapons out and the smoking remains of the rock wall in front of them.

"Wow," I say. "Nice job, guys."

Except the way ahead is blocked, I have no clue where Murray and Jared went, and dragging the others through a collapsing building is a stupid move. But then, half the place has fallen down already.

And Cas has disappeared again. Damn him. I'm *not* leaving him behind again.

"Cas!" I yell.

"Through here."

He stands on a pile of rubble, covered in dust, but appears unhurt. I check the ground's stable and nothing's about to collapse, then beckon the others to follow.

It's hard to tell where one lab ends and the next begins, let alone what they used to contain. Smashed glass litters the rock-strewn floors, and the fiend's left monster-shaped holes in most of the walls. Too many for one fiend alone.

"The others are loose in here," I say, in a low voice.

"Be careful, guys."

"Famous last words," Cas mutters from behind.

22

N o sign of anything useful. Worry is clawing at my chest once we've passed by the main set of labs, leaving the ones on the other side of the fiends' cages. The rampaging noises are louder than ever, and it's only a matter of time before the whole ceiling comes crashing down.

I can see the stairs on the other side, leading me to wonder if they're connected up with the other pathway out of here. But it's impossible to see.

"Uh, Leah, do you think this is human blood?" says Tyler, shooting me an anxious look as he hands me a test tube.

It's beyond me to tell the difference. "Not sure. Better take it anyway, just to be sure."

Cas had run ahead, supposedly to check for dangers. The rattling, shaking and falling rock becomes background noise, but worry for the people on the surface intrudes. Will I really have to choose between stopping the visions and saving my friends?

I already know the choice I'll make. And yet some part of me wonders what choice *Cas* would make. He stayed back here to find the cure. Because I'm the only person like him? Or because… it's me? Would he stay behind for my sake again?

Now isn't the time to wonder about that. We're at the final row of labs, and by the trail of destruction, it's obvious the fiends have destroyed everything worth salvaging from here.

I sag against a half-collapsed wall, trying to push down the despair clawing at me. The lab's finished. Jared and Murray are fighting for their lives, the fiends are pounding on Earth's doorstep… and yet, as self-centred as it is, the only thing I can think of is being consumed by visions, unable to protect anyone.

Just like when Lissa died.

Even as a Pyro, even as a Transcendent, I can't save the others.

Enough. I grit my teeth and dig through the trashed remains of the lab, throwing bits of crumbled wall and ceiling aside. A row of test tubes has smashed over the back wall and I run over, cutting my hands on the broken glass as I try to find something worth salvaging. Nothing left.

The trembling under my feet becomes difficult to ignore. Especially as it's now coming from all around us. I can barely walk steady.

Crash.

I brace myself against a doorway as a fiend charges through the ruins, leaving a hole in the wall. I swear as another chunk of ceiling comes down.

"Tran—scen—dent…"

I blink through the dust at the fiend.

"What?" I say. "You win, don't you? You're free."

"Only as you command, Transcendent."

I stare. Is this the fiend I controlled before? No way to tell, especially with the falling dust and the shaking…

Oh, God. The others. If the ceiling falls, if this place falls apart, I can't protect them.

"You. Get Ty and Poppy out, you hear me?"

I don't know if the fiend heard me. Because a tremendous cracking sounds overhead, and the world goes out in a cloud of red smoke.

———

They're coming to Earth. A distant army of fiends marching towards the divide. We're closer than ever, close enough to see the lava flowing through the breach, between scorched red sky and scorched red ground. Above, flames form a gate I recognise clearly now.

This is the bridge. Somehow, in the present day, I know this is the first time it appears.

The fiends wait restlessly. At the head of the monsters, a group of smaller figures march. Smaller figures dressed in black. Like humans.

Fiordans.

"I'll close it," I whisper. "I can close it. Let me..."

"Wait," says Cas from beside me. "Don't you think there's something odd going on? Where's Murray? And Jared? They were with the army just a second ago."

"I don't know. Cas, they're right there. *I could close it from here." I'm standing before he can reply, darting from our hiding place to another rock closer to the divide. The Pyro army stands in lines alongside us.*

Cas appears beside me and grabs my arm. "What happened to staying inconspicuous?"

"We're so close, Cas," I whisper. "So close to shutting them out for good."

Close enough to see the figures crossing the bridge, to make out the features of the Fiordan leading the group.

"No way. Jared's with them."

———

I blink awake. My head's pounding, and pain shoots through my limbs as I struggle to sit upright. Another blink tells me it's because half a wall's collapsed on me, and my chest feels like it's caved in.

"Don't move." Cas's voice comes from nearby, but I can't turn my head. "I'll shift it. We're gonna have to move fast."

I cough. I'm pretty sure I've broken ribs, but then again, I healed from certain death in less than five minutes. I concentrate on breathing instead of the pain, and the pressure lifts from my chest and legs. Cas appears, throwing the fallen ceiling piece aside, and I struggle upright.

"Hold on," he says. "You might not be able to stand yet."

Is he concerned for my safety? Maybe I got hit on the head harder than I thought. But I'm careful as I slide out from underneath the remains of the collapsed ceiling and stand shakily, trying not to look at the smeared mess of blood on the floor. Breathing becomes easier by the second. Once again, I'm a walking miracle... with a ticking time bomb over my head.

I look up, and my jaw drops. "What happened up there?"

"That fiend took Poppy and Tyler."

My heart misses a beat. "Which fiend?"

"One of the winged ones."

"Oh shit. I hope it was the one I told to get them out..." And now I have to explain this. I quickly give Cas a rundown of what I did to the fiend, controlling it with my blood, while he watches me, genuine shock on his face.

"You seriously controlled... that was *stupid*, Leah."

"What was I supposed to do?" I counter. "It probably

saved my life. And the others, too." *I hope.* "We need to get out."

"I'm aware." Cas points up over the ruins of the lab. "That way leads to those hidden stairs. It's not ideal, but it's the only way out now, unless you want to climb the cliffs of the divide."

"I'll pass."

So we climb through the ruins. Ignoring the shaking, the tremors that suggest something is happening on the surface. Or over the divide.

That army...

But I can't remember whether it's something I actually saw, or just the vision.

After several minutes' precarious climbing, we stumble onto the stairs. They're littered with rubble, too, but it's easy to climb over. I pick up speed, trying to forget that leaving this place is condemning myself to madness. But I have to make sure the others are okay.

There was nothing left in the labs. Nothing you could do.

Damn Jared. Damn Murray for not telling me the truth. If I'd known from the start, this might never have happened.

Then I remember Murray might be dead.

At last, sunlight streams down, through breaks in the ceiling. We're close. So close, the smell of burning catches in my throat, making me cough uncontrollably. Eyes watering, I push on, until we break the surface.

Burned ground. Fiends swarming overhead. The divide, only metres away.

Murray's poised over the edge, with Jared's knife at his throat and surrounded by Transcendents.

I freeze. *Crap.*

Murray's in a bad way. He's lost both his weapons, and the slightest movement will send him falling over the edge. My heart climbs into my mouth. How can we distract Jared?

At least the general racket covered the noise of us climbing, but if he moves, he'll spot us in a second.

And where are the others on the surface?

The cries of fiends echo from above. They're circling, enjoying the spectacle. Even with my dagger ready to leap into flame in my hand, I feel utterly powerless.

The twelve Transcendents are armed, too, and are spread out in a line, completely cutting off Murray's escape. The Pyros' leader sways on the spot, the side of his face crusted with blood. Jared moves with a slight limp as he pokes Murray with his sword, suggesting he's hurt, too.

"What'll it be, Murray?" Jared asks, pressing his blade to Murray's neck. The sword gleams as it catches the light. "You know you can't beat a true Transcendent blade."

"That weapon wasn't yours to take," says Murray.

"But I wield it brilliantly." He steps forward. "Death now, or would you rather I offer you up to the fiends? They're getting quite impatient over there." He indicates the other side of the divide.

So he does know. Of course he does. He has spies, after all. He's been right up close to them, gathering intelligence.

"You won't win this, Jared," says Murray. "I told you, you're underestimating the Fiordans if you think they'll let you get away with trespassing on their territory any longer." Murray shakes his head, almost calm, considering he's on the brink of falling off the edge.

"I have my reasons," says Jared.

"Madness," says Murray. "When will you give up this madness? It's not too late to accept there are other ways to defeat the Fiordans."

"There is no way to win this war without sacrifice," Jared snarls, pressing the tip of his knife to his brother's chest. "Different levels of sacrifice—what does it matter? Luck determines human survival, and the same for us Pyros, unless we use every advantage necessary to ensure our continued existence. It's all very well wanting to go out in a blaze of glory, but I intend to survive. This world is *ours.*"

"You mean, *yours.* Is there anyone you wouldn't kill to ensure your own survival? I know you couldn't give a damn about the rest of the world."

Jared shakes his head, a pitying expression crossing his face. "You're too cruel, brother."

"Look at yourself," Murray says, simply. "Look at what you've done."

Cas is edging stealthily towards them, blade at the ready. What's he thinking? We can't fight off all twelve Transcendents *and* Jared—and then there's that army waiting on the other side…

Cursing inwardly, I follow him.

"I do what's necessary, no more." He presses the blade harder. Is his hand shaking from tiredness, or does he really not want to kill Murray?

"Enough with the theatrics," says Murray. "You could have easily killed me a hundred times over by now. There's nothing I can give you that you don't already have, except a certain lack of conscience, but I suppose you don't feel the absence. You have your army, you have your mutants. There are your enemies. You always liked to see things in black and white."

"Lack of conscience? Yet you trust me enough to spare *your* life?"

Cas remains still, sword still held ready to strike. *Cas, what are you doing?* Even he wouldn't do something so stupid. Why…?

Then I see them. Hidden in the shadows of a cluster of rocks not ten metres away from Jared and Murray—even the fiends circling above haven't spotted them.

The other Pyros. I can't tell how many, but there's at least two, including Val. And if they moved fast—the Transcendents are that close to the edge—

Would they risk Murray's life to try and take out Jared?

I don't know if they have a plan, but it's all we've got. I stick close behind Cas, relieved that the sloping ground is dotted with rocks big enough to hide behind. I don't know why the fiends in the air haven't taken us out yet, but—from what I can tell, based on each time I dare to glance up at the sky—their attention is fixed on the army on the other side of the divide, or on Jared and Murray's standoff.

Still, I keep my hand clenched on my dagger. Beads of sweat gather on my forehead. Even moving quickly, I brace myself, expecting claws to sink into my back, or Jared to turn around and see us.

One step after another, moving swiftly. Cas is tensed up, too, and shifts the knife in his hand.

Val spots us. Though it's silent, and we're all in danger right now. I give her a nod of acknowledgment. I'm assuming she has some kind of plan, but there's no way to find out without alerting the fiends, and the Transcendents, too. Who must be back under Jared's control.

It's so wrong. All of this. Will destroying Jared really bring an end to the madness?

Val mouths, "Don't move any closer."

Cas frowns at her, his free hand resting on top of his blade—if anyone else did that, they'd get cut. The look on his face says *why? Don't you want me to cut them down?*

Wait. She's holding something in her hand, something I can't see. But I can guess. *The bomb.* Jared's lot are right on the edge of the divide. It would take one push to send them over the edge.

But it might cost Murray his life. He might have lied, but I don't want him to die.

Jared presses his blade to Murray's neck, drawing blood. He's inches from the edge himself.

Everything seems to slow down. The bomb spins through the air. Jared's head jerks up. My heart drops.

Jared moves. Just slightly. But the bomb's already heading towards his face—even from here, I swear I can see disbelief flicker in his eyes.

And it's enough for Murray to leap, higher than I've ever seen him move. He lands several feet clear as the bomb flies past...

And hits the Transcendent next to Jared.

The Transcendent goes flying—for an instant he's suspended in the air, face blank even seconds from death—and falls. Jared curses, backing away from the bomb, but there's nowhere to run. He's boxed himself into a corner.

Someone screams my name, then all sound is smothered in a tremendous blast. Red smoke smothers the world—I'm flying back, flying, and there's a ringing in my ears, and then an arm's around me and drags me back.

Then my feet are on the ground. I'm running through dust, even though I can't see where I'm going, and everything is red and grey and hazy...

Flickers of another place, Jared's lab—*no!*—I shove the vision away, forcing my eyes to focus on the dust and running, stumbling... the world's tilting sideways, the ground giving way, and I remember, too late, what a sorry state the labs underneath were in...

And Cas...

He appears from the fog like a ghost, grabs my arm, pulls me along. A fierce light gleams in his eyes.

Running through dust, breath coming in gasps. The world tilts sideways.

I shake my head fiercely.

But it's not a vision. The ground's tipping upwards, as

though the earth has come to life under our feet, trying to throw us off. I stumble and trip, sliding down.

The ground turns vertical. I grab desperately for Cas's hand, but it's too late. We're both tumbling into nothingness.

Into heat.

Into the divide, which has split wider than ever.

The last thing I see is two skies, both burning red, merging into one. Light fills my vision, blurring out the world.

Hot air slams into me at the same time as I crash down onto a hard surface. I blink, but only see red.

Red sky. Red ground. Cas at my side, shouting my name.

Shouting another name. One that should be impossible.

A figure stands opposite us on the scarred ground, a twisted smile on his face.

Nolan.

23

For an instant, all I can do is stare. *Impossible. You died.* On my right, the river of lava flows like in the vision, flames flickering above it. No gate, this time. No way out.

Impossible. We had to get through here somehow.

Nolan watches us, still smiling that insane smile.

Cas steps forward, blade held out, flames already leaping from the edge. Here, the air smells of burning, and the heat's starting to rise.

"I'm gonna give you one warning, Fiordan scum, then I'll run you down."

Fiordans. He's one of the shape-shifters. There's no other way.

Something isn't right. Not just the fact that we stand in a world not our own, with a burning sky overhead. Past Nolan, I can see the distant shapes of hills. But the divide draws my attention. Flames swirl above it in waves and patterns, but I can still make out hazy red ground on the other side. *It didn't look like that before.*

"You see it, don't you?" says Nolan, or whatever he really

is. "The divide is opening. And that's not all…"

"Enough." Cas takes one step towards him, pointing the sword so the tip rests inches from his heart. Nolan doesn't move.

"It's me, Cas," Nolan says quietly, and raises his hands in surrender. Both palms look burned-red. Sure, it sounds like him, but he *died.* I saw him lying broken on the ground before the fiends carried him away.

"A likely story."

"I've met one of your kind before," I say. "So you've been spying on us. Thought you'd screw with us by pretending to be someone who died."

"I'm not…" Nolan hesitates. "I'm really Nolan, Leah. I didn't die. The fiend carried me over here."

They'll say anything. Tell any lie. Rage at the Fiordans leaves a bitter taste in my moth. "Liar."

Nolan flinches as Cas's knife nicks the skin of his throat. "I wouldn't do anything I'd regret."

"I won't regret killing you whether you're the real thing or not," says Cas smoothly. "The Nolan who died was a traitorous bastard either way."

"Even if I helped Leah find you?" says Nolan.

How can he know that? Maybe the fiends were spying on us the whole time. Like Jared's.

Cas glances at me, then back at Nolan. I can't read the look on his face. "It's irrelevant. You're a monster."

"Speak for yourself." Nolan's mouth twists. "The fact that the two of you are still standing here is proof you're as unnatural as the fiends."

"What the hell are you talking about?" I ask.

"Ignore him." Cas's blade shifts. One movement and he can cleanly slice through Nolan's neck.

"Surely you've worked it out?" Nolan tilts his head away from the sharp point. "You can pass unharmed through the breach because you share fiend blood. *Our* blood, Leah."

"You're a liar," I say, my heart thudding. *No. He can't know that.* Nolan can't. But if the *Fiordans* know about my blood… then they must know about Jared's experiments.

"There's no other way it could be possible," says Nolan. "Believe me, I've seen some strange things here. Nothing's too strange in this place."

"I don't give a shit," I say. "You're a liar, and you're gonna go up in smoke." For emphasis, I send a flare to my right hand, and the blade, which immediately ignites. Fire waits beneath my skin, burning for a fight.

"Leah, wait!" he says, in the spitting imitation of Nolan. Now he's making fun of me. "I'm not who you think I am. They kidnapped me. You have to believe me."

Not before Cas strikes. The knife comes down, but Nolan's already jumped, impossibly quick, drawing his weapon.

I hesitate, but Nolan moves too fast for me to take aim from a distance, let alone close up. I stalk up to him all the same, weapon aimed low, prepared to take him off balance.

Nolan and Cas exchange blows, circling one another. For Nolan to be able to stand up to Cas must mean he's one of the enemies. It's the only explanation.

I barely breathe. Fire swirls around the pair of them, leaping to the end of Cas's blade. Blood spurts and Nolan cries out and falls back.

"Stop!" he gasps. "You can't kill me."

"Really, now?" Cas lunges forward, and Nolan barely dodges, stumbling. He lets his weapon hand drop, his dagger glowing with a series of patterns I've only seen once before.

There's no mistaking it. He definitely has Nolan's weapon. It's supposed to be impossible for anyone else to use a Pyro's weapon. Right?

"Wait!" Nolan gasps. "It's my sword. It has my blood. Only I can use it."

"Sure it is," says Cas. "You Fiordans have a thing for messing with blood and genetics, don't you? Nolan's dead, and even if he wasn't, he'd never come here. He'd be in the fight, or he'd be running away."

"That's what I'm doing. Running away."

Cas steps forward and presses the blade to his throat. Nolan raises his arms in surrender, but keeps hold of the weapon. If it's his true blade, he won't be able to let go of it.

"Honestly," Nolan chokes. "It's me. I'm on your side!"

"You're dead," says Cas, without emotion.

"I thought I died," says Nolan. "But I woke up here. They took me into their city, healed me. I'm Transcendent now."

"You're doomed," says Cas, flatly. "Don't you know what Transcendent blood does? It kills you slowly."

"They gave me *their* blood," says Nolan.

"As if," says Cas. "And that makes you our enemy by default."

"Jared is our enemy," says Nolan quickly. "We can work something out."

"He's dead," says Cas, and I stare at him.

"He is?" I'm betraying my own ignorance here, but I haven't a clue what happened when we crossed over the divide.

"He's not here," says Cas. "So he fell into the divide."

But that means Murray's…

It's Nolan's turn to look stunned. "You—you what? Jared? For real? You killed him?"

"If he lives," says Cas, "then we have bigger things to worry about than your lies."

"Not him," Nolan counters. "The Fiordans are amassing their armies. Even Jared won't be able to stand up to them, not on his own. You know the real reason he has spies over here? He thought the other Pyros survived."

Cas makes a choked noise. For the first time since I've known him, he appears lost for words.

I've no idea what Nolan's talking about. "Other Pyros? You mean Murray…" My heart twists at the thought of the others. Poppy. Tyler. Val. Did they make it out? *Please. Please let them be alive.*

"She doesn't know?" Nolan's mouth twists. "I suppose I can't say I'm surprised by this point."

"Enough of your bullshit, Fiordan," I snap.

"I'm not," Nolan retaliates, "but they'll be back. The only reason they haven't found you already is because their army's marching that way." He points to the left, over the horizon. I squint, at first unable to see anything unusual. A hazy pattern becomes visible. Like hills.

No. Not hills. Giants.

Ice slides down my spine. "No way," I whisper, Nolan's treachery forgotten. "There must be…"

"Thousands," says Nolan. "The Fiordans don't normally come this close to the divide. Energy blasts tend to take them unawares."

"Where did you come from, then?" I ask, no longer caring about fighting him. Right now, all I want to do is make sure that army never makes it over the divide.

Never makes it to Earth.

"Over there." He points across the divide, and a jolt of shock goes through me. The other side isn't Earth, not anymore. It's more wasteland, more of this broken world. And there's a vague line of shapes on the horizon to the left, like… buildings. "I got out because they're mobilising their army," he adds quickly. "They're abandoning all their posts."

"More's the pity," says Cas, coldly. "Give me one good

reason why I shouldn't kill you." And once again, his blade finds Nolan's neck.

"I can give you the cure," Nolan chokes. "The cure for what's killing her."

"You're a liar."

"It's true. And it's true Jared thought the others survived. The Fiordans don't know that. I never told them. I pretended to work for them because I had no choice, then slipped away when they left the city."

"Bullshit," says Cas.

"Why do you think he'd risk his neck here? He wasn't just stealing Fiordan technology. He was having his spies watching out for the rest of his army. You know how many died."

"Enough," Cas snapped. "Murray declared them dead, isn't that enough for you?"

"Murray... knows the Fiordans?" I ask, totally confused.

"No," says Nolan. "Murray had no idea what his brother was really doing over here. I guess I thought you two would have found out at Jared's place, unless he destroyed his research, or..." He trails off.

"Finish your sentences or I'll do it for you," says Cas.

"Murray doesn't know Jared's plans," Nolan says quickly. "At least, I don't think he did. It was one of Jared's fiends that brought me over here. The Fiordans caught us and killed the fiends for serving Jared. They were going to kill me, but figured they'd pay Jared back for capturing and corrupting their fiends."

"If it's true, they wouldn't have kept you alive," says Cas evenly.

"Maybe not. But there are only a few of them left. The Fiordans were too busy building their army to pay much attention to me once they'd injected their blood in me."

"So Jared was spying on them?" I ask, still feeling like I'm missing something.

"No. Well, he tried, but his fiends usually don't come back if they try to go near the Fiordans' places. It's like I said. He thinks there are surviving Pyros here."

"What the hell do you mean?" I cut in. "Pyros? Did you mean Fiordans?"

Cas shakes his head tightly. "What he means isn't possible," he says. "There were... others, in the original war with the Fiordans. They died, all of them did, when the divide closed. Like I said—we lost half our army."

"Jared thinks they lived." Nolan stumbles back. "Don't you think I'd tell the truth with a freaking knife pointed at my throat?"

"I don't think you'd tell the truth if you had less than a minute to live," says Cas smoothly. "Which you don't, as it happens."

"Wait," I say quickly. "I'm not saying I believe him, but I find it a little hard to believe that we've lasted this long here without being trampled by an army, if they really are invading Earth again."

"They're mobilising," says Nolan. "The last war scattered the forces, and the Fiordans have been rebuilding the past two years. But now they have..."

A choked noise escapes him, blood spraying the ground. For a second, I think Cas stabbed him.

Then I see the figure climbing out of the divide. At first, only its head and hands are visible.

One hand is clawed. The head is burned beyond recognition, a hairless mess of red and black. But horrifyingly familiar.

"Jared," I whisper. "No way. He survived..."

But does that mean Murray...?

Nolan slumps forward. Cas stares at Jared with more horror in his expression than I've ever seen.

"You fell," he says.

"I can't die," says Jared. Half his face has melted off, and his teeth gleam between the gaps in a ghastly grin. I want to run for my life. But I can't move, not even to raise my weapon.

"I've tolerated the pair of you for too long," Jared hisses.

And he raises his hands. I'm thrown back, head over heels. A gasping sounds in my ears, but it's not me. I raise my head and see Cas has collapsed, writhing in pain. Damn. Even falling to pieces, Jared managed to activate the tattoo.

"It's time to end this, Leah," says Jared. "My fool brother thought he could best me, but he was mistaken. You're the Transcendent, Leah, and I want you to join me of your own will."

"You're mad." And he is, more than ever before. Not just because half his face is falling off, but because of his uneven tone, shaking hands, unsteady steps. I'm pretty sure the only reason he's kept hold of his weapon is because it's melded to his hand. The Transcendent blade.

"Perhaps."

And he pushes outwards with his hands, sending me falling into the dirt again. Crap. He might be mad, but he's using his Transcendent powers, and Cas isn't getting up any time soon.

So be it.

I roll to my feet, my own weapon outstretched. It's time for revenge on the man who tormented me, who tortured Cas, who was responsible for the sick experiments and God knows, he's as much to blame for what happened to Earth as the fiends are.

That's more than reason enough to finish him off for good.

Last time I was here, I used my Transcendent powers to close the bridge. Even now, they wait under my skin, flaring to life as I push him back. He's close to the edge, but the hit doesn't do any damage to him.

"I'm Transcendent, Leah," he says.

"You're a bastard," I counter, advancing on him. "You're a cowardly, sick bastard who as good as destroyed our world. You deserve to die alone out here on this dead planet." I scream the last part, as I clear the last distance and leap at him.

This time, he doesn't hit back with an energy blast, but raises his blade to meet mine with a resounding clang. Though he looks like he can barely stand, my cut doesn't knock him any closer to the edge.

But he's close enough.

I send a burst of fire up my right arm, through the connection to my dagger, and the air goes up in flames.

24

For an instant, or maybe minutes, we're suspended, blade on blade, neither giving ground. Sweat drips down my forehead, my arms ache, but I've never felt more alive.

Fear flashes in Jared's eyes.

At last.

I scream, driving my knife downwards, and feel his give way.

"Give it up, Jared," I hear myself saying, but the words are muffled by the crackle of flames in my ears. I think Jared's screaming, too. But everything's blurred, like through smoke.

Like a vision.

Not now!

I focus on the fire, but it wavers and sputters. The smell of burning might be coming from far away, not right in front of me.

Jared's blade whips down and I'm forced to jump back, shattering the illusion. But he's nowhere near as fast as a Transcendent ought to be, even with the ugly claws sprouting from his hands, the wings hanging limp at his sides.

A fresh wave of anger crashes over me and I launch into an attack. What right does this pitiful man have to decide if my friends live or die?

I strike again and again. Blood spurts from small cuts on his arms. He raises the sword one final time, and my knife crashes into it like an avalanche. White light flares up all around me, but it goes through Jared in a worse way. I can see through his skin, see the veins pulse bright white, as he staggers, falling, his weapon cracking to pieces in his hand.

Gasping for breath, hanging onto the last threads of sanity, I drive the blade into his heart.

He shatters, like a boulder dropped from on high, breaking to pieces on the pockmarked, barren ground.

I stare, the image of Jared imprinted on my eyelids. But he's gone. Dead.

The world blurs out.

A hand rests on my shoulder, and I make a feeble lunge with my dagger. But it's Cas.

"Leah. He's dead."

"I know." I stagger back, somehow not caring that I'm leaning against him.

"We have to go."

"I know," I say again, mechanically. Then something snaps into place. "Nolan?"

"Not moving," says Cas. "Leave him here. We need to find a way out."

"The bridge." *Think, Leah.* "That's how I got out last time. But it's gone."

"Last time," he repeats. "There's always a last time. Murray… he's probably dead." He says this matter-of-fact-ly. But I'm not fooled.

"Cas, it wasn't your fault," I say. "If you hadn't—Jared

would have killed everyone, started another war. You've ended that."

You're free, I think, and with that, it all slams on me at once. Murray's dead, but so is Jared. His tattoo bindings don't work anymore, on Cas or anyone else.

Cas doesn't have to answer to him anymore.

Tears are running down my cheeks before I'm aware of it. I sway again, overwhelmed.

"Leah—dammit, Leah." He shakes his head, grabbing my arm to steady me. "We need to get back. Do you remember where the bridge was? It's not safe to cross over here, not now that bomb's probably destroyed Jared's lab."

Even though he's nowhere near as snappish as he used to be, those words are more than enough to jolt me out of my trance, and I furiously wipe the tears away. I point, hesitantly, though I'm not at all sure from this side. Assuming the two worlds run parallel, we need to walk alongside the divide.

Nothing to do but walk. At least we have the advantage of Transcendent speed, because God help us if we run into the army.

Worse, shadows are prickling at the edges of my vision again. If I pass out now, we're finished. Unless Cas finds a way back. He must do.

"Nolan, if it was him, he said we survived passing through the divide because we have Fiordan blood. Is that… true?"

Cas says nothing for a long moment. "Yeah. Guess so."

"Do you think it really was him?"

Cas walks faster. I have to speed-walk to catch up, but of course, getting the hell out of here is our priority. Things look different from this side. The bridge *has* to be here somewhere.

Shadows creeping in my vision.

An army on the horizon.

Blood. Screaming. Swords and fire and blood…

"Leah." A hand on my arm. "Focus."

"I'm trying," I snap, angrier with myself more than anything. "Don't you think I'm fighting with everything I have?"

Silence.

Apparently, someone hasn't learned any manners from this whole ordeal.

It's his fault I'm dying, says an awful, selfish voice in the back of my head. Never mind that the fiend in the woods all those weeks ago would have killed me if not for his healing me.

Blood sprays. A heartbroken scream.

I jerk back and slam into Cas. "Sorry," I say without thinking.

"What are you reliving?" He gives me a sideways look, for once not disdainful. More like… when he realised I was dying.

"The war, I think. I get flashes. You were friends with the other Transcendent."

Cas's expression turns icy. "I was."

"And?"

Nothing.

"If I'm dying, there's no harm in talking to me. Seeing as we're the only two humans here."

"Doesn't seem a good enough reason."

"Whoa." I step away from him. "That's kinda harsh for deathbed talk."

Not a word in response. What a way to die, on a hostile alien world with a guy I might just kill before the visions drive me to madness.

"It's not deathbed talk," he says. "But you're unlikely to last the day. You know that. Accept it."

"Been there, done that," I say. "I did tell you manners cost nothing, you know."

I turn away. There appear to be flames on the horizon, above the divide. Some trick of the fiends, or Fiordans, I guess.

Wait.

"There." I point. "I think I recognise it. That's the spot where I crossed the bridge last time."

We're going to make it. Hope rises in my chest before I can stop it. I won't die before setting foot on my own planet again.

Before I see the others. Before I find out if they survived.

The flames waver and flicker. I fix my gaze on them, though it doesn't make the dizziness any easier to bear. Every step becomes a battle of wills.

Screaming. The shimmering fire above the divide flaring up, a bridge covering the entire path as fiends beyond counting swarm across. An ugly, noisy struggle.

People screaming. Running.

Red-cloaked figures falling into the divide.

"Leah."

Screaming.

No. I can't...

Scenes of devastation play out before my eyes. The army marching on Earth, breaking into chaos as they set foot on our world. The sky's on fire, the ground's splitting open, and red-cloaked figures are falling into the gap.

Now I'm in a town. A line like an earthquake splits the street, growing by the second. Red figures fight on either side of it. One pulls a companion out of the gap just in time. Fiends are materialising one at a time, swiping at any target they find. The Pyros run up and down the widening split, trying to hit back. On this side, it looks like the fiends are appearing out of thin air.

Then a cracking rends the air. The divide splits like a lightning bolt, half the street disappearing in a split second...

And the army appears as one, a writhing mass, descending on the Pyros left on the other side.

I'm watching from behind a building, but I'm on the other side. I'm jumping through the gap.

Am I seeing this from the fiends' perspective?

Before I can wonder, I'm overwhelmed by pain. Agony splices my entire body, and once again, I'm looking at a familiar lab...

And I'm powerless to stop the visions as they crash into me, one at a time. The pain. The repeated attempts to see if I, Cas, am Transcendent.

Time blurs to nothing.

———

"Dammit, Leah, wake up."

I struggle, expecting pain to explode all over my body, but I can't feel anything but numbness.

"She's awake." Murray's voice. Impossible. He died. Right?

My eyes flicker open. And I almost jump a foot in the air. I'm in a lab. Again.

But Murray's here.

"What...?"

"Don't try to move," says Murray. "We've got you."

"What the hell... where am I?"

"Home."

The base. Impossible as it seems, I'm... home. In the sickbay, by the look of things.

And I'm not alone. Cas walks towards me. Did he carry me all the way here? There are other people outside, but the door's closed, and Val stands nearby.

"We'll have to act fast," says Murray. "The effects are... Leah, it's lucky you woke up."

"About that," I say. "I have a lot of questions…" But before I even finish speaking, my vision blurs over again. A pattern, like flickering flames, overhangs everything.

"I'm sorry, Leah," says Murray.

My heart drops. I'm actually going to… die.

"Tell me quickly," I say. "Did Poppy and Tyler make it? Who…?"

"They're alive," says Murray quickly. "And Elle. We had minimal casualties. We were very lucky."

His words become a hum as the flames dance and my head flops back. I no longer have the strength to lift it. Not even to look at Cas, who brought me back here even though I'm a lost cause.

"Guess this is it," I say.

"Perhaps not," says Cas, and holds up a test tube.

"Whose…?"

"Nolan's," says Cas. "I grabbed a few samples from the lab, too, but I've no idea if they were Fiordan or what. I just took everything that wasn't damaged.

"Well." I draw in a breath. "Let's find out."

I've nothing to lose. We got home safely. Murray somehow survived, and so did Val and the others. They'll survive without me.

They can win this fight.

And yet somehow part of me can't believe it's really happening. I have to make myself lie still and breathe calmly. Being in the lab is a bit too reminiscent of what I went through with Jared.

Relax. You're safe.

And if this doesn't work… then I can't think of a better place to die. Jared's experiments died along with him. My blood is my own again, and the enemy will never get hold of it.

"Leah? We're going to put you to sleep. If you wake up… you survived. You beat it."

I nod. I can't say any more. I don't want to spend my last few seconds crying. I've done enough of that already.

A few tears slip out anyway. I wish it could have been this painless for Lissa. But she'd be glad I'm happy. Glad I managed to find friends, in what's left of our world.

I close my eyes. This time, no visions rise to claim me.

———

"Leah." Murray's voice, close by. "Can you hear me?"

I nod. My eyes are sticky, but I force them open. Blink a couple of times. Murray leans over me, concern etched on his face.

"Did you black out?"

"Kind of. I didn't see anything, though."

Murray looks at someone behind me. "If the curse was breaking down, she'd have seen the battle again for sure."

"You think?"

Cas. The other person is Cas.

I manage to twist my head around. "Is that true?"

"It's been the case with all the others," says Murray, and Cas's expression goes hard.

"No proof," he says. "Other than experience."

"What other proof is there? She was sedated. She survived."

I survived. Despite the dizziness, I sit up. More to reassure my body that I can move. I'm here, at home, and I'm alive.

I break into a grin. "I'm… really alive."

"You are." Murray smiles at me. "And there are a lot of people who want to see you."

"Yeah, they're breaking down the doors." Cas appears

unimpressed. But he's not aggressively holding his weapon, like usual. And he's so close to me, I can hear him breathing.

A shiver runs through me.

We survived...

"Let me see them," I say quickly. "I bet I had Elle worried."

"Of course you did," says Murray. "Just in case, I'll tell them not to swarm you."

"Oh, come on." I let myself have this moment of triumph. "I'm pretty much indestructible."

Though my Transcendent powers are put to the test when ten people pile on me and hug me at once. I attempt to explain through the writhing bodies and shouts of, "Leah, you're alive!" But I'm pretty sure no one can hear the details.

There'll be time enough for that later. Time to celebrate being alive.

I have a permanent smile on my face as I talk to the others, even people I don't know. That this many people were worried about me is... unexpected. Different.

Hours of celebrating later, I have the headache of a life-time. Which, considering my Transcendent state supposedly makes me able to heal any pain, is saying a lot. I haven't seen Cas in a while, so I wander out of the recreation room and walk around the lava pool. If he's not there, he's probably stabbing targets or something.

But he's there, standing on the same rock formation where he told me the truth about being Transcendent.

I jump soundlessly down to join him, but he immediately turns around, no surprise in his expression. "Thought you'd come back."

"And thank you for carrying me here? Even though I'm a lost cause?" I can't stop smiling. Of course, Cas is as expressionless as ever, which is why I want to poke him until he joins in the fun. Not that I can in any way imagine Cas being the life of the party.

"You're not a lost cause."

I blink. "Wow. Almost a compliment. Maybe I really did wake up in an alternative world."

"Why would you think that?"

I shrug. "We all survived, right? We walked out of the fiends' world without a scratch. You carried me over the bridge, right?"

He nods.

"So," I say, shifting, the silence getting to me. "I guess that's it. You get to keep your secrets now."

Still, no answer.

"So we're back to me having to guess whether you're being an asshat on purpose or not." Inwardly, I wince at my own harsh tone. I don't even know why I'm so annoyed. What did I expect, him to hug me like my friends did?

Are we friends? I mentally kick myself for the stupid question. Like it matters. Isn't it enough that the rest of us got out okay?

"Never mind." I back up, prepared to jump for the surface.

"Hold on." He hesitates, looking at the floor, rather than at me. "I was trying to figure out what to say to you."

"About what?" I have goose bumps for some inexplicable reason. Seeing as I'm standing next to lava, that makes no sense whatsoever.

"What you saw."

I tense. "Which part?"

"Any of it. I'm sorry you had to live that. I knew when I healed you, and I did it anyway."

Wow and wow again. I've never heard Cas say so many words to me.

"What, you regret saving me?"

He shakes his head. "No. But if you'd died—"

"Then I'd be dead either way. I thought you saved me because Nolan told you to."

A pause. Then he shakes his head. "I lied. I didn't want you to know there was a possibility the blood connection might transfer over. Every time I did it to the other test subjects, I hoped it wouldn't. Then when it did the same to you, I couldn't face the responsibility."

My God. Is he actually apologising to me? It's understandable how he acted, if nothing else. Doesn't make it right, but who am I to judge?

"Is that why you kept treating me like crap?"

He looks away. "I'm not proud of it."

More wow. An actual apology. I half expect the fiends to show up and beg for forgiveness for invading our planet.

"Right," I say. "Then why not trust me enough to tell me your plan?"

"Because I knew you'd stick around and get yourself killed."

I release a breath. "I'm the Transcendent, you know."

"I think I know that."

So much for apologies. "Yeah, that attitude of yours needs adjusting."

"Says who?" His eyes narrow. "I don't think anyone's ever annoyed me as much as you have."

"Wow." My eyebrows lift. "You sure know how to compliment a girl."

"They don't cover that in basic training."

A laugh escapes before I can stop it. "I guess not."

He tilts his head up to meet my eyes—and the ground shakes. I brace my hand on the wall to keep from falling into the lava.

"What the hell?" Cas's eyes widen.

"What's going on?" I look up to see people coming out of the recreation room, and Murray crossing the corridor from his office. Shouts ring out.

Another tremor shakes the floor and lava spills over the

platform Cas and I stand on. Only instinct makes me jump out the way to avoid burning the soles of my shoes off. Cas follows, calling to Murray.

I hang back, disconnection and shock rooting me to the spot even as cries ring out.

Not only human cries. Fiends.

"We're under attack!"

Screaming. A siren-like wail kicks up, adding to the racket and making it impossible to tell where everyone's running. My thoughts spin. *Not the tunnels around the back... the fiends got in that way before.* Have the defences even been fixed since Jared's invasion?

The floor trembles. *The volcano's extinct,* I remember. Coming to my senses, I run to Murray, but I'm caught up in the jostling crowd.

"What's going on?"

Murray's shouting something, but I can't make out the words. Raw panic washes over me. A creeping sensation of eyes on the back of my neck.

A dark, winged figure drops from the ceiling. Then another.

The panic turns to terror as the crowd turns to the weapons room. Cas already has his sword out, slicing at a winged fiend.

How...?

Lucky I still have my blade. I grab it, cursing the narrow platform for slowing me down.

Another figure drops, landing right in front of me, warped and winged with razor-like claws. Jared's fiend.

There are too many of us crammed into a tight space, and the ground shakes like the mountain itself is moving. Panic erupts along with Pyro fire.

I slash at the fiend, fighting to get to Murray. He shouts,

loud enough for me to hear over the noise: "Get out! We need to evacuate now!"

A wrenching tremor cuts through the ground, sending everyone sideways, mid-fight. Fiends and humans fall into a writhing mass as a crack splinters through the floor, fanning out from the lava pool.

Growing by the second.

Too quick to stop two people sliding over the edge.

"NO!" I cry out.

But it's too late. The mountain splits with a roar, leaving half of us on one side, the others sliding further away with each passing moment. I dig my hands into the floor, inches from the edge, close enough to see the bubbling lava.

The wavering shape of flames.

A fiend soars out of the gap, slashing at the hands of the people hanging onto the edge.

Impossible. *Another divide is opening.*

I reach out with my dagger hand and stab any enemy within reach. On the other side of the breach, Val's hurrying people away towards the back tunnel. But on our side, the ground's tilting and it's all I can do not to fall over the edge.

Then it stops. A gaping line divides our home in two, tremors still rocking through the ground.

"Everyone out!" Murray shouts. With shock, I realise there are only a handful of us left, including Cas, who's speared one of the fiends with his blade, withdrawing it in a spray of blood.

"Out!" yells Murray, and we run for the tunnel. Worry for the others rattles through my head, but the shaky ground brings a renewed fear that the whole mountain's going to collapse.

We climb down the rocky mountainside in panicked single file, Murray rushing up and down making sure everyone can walk. *And the others?* I want to ask. They used the back exit. Val was amongst them.

My legs burn with the climb, my heart beating fast, fast. *Please. Please let them be all right.*

The ground's stopped shaking by the time we reach ground level. From this angle, the mountain looks the same as ever, not like it's split in two down the middle.

"Another divide," I say to Cas, who's nearby, anger etched on his face. "It's another divide. That means…"

"The Fiordans," says Murray, confirming my worst suspicion.

The second invasion of Earth has begun.

ABOUT THE AUTHOR

Emma is the New York Times and USA Today Bestselling author of the Changeling Chronicles urban fantasy series.

Emma spent her childhood creating imaginary worlds to compensate for a disappointingly average reality, so it was probably inevitable that she ended up writing fantasy novels. When she's not immersed in her own fictional universes, Emma can be found with her head in a book or wandering around the world in search of adventure.

Find out more about Emma's books at
www.emmaladams.com.

www.ingramcontent.com/pod-product-compliance
Lightning Source LLC
Chambersburg PA
CBHW020316200626
46814CB00006BA/2266